S0-AWD-548

MASSACRE AT POWDER RIVER

"You want things to be as they were," Logan whispered. "The soldiers will protect the road because gold has more value than promises made to Indians. It's a *Wihio* truth, old friend . . . I wish I could change somebody's mind. I admire your people, and I value our friendship . . ."

"Then there will be no peace," Wolf said, sighing. "Red Cloud will be gone by morning. I'm sick of war, of fighting and killing, but I'll ride with him. I'm tired of watching the women cut their hair and the children starve. That's what my people will find on Powder River, death and starvation."

"What will my people find?" Logan asked.

"The same," Wolf vowed. "If they come, we'll fight them . . ."

MASSACRE AT POWDER RIVER

G. CLIFTON WISLER

BERKLEY BOOKS, NEW YORK

MASSACRE AT POWDER RIVER

A Berkley Book / published by arrangement with
the author

PRINTING HISTORY
Berkley edition / March 1997

All rights reserved.
Copyright © 1997 by G. Clifton Wisler.
This book may not be reproduced in whole or in part,
by mimeograph or any other means, without permission.
For information address: The Berkley Publishing Group,
200 Madison Avenue, New York, New York 10016.

The Putnam Berkley World Wide Web site address is
http://www.berkley.com/berkley

ISBN: 0-425-15675-3

BERKLEY®
Berkley Books are published by The Berkley Publishing Group,
200 Madison Avenue, New York, New York 10016.
BERKLEY and the "B" design
are trademarks belonging to Berkley Publishing Corporation.

PRINTED IN THE UNITED STATES OF AMERICA

10 9 8 7 6 5 4 3 2 1

FOR GARY GOLDSTEIN,

*whose friendship, patience, and consideration
made this book possible*

MASSACRE AT POWDER RIVER

chapter
1

WOLF RUNNING SHIVERED. WINTER THAT year was numbing cold. It had come early, too. Hard Face Moon had yet to grow full, and already the snowdrifts stood waist high!

It's appropriate, Wolf thought as he kindled a small fire and waited for the sun to rise above the mist-shrouded eastern horizon. Winter had always been a season of death, of darkness, of despair. That year had been no different—only worse.

He'd seen part of it in his dreams. It had been a morning not unlike that one. Fog clung to the stream across from the *Tsis tsis tas* lodges, concealing the enemy. Snow Wolf, his spirit guide, had howled a mournful refrain, and Wolf Running had rolled out of his elk hide covering, trembling with dread.

"What is it?" Sun Walker Woman had cried.

"Ne' hyo?" Wind's Whisper, their oldest boy, called.

"Only a dream," he told them. "Only a dream."

Four days later a young *Omissis,* Snow Bear, appeared with sad news. *Wihio* soldiers had attacked the peaceful

camps of Black Kettle and White Antelope down near Ar-
kansas River, along a little stream called Sand Creek.

"Why?" Wolf demanded to know.

"When did the *Wihio* need a reason to kill us?" Bear
screamed. "Once you told me that Sweet Medicine warned
the people to avoid those crazy white people. He was right.
They've brought us only sad times."

For days thereafter *Tsis tsis tas* and *Lakota* rescue parties rode south to help the survivors. It was only later, after
a band of *Oglalas* visited the massacre site, that Wolf
learned the worst. He had relations among the dead. Pony
Leg, his cousin's uncle, died trying to protect the helpless
ones. Sun Walker Woman's aunt had been slaughtered
with her little granddaughters. *Wihio* soldiers cut the bodies, carrying off pieces for trophies! It was a thing that had
torn the harmony of Wolf Running's world.

"We must punish the ones who did it," Snow Bear had
urged as he tore at his hair. "To fight warriors is one thing.
To cut up little children . . . *Heammawihio,* give us the
eyes to find these men and the power to drive them from
the sacred earth."

Two moons had come and gone since the southern people had brought a pipe to the *Suhtai* camp where Wolf
dwelled. Parties of *Lakotas* began raiding the white settlements on Platte River. Left Hand's *Arapahos* had also
camped on Sand Creek, and their relations eagerly joined
the fighting. Now the northern *Tsis tsis tas* and *Suhtai*
camps added their young men to the struggle.

"I go to fight with a heavy heart," Wolf had told Sun
Walker Woman. "Our sons are still small. I want to swim
with them in the rivers and watch them hunt Bull Buffalo."

"You'll do those things," she assured him as they gazed
upon the three sleeping children. Whisper was passing his
sixth winter upon the earth. Winter Pup was only four, and
Deer Foot was just three.

"I have little taste for killing *Wihio,*" Wolf Running
confessed. "I have known some among them who have
been good men. These soldiers who wore the blue coats

at Sand Creek and cut up little children are another matter.''

It was much the same with many other *Suhtai,* even those with slain relatives. Winter was a bad time to wage war. Many of the northern people had grown used to trading hides with the fort traders or selling ponies to the wagon people who journeyed west along Platte River. Who would trade with hostile bands?

"Even if we win, we'll only bring more of their soldiers down on us," Long Dog, Sun Walker's father, had argued. As he was a *Suhtai* chief, Long Dog's words carried weight. Even so, they had no power to silence the pipe carriers. They, after all, had seen the dead children. No man who had held his own little ones could ignore what the bluecoats had done at Sand Creek.

The sun chose that moment to burn through the mist, and Wolf tried to clear his mind. It was time to make the morning prayers. Once he had stood atop those same hills, flanked by a father and uncle who no longer walked the earth. The three of them had spoken the ancient words together.

> "Give us the struggles to make us strong,
>   *Heammawihio.*
> Brave up our hearts,
>   *Heammawihio.*
> Show us the sacred path,
>   That we may walk within the harmony of the Hoop,
>   *Heammawihio.*"

Wolf sang the prayer that morning. Stands Long Beside Him, Wolf's brother-friend, was busy gathering their ponies. The children remained with their mother in the *Suhtai* camp a day's ride to the east. They were too small to stand so long in the snowdrifts anyway. Buffalo Horn, his cousin, had once shared the morning ritual, but who could say if the Horn still walked the earth? He, too, had erected his lodge among Black Kettle's *Wu ta piu.*

"Man Above, help him, too, to walk the sacred path,''

Wolf whispered. "Too many good men have climbed
Hanging Road."

"More will follow," the wind seemed to whine in answer.

Wolf closed his eyes for a time and imagined his cousin
riding the hills to the south. Horn was a man of power.
He had warned the people of the peril, Snow Bear had
explained, but the peace chiefs had been too blind to see
the truth of Horn's vision and too deaf to heed his words.

"Nothing changes," Wolf grumbled. How many good,
wise men had died because some fool chose to ignore such
a dream? The old man who had given Wolf his name had
fallen fighting alone because young big-talkers had broken
the medicine power. Raven Heart, Wolf's adopted father,
had similarly died.

"This time it will be different," Stands Long had
vowed.

Wolf hoped so. Certainly the camps that spread out
along Platte River that morning were filled with determined warriors. Hundreds, perhaps a thousand, men stood
ready to strike a hard blow against the *Wihio* at the town
they called Julesburg. In addition to the *Tsis tsis tas* and
Suhtai, Arapahos and *Lakotas* were there. Each band had
made their prayers. Soldier chiefs vowed to hold back the
hot bloods. Now individual warriors painted their faces and
prepared their ponies for the coming fight.

"*Nah nih,* the others are waiting," High Flyer, Wolf's
younger brother, called from the path leading to the river.
"The ponies are ready, but we need your help with the
paint."

"It's not a proper thing, hurrying prayers," Wolf explained.

"I heard nothing," the Flyer replied. "I feared you were
asleep."

"Not all prayers are spoken, *See'was'sin mit.* If there's
going to be a fight, we'll need power."

"We'll also need to be there," High Flyer added im-
patiently. "Red Hawk, our brother, has collected the weapons. If we're to lead the way, we have to hurry."

"And the shield?" Wolf asked.

"Yes, that, too, *Nah nih*. All that's required is for us to join him."

"We'll do it then," Wolf said, turning back to the fire. He spoke a few final words to the flame and then extinguished it with handfuls of snow. The brothers watched the dying smoke spiral its way toward the sky a moment. Then they turned down the path and made their way to the river.

Stands Long had painted the ponies with lightning bolts and hailstones. Red Hawk was helping Wolf's youngest brother, Morning Hawk, to tie the tails in the *Lakota* fashion their father had taught them. Wolf took his medicine bag and mixed some blue paint. He then drew small blue snakes on each horse's flank. The snakes were as much the mark of Elk warriors as the crooked lances carried by their ablest fighters. Wolf also oiled his shield so that it would catch what little sunlight penetrated the hazy winter sky.

It was the shield, of course, that protected him from harm, that attested to his power. He had carried it almost ten winters now, from the time Snow Wolf first visited his dreams. It was Snow Wolf's terrible red eyes that seemed to glare from that shield. The edges were black, but the coloring lightened as it neared the center. Snow Wolf itself was white, of course, and that made the hungry eyes even more daunting.

Wolf Running waited until the final moment to apply his war paint. He had hoped to receive a dream that might help him plan his fight. It didn't come. Stands Long always painted the white hailstones that adorned his shield onto his face. Wolf relied on his dreams to indicate the appropriate paint. Lacking spiritual guidance, he chose to color his face dark blue, leaving only a stripe of yellow across his eyes. When he finished, he painted his brothers' faces in the same fashion.

"I want them to see us today," the usually modest Wolf explained as he tied three eagle feathers in his hair. He had counted coups enough to merit a war bonnet, but he disdained such ornaments. He continued to trust the elk tooth charms tied behind his ears and the silver eagle he wore on a thong around his neck. That eagle, the gift of a *Wihio* trader's son, commemorated his first rescue.

"You should set that *Wihio* trinket aside," Flyer scolded.

"No, *See'was'sin mit*," Wolf countered. "It reminds me that nothing is ever what we expect. It makes me cautious."

"Today's no day to be cautious," Morning Hawk insisted. "We're going ahead, aren't we? To strike the enemy first?"

"You'll stay behind with the other pony boys," Red Hawk scolded the thirteen-year-old.

"None of us will count the first coup," Wolf explained after Morning Hawk left. "It's our task to draw out the enemy."

"Yes," Stands Long said, studying the faces of Wolf's remaining brothers. "Two *Lakotas* are also coming. It's only right since they first accepted the pipe. Big Crow will lead us."

"Only seven then?" Flyer asked.

"That's enough," Stands Long observed. "The *Wihio* won't ride out if they see a large band."

"The people rely on their shield carriers to do what's necessary," Wolf added. "I vowed my brothers were reliable men. No hot bloods are going this time. Too often they've broken the medicine power and ruined the plan. We'll lure the bluecoats into the hills, and the others will fall upon the enemy and count coup."

"We'll share in the fighting, though?" Red Hawk asked.

"We're only decoys," Wolf explained. "If you want, you can join the main band. Long Dog and his sons are there. They would welcome you."

"Our place is with our brother," Flyer declared, clasping Wolf's hand. "This time Red Hawk and I may be the rescuers."

"It's a warming thought," Wolf said, nodding with

pride at the strong young men his brothers had become. "Maybe we'll strike the *Wihio* hard, and only the bluecoats will require rescuing."

They grinned at the notion, but none of them really believed that would happen. Stands Long turned and led the way to where Big Crow and the two *Lakotas* were waiting. Big Crow welcomed his fellow Elks and then indicated the huddle of buildings and the strong stockade that were gradually emerging from the snowy mist.

"The bluecoats are there," Big Crow announced. "It's our task to bring them out."

"It won't be easy," Flyer pointed out. "*Wihio* like their warming fires on winter days."

"I do, too," Big Crow confessed. "Let's wake them up."

The decoys approached the little fort with considerable difficulty. The country was scarred with ravines and shallow streams. Even without the winter chill and the deep snowdrifts, it was slow going. Wolf soon found himself at the head of the column. As was his custom, he rode a pale horse. The white war shirt that usually marked him amid the other riders made him little more than a phantom that misty morning, though. High Flyer and Red Hawk, sitting atop their buckskin ponies, contrasted sharply with the snow-clad landscape.

"*Nah nih,* it's as I feared," Flyer remarked when Wolf paused a stone's throw from the fort's corral. "White men don't leave the comfort of their fires on days like these."

"It was a day like this that the bluecoats killed the people at Sand Creek," Wolf reminded his brother. Speaking the words left a bitter taste in Wolf's mouth. Enemy country? Hadn't his father and his grandfather hunted Bull Buffalo along that very river! No other enemy, not even the crafty *Pawnees,* had been strong enough to steal the buffalo valleys. The *Wihio* weren't like other people, though.

Wolf Running reflected on the sweet words spoken at treaty councils. How many papers had the people signed? Wolf himself had been at Horse Creek when the first great treaty agreement had been made. Old Broken Hand, the trader Fitzpatrick, had organized that peace gathering of the *Wihio* and the plains peoples. Even then some of the chiefs had voiced concern. Black Kettle and White Antelope had both spoken loudly for peace, and what had it won them? Butchery!

It will be different now, Wolf vowed as he studied the fort. A pair of sentries scurried about, and soon a handful of *Wihio* soldiers dressed in heavy buffalo hide coats gathered.

"They have many ponies," Stands Long observed. "Maybe we should try to take some."

"We're here to punish the child killers," Big Crow insisted.

"We're not good at fighting forts," Wolf lamented.

"We won't," Stands Long replied. "We'll take their animals and stop their supply wagons. They'll starve inside their walls or come out and fight us like men."

"It won't be easy," Wolf insisted. "How long can so many warriors stay here?"

"Long enough," Stands Long barked. "The wind carries the mourning chants of the weeping mothers and fathers. No one can ignore them."

The debate ceased when a party of white men stepped out from the stockade and approached the animal corral. Big Crow raised his crooked lance, howled furiously, and charged. Wolf and the others followed, and the *Wihio* scattered. Big Crow was careful not to get within rifle range of the fort, and the frightened soldiers escaped. The decoys had accomplished their purpose, though. Soon a party of bluecoats, accompanied by some ranchers, rode out to chase Big Crow's little party.

"Ayyyy!" Wolf shouted. "Let's ride!"

Big Crow and the *Lakotas* had already turned away. Wolf and Stands Long, as was their habit, lingered until they were certain the others had gotten away. Then they, too, rode south.

Big Crow's plan was to lure the bluecoats into the Sand Hills. The main war party was waiting there, concealed in ravines and behind the low hills. At first everything went well. Fifty or so bluecoats and ranchers charged recklessly after the decoys. Big Crow took care to hold his pony in check, allowing the bluecoats to close the distance. The eager *Wihio* hurried toward the ambush. Then the trap disintegrated.

It was the same old story. A few overanxious hot bloods raced up out of a ravine and alerted the bluecoats. Instantly their commander halted his pursuit and turned back toward the fort. Big Crow muttered in disgust and waved his lance at the fleeing enemy. Wolf, too, turned. Screaming at the top of his lungs, he raced after the fleeing bluecoats, hoping to strike their column and turn them back toward the others.

Actually some of the hot bloods were the first to strike the fleeing *Wihio* horsemen that morning. On fresh horses, they hurried past the decoys and struck individual soldiers. Some of the bluecoats turned in an effort to defend themselves. Others tumbled off stumbling horses. At least half the soldiers never glanced back. Instead they galloped wildly toward the fort.

Wolf Running struck the middle of the bluecoat line. A big, hairy-faced *Wihio* pulled a pistol and fired. The bullet struck the heavy bull hide shield and lodged in the willow frame. Wolf then clubbed the *Wihio* with his bow, nocked an arrow, and shot the man through his belly. The *Wihio* somehow remained atop his horse, but Wolf's second arrow tore through the bluecoat's heart, and he fell.

Stands Long Beside Him cut off a small party of young bluecoats and turned them back toward the main body. Three of the bewildered soldiers jumped off their horses and produced rifles. A fourth *Wihio* tried to shield them a moment. A shower of arrows knocked him from his horse. Then the main war party arrived, and a line of *Lakotas* overwhelmed the dazed soldiers.

It was hard to know exactly what happened next. Wolf counted coup on a *Wihio* leader, but the man managed to get away when two *Arapahos* blocked Wolf's path. In the end only eighteen *Wihio* bodies lay in the snow. Others, bloodied and battered, escaped to the fort.

The fighting didn't end there, though. Young *Arapaho* and *Tsis tsis tas* warriors fell upon the dead men with a new manner of viciousness. Perhaps the memory of the dead children at Sand Creek drove them. Maybe it was frustration that hot bloods had spoiled the trap. Soon blood stained the snowy ground.

The main war party never reached the fleeing bluecoats. A few warriors charged toward the *Wihio* fort and hurled insults at the cowering garrison. Most turned away and galloped toward Julesburg, the little town located down-river of where Lodgepole Creek emptied into the south fork of Platte River.

Wolf didn't know exactly how it happened, but Long Dog's second son, Spring Fox, insisted that a mail wagon attracted the warriors to the town. Others said it was the stagecoach from Fort Laramie. No one was certain. Warriors broke into the stage depot and plundered its supplies. Spring Fox boasted that he had eaten the hot food prepared for the *Wihio* passengers.

Large parties of *Arapaho* and *Lakota* warriors next began breaking apart the wooden doors of the houses and stores in Julesburg. The *Wihio* inside fled to the river, and most escaped unhurt. Some of those people were traders well known to their attackers, and some even had relations among the raiders. Chiefs and even individual warriors protected the innocents, but no one spared the warehouses and their shelves of trade goods. Women began arriving from the nearby camps with extra ponies, and the raiders gradually emptied the buildings of every sack of flour, bolt of cloth, and flask of powder.

On the far side of Platte River, a large herd of *Wihio* cattle grazed. It escaped attention at first, but soon small bands of warriors crossed the river and began running off the cows. Others took the ponies of the herders. The soldiers began firing off their howitzers from the safety of the fort, but the noise only stampeded the cattle. It did little to deter the raiders.

All that day the raiding continued. Only when no one had a spare pony left to carry anything did the raiders begin to move away. When they did, the remaining blue-coats lacked supplies, mounts, and pride. A band of *Tsis tsis tas* even found the soldiers' paymaster and captured the boxes of paper money used to pay them. Young men, ignorant that paper money could buy rifles, powder, and iron pots at the trading posts, threw that paper into the air, and the wind scattered it across the countryside.

"Platte River is full of it," Flyer declared.

No one doubted that it was a remembered fight. The raiders traveled east three days, stopping only when darkness made continuing impossible. They finally halted when they reached Black Kettle's meager camp of survivors at Cherry Creek. The captured ponies and supplies helped restore the strength of the hollow-eyed victims of Sand Creek. Various bands celebrated the success, and young men recounted their coups around the council fires of the soldier societies.

"We punished the *Wihio* this time!" Flyer boasted as he rode alongside his elder brother.

"Did we?" Wolf asked. The *Wihio* fort remained on Platte River, and only eighteen bluecoats were dead. The white people had plenty of flour and powder and ponies. The hot bloods had once again thrown away a chance a strike a hard blow. Who knew if another such chance would come?

chapter
2

WOLF RUNNING, HIS BROTHERS, AND Stands Long
Beside Him were among the last of the warriors
to reach Cherry Creek. Wolf was tired, and he left his
brothers to tend the ponies while he sought out Sun Walker
Woman and the children. Their lodge stood in its accustomed honored place beside her father's. Long Dog, as a
Suhtai chief, camped at the center of the band.

"You've had a hard fight," Sun Walker observed as she
rose from beside a crackling fire. Smiling, she took his
hands in her own and led the way to the fire. The night
was cold, and their breath made little clouds as it left their
mouths.

"Yes, it was difficult," Wolf muttered. "War's better
made in summer."

"There was need, though," Sun Walker noted. "The
camp is rich with things taken from the *Wihio* town. Did
you bring us something?"

"Only myself," he told her as he set his shield on its
framework. He rested his bow and quiver of arrows
nearby.

"Snow Wolf's nose is torn," she pointed out.

"The shield took a bullet intended for me," Wolf explained. "Once it would have blinded the *Wihio*. I must restore its power."

"After you rest," she argued. "You have other obligations."

"Oh?"

"Your cousin's wedding feast," she said, grinning.

"My cousin? Which one?"

"Buffalo Horn. He has invited Bright Swallow Maiden to share his life. Her father and brothers are gone now."

"But Horn is alive?" Wolf asked. "That's warming news. No one knew for certain whether he had fallen at Sand Creek or not."

"He has a new scar," Sun Walker explained. "New brothers, too. He was always one to draw company, after all."

"He understands suffering," Wolf said, frowning. He recalled how, as a small boy, Horn had struggled to run in spite of a mangled foot. "He's an Elk, too. We are responsible for the helpless ones."

"His wife's people are gone, Wolf. You could invite him to ride with us. Another good man would be welcome."

"I'll ask," Wolf promised. "I don't think he'll come, though. He follows Black Kettle."

"Some who followed the Kettle to Sand Creek won't listen to his words any longer," she grumbled.

"Black Kettle's had a different road to walk," Wolf noted. "Horn remembers the warrior who saved a small maimed boy from the trappers. I expect him to stay."

"You *will* ask him?"

"I will. I'll also make the giveaway at his wedding feast."

"Can we spare the horses?"

"We have many, and the southern people need them. We'll be generous."

"One day you'll give away everything we have," she said, laughing. "My father worries about that."

"Do you?"

"No," she declared. "I tell everyone that my husband's a man of the people. His power grows from his sacrifices. Soon the Elks will offer you a chief's bonnet."

"More likely I'll carry one of the lances," he told her.

"You already hold back to protect the helpless ones. And the foolish ones."

"Do you disapprove?"

"How could I?" Sun Walker cried. "You're the man I love, and it's your devotion to the people that first drew me to you."

"I have sons now, though."

"They aren't starving. They have warm coats and a good lodge."

"I didn't come back with trader blankets or flour," Wolf reminded her.

"Trader blankets make me itch," Sun Walker complained. "Flour? I have lots of cornmeal, and I like its taste better."

"Me, too," he told her.

They sat together a little longer as the fire burned down to embers. Then Wolf escorted his wife inside the lodge, and they prepared their beds. For a time after Deer Foot's birth, Sun Walker had kept herself apart. Once the child began walking, though, she drew her husband to her side. That night they both seemed to realize a chill had filled their hearts during the four days they had been apart. Wolf stripped himself and smoothed a place for Sun Walker on the thick bear skin beside him. She slipped her dress over her shoulders, smiled, and crawled over.

As they merged their separate beings into the oneness that always cast away even the bitterest grip of winter, Wolf heard Wind's Whisper talking softly to his brothers.

"We should be quieter," he told Sun Walker.

"No, they should know their mother loves their father."

"He loves her, too," Wolf announced as she tickled his ribs. "And them."

That next morning Wolf located Buffalo Horn and his brother-friend, Otter, in the crude mixture of stick shelters and skin huts that housed the remnant of Black Kettle's band. It troubled him to see so many hungry faces. There were children there who scarcely had clothes enough to offer some modesty, and Wolf saw for himself how the icy wind tore at their exposed flesh and bare feet.

"This can't continue," he told Horn. "There are plenty of blankets in the other camps, and most of our people can spare buffalo hides. There are enough for new lodges."

"Women are already at work on the lodges," Horn assured his cousin. "Soon we'll have moccasins and shirts for everyone."

"It's been a long time since the *Wihio* attacked," Wolf muttered. "Time enough more could have been done."

"We've never lost so much," Horn explained. "Or so many. Not so long ago we marked each morning by remembering an old person or a child who walked out into the ice to reduce the people's burdens. Perhaps, too, to stop their own suffering. Now even the weak are getting stronger. The boys talk of carving courting flutes and hunting Bull Buffalo. The world goes on."

It certainly did for Buffalo Horn. The camps moved north, back toward Platte River, but that didn't deter women from sewing a fine lodge covering for him. Otter cut pine poles for the framework. When the *Tsis tsis tas* and *Suhtai* paused briefly at White Butte Creek, Wolf Running and his brothers provided horses and buffalo hides for the giveaway. Each animal went to a family in need, and the hides provided good winter coats for people who needed them. The wedding feast itself fattened the hungry, and the dancing and singing that followed sealed the old bonds of kinship between the cousins.

Others, too, chose wives that winter. Summer Cherry Woman, whose little son Mole was also Buffalo Horn's cousin, ended her mourning for the fallen Pony Leg and accepted the *Oglala* Storm Eagle's offer of marriage. The Eagle had lost a wife and son to summer fevers, and he declared his heart once again whole. The gathering of so many separate bands provided a rare opportunity for young men to court wives, and the large number of fatherless girls among the *Tsis tsis tas* and *Arapaho* camps attracted numerous offers. Children once again had fathers, and those who considered themselves too old to follow their mothers into another band accepted adoption by friends of slain fathers or else joined soldier societies.

It was, Wolf supposed, only natural that harmony could not survive forever in such a large encampment. Some of the chiefs argued that the gathering offered protection against vengeful bluecoats. Others feared that it would only attract the attention of their enemies. When the weather warmed briefly, several northern bands broke away and crossed Platte River. Some of the Sand Creek bands turned south and east, hopeful that they could escape danger in that direction.

For Wolf Running, the choice of winter camp depended on whether he and the other men would continue to raid the *Wihio* ranches and settlements. The *Lakotas* had vowed to fight. The Crazy Dogs, perhaps the largest camp among the *Tsis tsis tas* after the Sand Creek killing, urged their brother bands to do the same.

"We sign treaties and we speak with the *Wihio* soldier chiefs," Weasel, one of their lance carriers, argued. "Then, when we make our winter camps, they come and kill us. Now's the time we should show them that white men can also bleed in the snow!"

Weasel, being a young man, had only a small voice in the council. Black Kettle, in spite of Sand Creek, was an old and honored leader. He insisted fighting would only bring death to everyone.

"Already we're hearing from good-hearted *Wihio*," the Kettle explained. "They have promised to punish the men who killed our brothers and sisters. If we strike the people on Platte River, we're no different from the crazy ones."

"Which path will you walk?" Wolf asked Buffalo Horn when Black Kettle decided to break away and turn east.

"I'm troubled by the killing," Horn explained. "Black Kettle's right about that. Too many helpless ones are being killed."

"Your wife's father walks on the other side," Wolf

pointed out. "Your uncle, too. We've turned away too often. Come and join us. The *Suhtai* would welcome a man with far-seeing eyes. We won't ignore your dreams."

"I have an obligation," Horn insisted. "Black Kettle's too old to carry the load alone."

"I understand, Horn," Wolf said, sadly clasping his cousin's hands. "Do you remember that time when you, I, and Curly raced ponies along Horse Creek?"

"Yes," Horn admitted. "That was a remembered time."

"We three were once like the branches of an oak, that strong, but now . . ."

"We each have our path to walk. If yours leads you along Platte River, be careful. The hot bloods will get good men killed."

"We're running out of good men," Wolf observed. "I'm sorry to see another ride away."

"Not so far," Horn vowed. "Maybe we'll hunt Bull Buffalo together this summer. You, me, our brothers. Ayyyy! It, too, will be a remembered time!"

"Yes," Wolf agreed. He doubted it would happen, though. There was an odor of death in the winter air.

It wasn't long after Black Kettle's departure that raiders set off to strike the ranches along Platte River. The main bands crossed the river and worked their way north, into safer country less vulnerable to *Wihio* soldiers. Wolf later learned that one party of soldiers had actually followed the big camp and attacked Cherry Creek only a day after the last band departed the place.

Big Crow organized thirty Elks into a war party. He intended to strike a small trading post along Lodgepole Creek.

"Come and lead us," Crow said, offering a pipe to Wolf Running. "This time we have no hot bloods along."

"I have no power to offer you," Wolf explained as he declined the pipe. "You saw how the *Wihio* bullet tore my shield. I have to restore its power."

"We understand, brother," Big Crow answered. "Do what's needed. We'll wait for your return."

Many younger *Suhtai* grumbled about the delay. Red Hawk and High Flyer quieted such complaints, though.

"Remember, our brother always rides where the danger's greatest," Flyer boasted. "Who's the first man to help someone whose horse is killed? Who makes charms to protect the youngest of us? Who suffers so that his dreams can guide the people?"

The other young Elks hung their heads. Half of them recalled such a rescue, and all of them wore Wolf's elk tooth charms behind an ear.

"*Nah nih,* we trust you to do what's best," Red Hawk explained when Wolf prepared to leave the camp for the isolation of the nearby hills. "I'll go along to watch."

"Not this time," Wolf replied, resting a hand on his younger brother's shoulder. "It's my sons who need watching."

"Flyer and Morning Hawk can do that."

"I have three sons," Wolf pointed out. "With three uncles nearby, one can watch them while the others hunt."

Or escape, Wolf thought.

"Then take Stands Long," Red Hawk suggested. "At least invite some boy to tend a fire."

"Long ago, in the grandfathers' time, Sweet Medicine set off alone to craft the first medicine shield," Wolf explained. "Solitude is a powerful thing. It's power I need to remake this shield, to help me find a path for us to walk. My dreams have been empty too long."

"You always know what's best, *Nah nih.* Remember, though, in Sweet Medicine's time, the *Wihio* were far away."

"Few ride where I'm going," Wolf assured his brother. "Very few."

In truth, Wolf was less than certain just where he *was* going. He knew the high country north of both forks of Platte River, though, and there were many high, lonely places there. Once he would have consulted the old men or invited a dream, but the old men he had once trusted were dead, and the dream didn't come. He chose to allow *Heammawihio,* the Great Mystery, to direct him. He sensed there would be signs. He only had to follow them.

When he told Sun Walker Woman that he was leaving, she didn't argue. She was a chief's daughter and understood some of the mysteries of the medicine trail. The boys only reluctantly let their father go, though. He had been gone too frequently that winter—hunting or raiding. They were young, and even a few days seemed like a long time for their father to be gone.

"It won't be a few days, will it?" Sun Walker asked when Wolf placed his shield in its heavy elk hide cover.

"I don't know," he replied. "Only *Heammawihio* can know the length of my path."

"Come back to us, Wolf," she pleaded.

"I will," he vowed. "When I have restored the harmony of my world."

That afternoon when Wolf Running left the *Suhtai* camp, the sun was shining brightly in a cloudless sky. Wolf saw this as a hopeful sign. By nightfall he regretted the clouds' departure. The ground was frozen hard, and the air had an icy bite to it. He managed to make camp in a crevice between two boulders. Shielded by the wind there, he kindled a fire and sang an ancient *Suhtai* prayer.

"*Heammawihio,* hear me.
 I'm nothing beside the great rocks and tall trees.
 A bird may fly and a fish may swim, but what can man do?
 Lead me to the path that will restore my harmony.
 Give me eyes to see the beauty You have placed all
 around me.
 Heammawihio, guide me."

He sang the prayer again and again. He danced beside the fire, fighting the cold as he stared overhead at the countless stars. He continued until exhaustion overpowered him. Then he wrapped himself in his warmest hides and huddled beside the fire.

The next morning he awoke with the sun. A snowy mist returned to the land, and he made little progress. The trails were icy, and his horse found no footing. For a time Wolf tried to ride through the snow, but the drifts there were too deep. He quickly found himself trapped, and it required all his strength to free his horse and return to the trail.

The third day a blizzard blew down from the north, and he was forced to seek the shelter of a cave. Fortunately the opening was large enough for his horse. The animal might have frozen outside. The storm continued for two more days. Snows deepened, and Wolf fought off a creeping despair. Each night he sang and danced, hoping to invite a dream. The final night he cut his flesh and ignored his growing hunger. The strips of buffalo meat he had brought with him were nearly gone anyway. He deemed it best to undertake the fast by choice.

Always before, suffering had hurried a dream. As Wolf ran the blade of an old flint knife along the scarred flesh of his chest, he felt the trickle of warm blood run down onto his belly. He made like cuts on his arms. The bleeding induced a fever, and as he danced, Wolf began seeing things. First there was a giant grizzly bear. Later a badger appeared. Finally Snow Wolf stepped out of the shadows.

"Brother, are you lost?" the phantom called.

"I'm confused," Wolf answered. "Once I knew what to do, but now I don't."

"Once man walked the world like the four-leggeds," Snow Wolf whispered. "He was nothing. *Heammawihio* felt sad, so He raised the pitiful thing onto its hind legs and gave him power over all the beasts of the earth. His was the bow, the knife. He had but to respect life, to make the appropriate prayers, and all would be his.

"Once you rode with far-seeing eyes, and you killed only reluctantly the creatures of the world. Now your heart is torn with anger. You strike hard at those you call enemy, even though they are your brother creatures, too. Renew yourself. Cast out the anger. Walk with harmony, and the old power will also return."

"And my shield?" Wolf asked.

"Sew the tear with the sinew of a brother wolf," Snow Wolf explained. "Suffer hunger while you mend it. The power will return."

Wolf felt his legs give way, and he collapsed to the floor
of the cave. His vision blurred, but he sensed something
nearby. His horse stomped the ground. Wolf felt something
warm touch his bare shoulder, but when he tried to touch
it, there was nothing there.

He fell into a deep sleep. In his dreams he saw Snow
Wolf racing through the snowdrifts, urging him again and
again to remember the old ways, to strike only out of need,
and to respect all living things. He finally awoke in a sweat
two days later. A terrible hunger gnawed at his insides,
but he disdained food. Instead he gazed in amazement at
the body of a great gray wolf.

"Brother Wolf," he whispered, touching the beast's
flanks. It was cold. The creature had crept in out of the
snowdrifts to die beside that fire. Wolf spoke the words of
a mourning prayer and drew out his flint knife. As Snow
Wolf had directed, he cut sinew from the dead wolf and
used it to close the tear in the hide. He wrapped the splin-
tered willow frame with sinew as well. Finally he drew
the two long canine teeth from the wolf and tied them to
the shield.

"I know you, brother," Wolf told the dead creature.
"You, too, are a warrior who has fought long and hard.
Now you're alone, and you've come to this place to begin
the long walk up Hanging Road to the other side. Ayyyy!
You've helped me restore my medicine."

Wolf Running was different, though. He could not ease
his own suffering while the helpless ones continued to
need him. Now there were sons to start up Man's Road.
Brothers to see married. A people to guide to a better future.

"I understand, *Heammawihio*," Wolf whispered as he
stoked the fire. "I had forgotten the old ways I learned as
a boy. I have remade the sacred shield. I have remade
myself. You have showed me the path to walk, and I will
keep my feet upon it."

chapter
3

THE MORNING FOLLOWING HIS VISION, Wolf Running
ate the last strips of dried buffalo meat that he had
brought along. He melted snow for drinking water and
smeared a healing paste onto the cuts on his chest and
arms. Gradually Wolf regained his senses. The following
day he mounted his horse and rode homeward.

He did not know precisely where Long Dog intended to
move the *Suhtai* camp, but as he made his way south
across the frozen hills and icy streams, he spied small parties of *Lakota* raiders. They directed him to where Long
Dog's band had erected their lodges along Lodgepole
Creek.

"Ayyyy!" High Flyer shouted when Wolf finally
reached the *Suhtai* camp. "Our brother's returned!"

Red Hawk and Stands Long rushed to where Wolf wearily rolled off his pony. Hawk took the horse in hand, and
Stands Long helped his brother-friend along to the camp
circle.

"You had the dream?" Stands Long whispered.

"I remade the shield," Wolf explained. "And myself."

"It's good," Stands Long declared. "The *Lakotas* brought us a pipe. We have a decision to make."

"To fight?"

"To join the raiding. To remain here or turn south. Or maybe to head north into the mountains."

"There's to be a council?" Wolf asked.

"Tonight," Stands Long explained. "I hoped you would return in time. The Elks rely on your strong voice. The young men listen to you."

"They may not hear what they expect," Wolf warned.

"They expect you to tell them what you've seen in your dreams. You'll say what you think's the best thing to do. Wherever you lead, plenty will follow."

Wolf sighed. That was the trouble. He didn't want anyone to follow. How could a man be certain of his own path? When others followed, it only became more difficult!

That afternoon Wolf Running sat beside a warming fire, sharing old stories with his little sons and filling his belly with broiled beef strips and fry bread. The pony boys also watched over twenty or thirty stolen *Wihio* cows, so there was fresh meat in the camp. Sun Walker also made a soup of peas and carrots.

"The raiders have shared their wealth," she explained, pointing to a group of children wearing bright shirts crafted from trader's cloth.

"Yes," Wolf said, nodding sadly. "The bluecoats will come and punish us for this. You know that."

"They'll attack us anyway," she grumbled. "As they did our relatives at Sand Creek. We might as well warm ourselves with their cloth and eat their cows."

That night as he sat with the other Elks and pondered what to do, Wolf heard his own words thrown back at him by Long Dog. The Dog, with young sons in his lodge, argued against joining the raiders.

"Our *Oglala* friends keep their winter camps farther north," Long Dog pointed out. "It's one thing for a man alone to strike the *Wihio* ranches. We have to consider the helpless ones."

"Yes," Wolf said, rising to speak. "We do. I have little

sons, your own grandsons, Dog. Are they safe here? I walk around and see few guards. Have the scouts gone out looking for bluecoats? It would be better for our women and children to be up north, too."

"Or with the peace people farther east," Long Dog suggested.

"I won't camp there," Wolf insisted. "If the bluecoats are angry, they'll strike those camps first."

"Are you for taking up the *Lakota* pipe?" Long Dog asked.

"Tell us what your dream told you," Stands Long urged. "Help us find our path."

"Yes," others added. "Tell us."

Wolf stared at their eager faces and closed his eyes. In his mind he saw Snow Wolf running through the clouds. No words came, though. Wolf would have to find his own.

"I saw many things," he explained. "Once, long ago, before Horse came to the people, before any of us saw our first *Wihio,* Sweet Medicine gave his power to us. He taught the Elks about the blue racer. He made our medicine rattles. He explained how we should carry the crooked lance."

"Yes," the others agreed. "We remember the stories."

"We've forgotten much, though," Wolf told them. "When *Heammawihio* first gave us the bow, he warned us its aim would be true so long as we walked the world humbly. We hunted in the old way, with stone tips on our arrows and prayers upon our lips. We killed with reverence. Our hearts remained free of anger, and we cut no pieces from our enemies' bodies to wear as trophies.

"Now I watch our young men cut the dead. I see people who never dared to count coup on a living enemy touch the dead and tie feathers in their hair. They tie scalps to their shirts and boast about the brave heart deeds they never performed. Ayyyy! It's a bad thing."

"You haven't seen the slaughtered children!" Broken Wing cried. He and his family had camped at Sand Creek. Although he had yet to mark his fifteenth summer, the Elks had invited him to join them. He had nowhere else to go.

"I've seen them," Wolf argued. "My own cousin told me of it. Like an eagle's claw, it tore at my heart."

"We've done nothing to the bluecoats that they didn't do to my brothers," Broken Wing complained.

"It's probably true," Wolf admitted. "Most *Wihio* are crazy. They don't understand how a man must walk the sacred path, living in harmony with his world. With them, killing is a hunger they have to satisfy. Is that how it is with you, brother?"

Broken Wing stared at his toes. A solemn hush flooded the Elk council. Finally Long Dog rose.

"Once we were strong enough to run every enemy," the chief declared. "Now, look at what we've become. We're not all of us, ten bands, as strong as the *Suhtai* alone used to be."

"I can't remember those days," Broken Wing said, speaking slowly and with a new respectful tone. "I have no grandfather to tell me the old stories. When we ride to hunt Bull Buffalo, I'll have no father to follow. Wolf Running says we must not hunger to kill these white men who have killed our relatives. How can I forget my pain?"

"You can't!" Big Horn, another of the younger Elks, shouted. "Look around you, brothers. Our camp is filled with good things. Why? Because we've taken them from the white ranches and traders."

There was a murmur of agreement, and Long Dog gazed helplessly at Wolf. It was Stands Long Beside Him who rose to talk, though.

"It's one thing to ride down on helpless ranchers," he observed. "We all know why there are so few bluecoats on Platte River. The *Wihio* are busy fighting each other in the eastern country. I've spoken with the mixed blood traders' sons about it. That war's coming to an end. Soon there will be more bluecoats than any of us can count with nothing to do but kill our people.

"Before they come, we can raid and kill. Afterward we must have a peace or see ourselves die. Not just you and I. We're Elks, and it's appropriate for us to die fighting our enemies. But what of the little ones? The women? Will it ease your hurt, Wing, to listen as I mourn my dead brothers? If Wolf cuts his hair because his sons are gone, will that help yours grow back?"

"It's a hard thing, knowing what's best," Long Dog observed. "We're warriors, and our blood grows hot to strike the enemy. We have obligations to the helpless ones, though."

"They'll die anyway," Big Horn insisted.

"It's easy for a man without sons to talk that way," Long Dog said, staring hard at Big Horn.

"Maybe he can capture a *Wihio* woman and make her his wife," Younger Dog, the chief's eldest son, said, grinning.

"He's failed to capture any *Suhtai*'s heart," Red Hawk added. "Even when he offered three ponies, he couldn't arrange a match with the Arapahos."

"We're not in a hunting camp," Long Dog scolded. "A council's no place for taunts."

"He's right," Wolf agreed. "We have serious decisions to make. The *Lakotas* have sent us a pipe."

"Your dreams have shown you a path, brother," Stands Long whispered. "Tell us what we should do."

"I can't speak for everyone," Wolf announced. "I wear no chief's bonnet. My way is a quiet way. I walk the world modestly, mindful of what I am. Our brothers, the *Lakotas,* are good men to follow. The fighting's here, all around us, and I don't see how we can turn away from it."

"Ayyyy!" Big Horn screamed. "We'll fight!"

"It's not enough, though," Wolf argued. "We must leave good men behind to watch our camp, to guard the helpless ones. When we fight, we must remember the old admonitions. We fight honorably, and we kill reluctantly, with reverence. We spare the helpless."

"No," Big Horn growled, rising. "We've heard all this before, and it always gets us killed."

"No, it's the hot bloods that do that," Long Dog barked. "I saw you spoil the surround at the fort. We might have celebrated a great victory in the Sand Hills, but you broke away and ran ahead. You killed nobody, and the bluecoats got away.''

"You would have waited for them to shoot us, old man,'' Big Horn replied.

"This is how it always is,'' Long Dog said, frowning. "We are no council. There's no harmony anywhere.''

"Sit here and smoke,'' Big Horn urged. "We'll bring you beef to chew and tobacco to smoke. Leave the fighting to us.''

As Big Horn and a handful of others marched away, Wolf Running turned respectfully toward Long Dog.

"I can do nothing,'' the chief announced. "You see how it is. They don't hear my words.''

"We're not all fools,'' Broken Wing declared, gazing around the council at his elders. "We only wait for someone to lead us.''

"I won't lead my sons to their deaths,'' Long Dog announced, folding his hands across his chest.

"The *Lakota* pipe still waits for an answer,'' Stands Long pointed out. "Wolf?''

"We'll smoke the pipe,'' Wolf said somberly. "I'll lead those who choose to go with me. We'll see to the safety of the defenseless ones, too, though.''

"Ayyyy!'' his companions howled. "It's a good plan.''

Wolf Running was far from certain of it.

Long Dog also had doubts. The next morning he announced that he was moving his camp farther north, away from Lodgepole Creek and across the northern fork of Platte River.

"I intended to keep half the warriors near your camp,'' Wolf explained when he learned of his father-in-law's decision. "It's not possible if you leave.''

"I know your heart is with us, Wolf,'' the chief said, clasping the younger man's hands. "There are too many hot bloods around here, though. They'll bring more trouble than either of us can hold off. It's no good fighting the *Wihio* when your thoughts are back in camp. You'll only find your death.''

"I understand your decision.'' Wolf felt a chill spread

through his insides, and he shivered. He felt cut off, separated from his wife and sons when he needed them most of all.

"Don't worry," Long Dog urged. "My sons and I will see to the needs of the helpless ones. We're only twenty lodges. Many of the men are keeping their families here."

"It's probably better to divide the camp," Wolf said, not really believing it. "We used to split apart when the hard face moons came."

"Yes," Long Dog agreed. "It was always a good idea."

As his father-in-law departed, Wolf prepared himself for the coming farewell. When he entered the camp circle, though, he saw that his own lodge remained erect amid the collapsed poles and rolled skins on either side.

"I'll ask High Flyer and Red Hawk to help break it down," Wolf told Sun Walker Woman. "Your father explained—"

"For a long time, I lived in his lodge," she broke in. "Now I have sons who need to walk beside their father."

"It's not our people's way for a woman to leave her band," Wolf argued.

"Perhaps not, but my father won't complain. His burden's heavy enough."

"And mine?" Wolf asked.

"You would worry anyway," she insisted. "You took up the *Lakota* pipe, didn't you? We're not without friends in their camps."

"Their camps are also in the northern country."

"Not all," Sun Walker explained. "There's an *Oglala* camp a day's ride from here. You have cousins there."

"You won't miss the *Suhtai* ways? *Lakotas* speak differently. They—"

"Hah!" she interrupted. "How many women in my father's camp came from the *Oglala* or *Sicangu* bands? I know their words almost as well as you. Our sons, too, will learn. Already our peoples share the same hunting camps. So many of us have both tribes' blood that it's sometimes hard to determine who isn't related."

"You're certain?"

"I am," she declared. "Now, ask your brothers to help break down the lodge if you're too busy, but understand. We're not going north."

"I'll send them," he explained. "Stands Long and I are riding to bring the pipe back to the *Lakotas*. I've heard that my cousin Curly's there. It's a good thought, riding with him again."

Sun Walker smiled and drew him close. He was glad she was staying, but he was also troubled by the thought that his family would be in danger.

Shortly after Wolf Running bid farewell to Long Dog and the main *Suhtai* camp, he helped his brothers load the last of his possessions onto a travois crafted from the long pine lodge poles and the heavy buffalo hide covering. Morning Hawk was hopping about with one nephew or another on his slender shoulders, and Wolf managed to laugh. His youngest brother had been little more than a child when Wolf and Sun Walker wed, and it was sometimes difficult for them to realize that he now dwelled in young men's lodge.

"He's plucked hairs from his chin," Red Hawk said, reading Wolf's thoughts. "You won't be able to leave him behind with the pony boys any longer. He's eager to win a man's name."

"Why shouldn't he come along?" Wolf asked. "He's nearly as old as Broken Wing. You two will be watchful, though? If I'm to lead, I can't hold his safety above that of the others."

"No," High Flyer agreed. "*Nah nih*, why are we joining the raiders? You have no heart for that. Everyone sees it."

"We have to do something," Wolf told them. "From the time I first stepped onto warrior's road, I've never turned away from an enemy. It's fine to talk of ranchers and stores, but there are bluecoats on Platte River, too. They're the true enemy."

"All *Wihio* are our enemies," High Flyer argued. "I know you still favor the traders' sons at Fort Laramie, but if it came to fighting, they would stand beside the other whites.''

"You don't know them," Wolf insisted.

"We know their kind," Red Hawk growled. "They sell us their goods at a high price. They grow rich and fat at our expense."

"Not many of them are growing fat or rich these days," Wolf remarked as he pointed to the stolen cattle Long Dog's people were herding north.

"Not many of us are fat, either," Red Hawk said, nodding toward Wind's Whisper. The boy's legs, sheathed in elk hide leggings, were like the brittle branches of willow trees.

"It's a hard thing to see," Wolf confessed. "Winter's always a difficult time, though."

"We'll fatten the little ones on buffalo meat this summer," Flyer vowed.

"Watch them while I'm away," Wolf said, clasping the hands of his two oldest brothers.

"Soon we'll be with the *Oglalas*," Red Hawk declared. "It will be good to see our cousins again."

"Yes," Wolf agreed. "It's been too long."

Once all the possessions were loaded and Wolf had spoken to his children, he located Stands Long. The two of them then set off toward the nearby *Oglala* encampment. As Wolf rode along Lodgepole Creek, he couldn't help sensing those were important steps he was taking.

"We've started down a new trail," Stands Long remarked as if to mirror Wolf's thoughts. "It's a good notion, having strong friends nearby."

"We may need them," Wolf replied. "If you're right about the bluecoats coming here, even the *Lakotas* will need friends."

"Yes," Stands Long agreed. "We all will."

chapter

4

SUN WALKER WOMAN HAD BEEN right about the *Ogla-las*. Their camps were only a short distance away. The smoke of their campfires betrayed their location, and Wolf had little trouble reaching them.

"No scouts," Stands Long grumbled as they approached the first of the camp circles. "We could run half their ponies."

"I won't entrust my children to these people," Wolf declared, turning away from the first circle. The second was no better, but farther ahead Wolf spied a small group of pony boys watching over a hundred good horses. The camp beyond was shielded by the banks of Lodgepole Creek on one side and protected by three wary horsemen on the other.

Wolf studied the faces of the riders as they rode out from the camp. "I know him," Wolf said, pointing to the one on the left.

"Yes," Stands Long agreed. "It's Storm Eagle, who married the wife of Horn's dead uncle."

"Hau!" Wolf called to the *Oglalas* in their own language. "We're friends," he added, holding up the pipe.

"Hau!" Storm Eagle shouted in reply. "You've come to join us?"

"Yes," Wolf told the chief. "Some of us. Others have gone north."

"Long Dog?" the Eagle asked. Wolf nodded, and the *Oglala* chief sighed. "I hoped that he would come. He's known as a good fighter. Dog's careful, and he holds the hot bloods back."

"He did once, but now he's tired of trying," Wolf explained. "He worries about his sons."

"He's not the same man I remember," Storm Eagle said, sighing. "When I was a boy in my mother's camp, he led the young men. Well, we're all older. How many *Suhtai* are coming?"

"Maybe twenty will follow me," Wolf said, gazing at the youthful faces of Storm Eagle's companions. "Most are young."

"Some young men are hungry to win honor," Storm Eagle noted. "Others rush ahead and spoil traps. Which kind ride with you?"

"I was with the decoys on Platte River," Wolf reminded the *Oglalas*. "I led the bluecoats to the Sand Hills. When the hot bloods went ahead, I stood and protected the reckless ones. Those who follow me will fight with honor, and they won't run away from their friends."

"That's good to know," Storm Eagle said, nodding with approval. "Come and follow me to our camp. We'll smoke that pipe and make plans."

"I'll ride back and bring the others," Stands Long volunteered.

"Be careful," Storm Eagle advised. "There's been a lot of raiding. Our scouts saw bluecoats on the river yesterday."

"I'll be watchful," Stands Long promised. He then turned his horse and rode away. Wolf continued on to the *Oglala* camp with Storm Eagle.

Several snows had come and gone since Wolf had spent time with his *Lakota* cousins. As he rode among the *Ogla-*

las, he saw a few familiar faces, but he had trouble putting names to the people. Only after dismounting and giving his horse to a pony boy did Wolf spy a recognizable body. Before Wolf could shout a greeting, Storm Eagle called the slim young man closer.

"Wolf, here's a man to know," the Eagle declared. "Crazy Horse."

Crazy Horse paused a moment before approaching. Wolf merely grinned.

"I once knew a strange boy fond of racing ponies against the Crows," Wolf noted. "We called him Curly, but that wasn't much of a name."

"My father gave me a better one," Horse explained as he gripped his cousin's hand. "His own. Now he's called Worm, a poor name for a man of the people to carry, but he says it brings us both power."

"Do you also have a wife?" Wolf asked.

"No," Crazy Horse said, staring out past the pony herd. "Tell me. Do you still talk with the white traders?"

"It's been a long time now," Wolf confessed. "My people have suffered."

"We'll punish the child killers," Crazy Horse vowed.

"Yes," Wolf agreed. "I've brought the *Oglala* pipe. Did you send it to me?"

"I sent it," Storm Eagle explained. "Crazy Horse advised it, though."

"It's appropriate," Crazy Horse added. "I'm a shirt wearer."

Wolf nodded his understanding. Each soldier society possessed shirts adorned with charms and carrying the hair of dead enemies. The man who wore such a shirt was a valued warrior who pledged, not unlike a lance carrier, to place the welfare of his brothers above his own. Crazy Horse, like his cousin, stood tall in the eyes of his fellow warriors in spite of his youth. Once people would have considered a man of twenty-two summers too young. No longer.

"We'll smoke later, when the others arrive," Storm Eagle said. "Cousins should talk."

"It's a good idea," Crazy Horse replied. "We'll walk along the creek."

"Yes," Wolf agreed. "There's much to share."

After they walked out past the last lodge, Crazy Horse stopped.

"I know most of it," he told Wolf. "Storm Eagle's wife spoke of the killing. She also told how our cousin, who now calls himself Buffalo Horn, chose to remain with Black Kettle. You didn't."

"I'm no chief to decide things," Wolf insisted. "My dreams guide me. I can only go where they lead."

"We've run the whites on Platte River," Crazy Horse boasted. "We've killed a few and captured many horses and cows. The hot bloods are growing foolish, though. They don't take precautions."

"Such as guarding their camp," Wolf observed. "Have you spotted *Wihio* soldiers?"

"Only a few. Some at Julesburg and some farther east. They're in no hurry to fight us."

"Their war with the graycoats continues?"

"I've heard that it does," Crazy Horse said, sighing. "The loafers at the forts say that, but who can know for certain? The *Arapahos* warn that more bluecoats will be coming soon, though."

"The grandfathers saw it all," Wolf declared with a scowl. "We should have fought them before, when we were strong and there were fewer of them."

"Maybe," Crazy Horse said, sighing. "If we had, they might have killed all of us by now. Who can say what's best?"

"Only Man Above knows."

"So, tell me of your wife. Is she pretty?"

"Yes," Wolf said, grinning. "She's called Sun Walker Woman."

"Ah, Long Dog's daughter," Crazy Horse said, smiling as he remembered her. "You have sons?"

"Three. Wind's Whisper, the oldest, will mark his seventh summer when the grass greens again."

"It's good that my cousin's bringing sons into the

world. The people will need good men to lead them.''

"You already lead," Wolf observed. "It's unusual for such a young man to be a shirt wearer.''

"Too many of the old, remembered men are dead," Crazy Horse observed. "It's often hard, putting the needs of all the others before my own.''

"Our family has always expected it, though.''

"We've had to prove ourselves.'' Crazy Horse sat on a large rock and stared into the sunlight glittering off the placid water. Wolf knew that his cousin was recalling the taunts that the older boys had once heaped upon them. *Light skins, Wihio hearts,* and others things besides. Even as men the cousins' skin remained lighter than their *Lakota* and *Tsis tsis tas* companions. Worse, Crazy Horse's hair retained traces of its old yellow-brownish tint.

"That's in the past now," Wolf declared.

"Is it?'' Horse asked. "I hear the whispers when I sit in council with the other men. Not so long ago, when I wished to take a wife, the others urged me to ride against the Crows. When I returned, the girl lived in the lodge of another man.''

"We'll find you someone else," Wolf suggested.

"I will never live with anyone else. I also have dreams, Wolf. I won't know happy times, and I'll have no sons.''

"That's a difficult path to walk.''

"When we were boys, we prayed that Man Above would send us the difficult things to do. I never expected it to be otherwise.''

"A man's path takes turns, though," Wolf pointed out. "Once, not so long ago, I only saw darkness. *Heamma-wihio* sent me a dream, and I hope to walk a brighter road.''

"You've come here with the pipe, Wolf," Crazy Horse reminded his cousin. "When did you ever find warmth on warrior's road? There will only be more fighting and more dying.''

"Those are strange words for a shirt wearer to speak.''

"Perhaps, but we two swam Horse Creek as brothers.

We've mourned our dead relatives together. There can't be any lies between us, Wolf.''

"No," Wolf agreed.

Later that afternoon, after the small band of *Suhtai* added their lodges to Storm Eagle's camp, the men met in council and smoked the *Oglala* pipe. Each man chose for himself whether to join the fight or remain in camp. The majority agreed to follow Storm Eagle, Crazy Horse, and Wolf Running.

"We'll make the *Wihio* suffer!" Broken Wing vowed.

"We'll do what's necessary," Wolf cautioned. "We'll also protect the helpless ones.''

Wolf Running also insisted that the warriors prepare themselves properly. The *Oglalas* erected a sweat lodge, and each man purified himself before making his personal medicine. Wolf painted his face yellow, like a morning sun, and he once again wore only the three feathers in his hair. He smiled with approval when Crazy Horse appeared. He wore only a single hawk feather in his hair. Except for a small stone tied behind one ear and a red-tailed hawk worn atop his head, the *Oglala* shirt wearer appeared no different from the young pony boys who followed to tend the spare horses.

"It's good that men of the people display modesty," Wolf remarked to his cousin.

"Yes," Crazy Horse agreed. "I wish my cousin wasn't riding a white horse. It marks him as a man the *Wihio* will want to kill.''

"On a summer day, it would mark me," Wolf argued. "In winter, it's nothing.''

"He rides that pony in summer, too," Stands Long observed. "He's not so easy to kill, though.''

"That's good," Crazy Horse said, grinning as he waved to his tardy companions. "We have too few good men already.''

Once the *Lakotas* and their *Suhtai* allies assembled, Wolf counted forty men. Seven pony boys followed along to herd the relief horses. A short distance from the *Oglala* camps Big Horn appeared with eight others. Storm Eagle rode out to admonish the hot bloods, and only when he was convinced that they would comply with his wishes did the chief allow the hot bloods to join the raid.

"It's good that we're together again!" Big Horn cried as he rode past Wolf. "Ayyyy! We'll count coup today!"

"The *Oglalas* should have driven them off," Stands Long grumbled.

"We're few enough," Wolf pointed out. "Besides, they would have followed anyway."

"You know they won't wait," Stands Long complained. "Look at them! They've made no preparations."

The newcomers attached themselves to Crazy Horse, but he turned and chased them away.

"My power's been broken by the hot bloods too many times," Crazy Horse told Wolf. "Let them follow the pony boys."

Wolf also worried about the hot bloods, but he said nothing. Storm Eagle had sent out the pipe, and he alone had the obligation to maintain the harmony of the war party. Wolf concentrated on the welfare of his brothers. Morning Hawk rode alongside young Broken Wing. The two youngsters betrayed both their eagerness to strike the enemy and the uncertainty that grew out of inexperience.

"We remember our promise," Red Hawk assured Wolf. "We'll watch them."

All that day the warriors rode south toward Platte River. Only at dusk did they approach the river road, and then it was too late to attack. Storm Eagle chose a nearby ranch as the target, but he insisted that it would be better to strike at dawn.

"We could take their ponies," Big Horn suggested. "See there. Only one man's watching."

"There are more in the houses and there, in the rocks," Crazy Horse argued. "You only see one of them. Tomorrow we'll be rested, and those men will be tired."

"They'll be able to see us, too," Rock Lizard, another hot blood, complained.

"Are you afraid then?" Broken Wing asked. "We've

painted our faces and performed the sacred prayers. Their bullets won't touch us."

"Dreamer," Lizard muttered. "Old men and dreamers, all of you."

"Be quiet," Storm Eagle demanded. "If you can't share our camp in harmony, leave."

Big Horn quickly interceded, and his companions grew quiet. The hot bloods slept together a short distance from the others that night, and the following morning they joined in the prayers and preparations.

"There's the enemy," Storm Eagle said as he organized the small band into three columns. "We'll strike him hard. We want the animals and the good things they keep in the log store."

"There are women there," Crazy Horse added. "Little children. Some of you are angry with the whites over the Sand Creek killing, but we will harm no helpless ones here."

Broken Wing scowled, and Big Horn argued no white man deserved to live, but Crazy Horse's dark gaze silenced the hot bloods. He then led the first group, a handful of *Oglalas,* toward the ranch. Wolf took the second column in hand and advanced upon a line of outbuildings. Storm Eagle directed the final group against a horse corral and the herd of cattle grazing along the river.

The attack began well. Crazy Horse's band exploded out of a ravine and took the two young white men guarding the main house by surprise. One got off a shot before Crazy Horse clubbed him senseless. The second *Wihio* died in a shower of arrows.

Wolf and his companions easily overran the outbuildings. A white-bearded old man was in a privy, and he jumped out, naked below the waist, and tried to fend off attackers with a hunting knife. It was a comical sight, and the *Suhtai* refused to strike him. Instead they circled around, jeering and touching him with the tips of their bows. Finally he sank to his knees, exhausted, and plunged the knife into his own chest.

"Stay away from him!" Wolf warned when Broken

Wing climbed down to examine the crazed *Wihio*. "He's touched by bad spirits."

Wolf and his little party tore apart the smaller buildings, but there wasn't much inside any of them worth taking. Some of the ranchers made their homes there, but their clothes and blankets were too worn to be of any value. No *Lakota* or *Suhtai* had use of the heavy cowhide saddles, so Wolf ordered the buildings burned. By that time Crazy Horse and the *Oglalas* had driven the surviving defenders out of the ranch house and along to the stronger store building.

The fighting there grew intense. *Wihio* riflemen kept up a hot fire from the small slits cut in the walls of the store, and two *Oglalas* fell, wounded. Wolf noticed the shooting was heaviest on the far side, and he waved his companions toward the back. With Stands Long at his side, Wolf Running charged the back door. Using their ponies for cover, the two warriors avoided a pair of rifle balls sent their way. They jumped from their horses, rolled across the snowy ground, and crawled to the back wall unharmed.

The *Wihio* ranchers faced a difficult choice. They had no chance of striking Wolf and Stands Long without coming out of the store. Wolf, meanwhile, drew a knife and began tearing the hinges from the store's heavy door. He could hear children crying inside, and a woman screamed. The door then opened, and a large *Wihio* stepped out. Stands Long shot an arrow into the hairy-faced storekeeper, and he fell facedown into the snow. Wolf then jumped into the store and slew the first rifleman he encountered.

It was all over in a matter of minutes. Stands Long, Red Hawk, and two others followed Wolf, and the last three white defenders had no chance to turn and fight. A woman huddled with two small children in the far corner. Big Horn stepped through the door and started toward them, and Wolf called to him.

"They're helpless," Wolf declared. "Leave them alone."

"They're white!" Big Horn insisted.

"No!" Broken Wing shouted, blocking Big Horn's path. "They're mine."

The fourteen-year-old approached the terrified woman and touched his bow to her forehead. "I'm first," he whispered. He then counted coup on the youngsters. "I'm an Elk," the boy explained, "and I'm pledged to harm no helpless person."

The whites gazed up in confusion. They understood none of the *Suhtai* and *Tsis tsis tas* words, and soon the *Oglalas* added their language to the discussion. The woman located a large knife, but before she could grab it, Wolf interceded.

"You're safe," Wolf assured the woman as he flung the knife away. "Enough have died already."

She turned sadly toward the hairy-faced man in the doorway, and Wolf nodded his understanding. The oldest of the children, a girl of perhaps twelve summers, stumbled to her father and began weeping. The second child, a boy a year or so younger, dropped to his knees and covered his eyes.

"He could be my brother," Broken Wing said, touching the boy's shoulder. "Or my killer," Wing added as he noticed an empty pistol on the floor. "How can anyone know what to do?"

"It's difficult," Wolf confessed. "It's probably best to trust your heart."

"Not so long ago I would have killed them myself," Broken Wing said, leaning against Wolf's side. "Cut them into pieces as the bluecoats did my mother."

"I understand," Wolf said, scowling. "But doing that would not have restored your family to you. You would have remembered it in your dreams, and even the sweat lodge would not have driven their ghosts from you."

"*Nah nih*, maybe Wing and I should go and help gather the ponies," Morning Hawk said, taking Broken Wing's hand. "There's nothing more to do here."

"You'll watch them?" Broken Wing asked, gazing from Wolf to where Big Horn stood, fuming.

"The killing's finished," Wolf announced. "These three are my responsibility."

"No longer," Storm Eagle said, finally entering the store. "I'll now see to their needs."

"Remember our pledge," Wolf warned.

"I remember everything," Storm Eagle replied. "No *Oglala* will bother these people. No one else will unless he wishes trouble with my people."

The threat clearly disappointed Big Horn, and he muttered something to himself. He then lifted a small barrel from a shelf, pushed the *Wihio* girl out of the doorway, and stormed on outside.

"That man will bring you trouble, *Nah nih*," High Flyer observed when Wolf followed Big Horn outside.

"Yes," Wolf agreed. "If he doesn't find his death first."

"Those are never the ones who die," Crazy Horse added. "They remain like a bad smell, and are just as hard to drive away."

"You're hurt," Wolf said, noticing a bloody slash on Crazy Horse's left forearm.

"A man should have some reminders of the fights he's known," Crazy Horse declared. "Other than the dark dreams."

"Yes," Wolf agreed. "The dreams always come, too."

chapter
5

T HE SMOKE FROM THE BURNING buildings soon attracted attention. First a band of curious *Arapahos*
appeared. Later a larger group of *Lakotas* arrived. Storm
Eagle was doing his best to apportion captured ponies
among the raiding party, but the newcomers began helping
themselves to bolts of cloth and other supplies from the
store. Big Horn spread the word that there were barrels of
whiskey in there, too, and men were soon becoming drunk.

Wolf Running held only contempt for warriors who
turned away from the sacred path and submitted to the
dizzying effects of *Wihio* whiskey. All too often he had
witnessed good men give away their possessions, sell their
daughters, and abandon their responsibilities in order to
satisfy a craving for the strong drink. Long ago he had
vowed to avoid the crazy liquid, and those closest to him
followed his example. Big Horn, unfortunately, was neither close to Wolf nor prone to following anyone's example.

The trouble started with two *Arapahos*, but it didn't take
long for Big Horn to step into the middle of it. There were

several barrels of whiskey in the store—enough for everyone—but Big Horn claimed it all.

"I found it here!" he insisted. "I was the one who
counted coup! Who are you *Arapahos* to make claims?
You came after the fighting was over."

Wolf also considered Big Horn a go-behind raider.
Stands Long wondered aloud what coup Big Horn had
counted.

"Touching your bow to a whiskey barrel counts for
nothing," Stands Long declared. "They're no different
from you, Big Horn. You take all you can without regard
for anyone else."

The whiskey drinkers paid no attention to such argu-
ments. They only knew there were three barrels left, and
each man intended to take all three for himself. A tall
Arapaho finally stepped in front of Big Horn while two of
his companions attempted to take the barrels. Big Horn
pulled a pistol from his belt and shot the tall man in the
face.

The *Arapaho* was dead before he struck the earth, and
his friends rushed to his side. One began singing a death
chant while others strung their bows or readied their rifles.
Big Horn remained behind only a moment. Then he ran to
his horse, mounted, and fled. The angry *Arapahos* remained behind.

"You've killed our friend!" one of them screamed at
the nearest stranger, a young *Lakota* called Elk Antler.
"Ayyyy! We'll punish you."

Broken Wing boldly approached the *Arapahos*, hoping
to prevent further bloodshed, but an *Arapaho* pushed the
boy aside.

"Brothers, we must stop this," Wolf Running called as
a line of *Tsis tsis tas* and *Lakota* warriors formed to face
the vengeful *Arapahos*. "It's a bad thing, this fighting. We
have enemies enough already."

"He's right," Crazy Horse agreed, joining his cousin.
"Take the whiskey. It's the cause of the trouble."

"No, that man was," an *Arapaho* insisted.

"He's not here," Wolf pointed out. "Why should we

fight? I hold no anger for my brothers. Am I the one you want to kill?''

''Remember,'' Crazy Horse added. ''There are many of us. Do you want to make enemies of us all?''

''No,'' the leader of the *Arapahos,* a smallish man called Blue Water, declared. ''We'll take the whiskey as payment. Also ten ponies.''

Many of the *Lakotas* grumbled that the price was too high, but Wolf offered his own horses.

''It is too high a price,'' Crazy Horse complained. ''You can have the whiskey and three.''

Blue Water nodded his agreement, and Crazy Horse sent for a pipe. The bargain was sealed, and although some of the *Arapahos* vowed that they would find Big Horn later, Blue Water silenced them.

''These good men have healed the injury done to our people,'' the *Arapaho* chief observed. ''We have to leave our bad hearts behind.''

Later, as the *Arapahos* emptied the three whiskey barrels, Wolf wondered if they would even remember their dead friend the following morning.

''Even when we run the *Wihio,* he brings us trouble,'' Stands Long noted when he and Wolf led the way back toward the *Oglala* camp on Lodgepole Creek.

''It wasn't the whiskey,'' Wolf argued. ''It was Big Horn's greed.''

''There are many like him among our people,'' Stands Long said, sighing. ''Sometimes I think they're more dangerous than an army of bluecoats.''

''Sometimes they are,'' Wolf agreed. ''I don't understand how we could have strayed so far from the sacred path.''

''It's hard to know,'' Stands Long replied. ''Harder still to understand.''

Wolf Running agreed. He was still pondering the matter the following day when he walked beside the creek with Sun Walker Woman. She shared his view.

''Not so long ago we honored men who walked the sacred path,'' Sun Walker said, leaning on his weary shoulder. "A man of the people placed the welfare of the helpless above his own interests. Our fathers often went hungry so that the children could eat. How many times have you provided ponies to poor young men?"

"It's expected," Wolf pointed out.

"You're no chief. You could do like most and ignore the poor people. This troublemaker, Big Horn, has never given anyone something they didn't already have. Those of us who walk the world in the old fashion are vanishing. When we're gone, the people will be as shortsighted as the *Wihio*."

"You're wrong," Wolf said, managing a faint smile. "We have sons."

"It's hard for us to walk the sacred path," Sun Walker pointed out. "For them, it will be an even steeper climb."

"Perhaps," Wolf admitted. "But they're our sons. You wouldn't want their walk to be an easy one."

"No, but I don't want it to be a short one, either."

He sighed. Another day they might have found a boulder and sat together beside the creek. Winter's chill still clung to the earth, though, and they continued walking.

In the days that followed, Wolf Running tried to take comfort from the love he shared with Sun Walker and their children. The *Oglalas* continued raiding the ranches and settlements on South Platte River, but Wolf often stayed behind, watching the camp with Stands Long or one of the brothers. Eventually, though, he painted his face, took up his shield, and joined the other raiders. *Oglala* scouts brought word of a party of bluecoats approaching from South Platte River, less than a day's ride away.

"It's best we keep these dark hearts from our camps," Crazy Horse declared.

"He's right," Stands Long argued, and so he and Wolf prepared once more for war.

Crazy Horse led the raiders that day. The *Oglala* shirt wearer insisted that the appropriate prayers be spoken, and he admonished his companions to let their leaders plan the attack. Because most of the warriors were *Oglalas*, Wolf deemed it fitting that Crazy Horse should take charge.

Stands Long and High Flyer complained that they should have been out front, leading the avengers, but Wolf only frowned.

"If the bluecoats are out here, you'll have your chance to kill them," Wolf told his brothers. "See how Broken Wing rides along with us? He more than anyone is entitled to strike the first blow!"

Actually no one struck a blow that day. The bluecoats were farther south than expected, and even when the party split up to scout the broken country, no one spotted a bluecoat. The sun stood high up in the midday sky the following day when the sound of rifles echoing along South Platte River betrayed the bluecoats' whereabouts.

"Ayyyy!" Wolf called, waving his bow in the air over his head. "Follow me!"

Stands Long, Broken Wing, and Morning Hawk, who were close at hand, did follow. High Flyer and Red Hawk came later. When the little band finally spotted a plume of smoke thrown skyward by a burning wagon, Crazy Horse and a line of *Oglalas* also appeared. Ahead, Big Horn and a few others fired rifles at a few bluecoats from the cover of a low sand ridge.

"For once Big Horn's found a proper fight," Crazy Horse observed when he joined his cousin.

"No one's doing much fighting, though," Wolf grumbled. As the firing continued, he identified eight, perhaps nine, *Wihio* shooters. Two still wore their bluecoat soldier coats, but the others had heavier clothes of buffalo or elk hides. They used their two remaining wagons as cover, along with a line of barrels and hides that formed a low wall between the wagons.

"Someone should run the ponies," Crazy Horse pointed out. The animals stirred restlessly behind the wagons. They weren't tethered, nor had the bluecoats bothered to hobble their feet.

"It's for me to do," Broken Wing said, solemnly tying his bow behind him. He then drew out a blanket and kicked his pony into a gallop.

"Once the horses are gone, they're trapped," Wolf noted.

"Even a fool like Big Horn can't spoil it," Stands Long added.

"No, but I have no patience anymore," Crazy Horse muttered. "I have the right!"

"I have the left!" Wolf answered.

"Nothing lives long!" Stands Long sang.

"Only earth and mountain," Wolf sang, finishing the death chant.

The cousins then led their separate columns in snakelike fashion toward the rear of the *Wihio* position. The ponies snorted in anticipation, and Wolf felt a rage rise inside himself. His brothers strung their bows and waited for a signal. Then Broken Wing raced out from a ravine, waving his blanket and screaming like a descending eagle as he chased the startled *Wihio* ponies out past the wagons.

"Look there!" one of the bluecoated *Wihio* shouted, turning to face the new peril.

One other *Wihio* managed to turn in time. The two men made a brave effort to stop their stampeding horses, but it was futile. The dust thrown up by the departing ponies had not yet settled when Wolf and Crazy Horse charged. The first *Wihio* managed to turn back. Had he started an instant earlier, he might have reached the wagons. Instead, Crazy Horse shot him through the chest.

The second man recognized his peril, but instead of fleeing, he aimed his rifle and fired two bullets at Wolf Running. The first struck the ground a few feet short of Wolf's pony. The other hit the hard hump hide of the medicine shield and broke apart.

Wolf never flinched. He raced onward, bent over, and struck his enemy across the forehead with his bow. The bluecoat fell to one knee, dropped his rifle, and clutched his face.

"I'm first!" Wolf shouted as he turned quickly and dashed back to the stricken bluecoat. By then Stands Long had also touched the dazed enemy. Morning Hawk counted the third coup, striking the bluecoat hard with a war ax.

Wolf jumped down from his horse and stared at the glazed eyes of the *Wihio*. The face was familiar. The bluecoat was one of the trappers who had ridden to Fort Laramie to trade.

"You!" the bluecoat gasped as Wolf approached. The *Wihio* was looking at someone else, though. Terror flooded the helpless man's gaze.

"It's for me to do," a young voice called from Wolf's side.

"He knows you," Wolf realized, stepping aside so that young Broken Wing could approach. The *Wihio*'s face was battered and bloody, and he had little chance of surviving. Instead of drawing a weapon, though, he tore open his tunic and grabbed a small skin pouch. He tried to fling it away, but Broken Wing easily located it.

"Tobacco?" the young *Tsis tsis tas* muttered, examining the pouch. Broken Wing's eyes darkened, and for a moment Wolf expected the boy to become sick.

"Wing?" Wolf called.

"This was part of a man!" Broken Wing said, angrily raising the pouch into the air. Wolf saw it, but he refused to believe such a thing possible. The shape, the color . . . No wonder the *Wihio* hoped to lose that pouch!

"Wing?" Wolf called a second time as the young man stumbled.

"Take him," Broken Wing pleaded. "Hold him."

Wolf grabbed one arm, and Stands Long seized the other. Together they lifted the whimpering bluecoat to his feet. Broken Wing tossed his bow aside and drew out a knife. He touched it to the *Wihio*'s throat, but instead of killing him, Wing cut the helpless bluecoat's tunic open. Inside were other trophies—rings, a silver bracelet, and two small ears cut from children! The bluecoat also possessed two scalps. One had tiny shells tied to its braids.

Wolf shuddered. Broken Wing fell back and dropped to his knees.

"He who was my father wore such shells," the young man cried. "That pouch! My father . . ."

Morning Hawk was the first to reach the stunned Broken

Wing. The two young men stared angrily at the terrified *Wihio*.

"Leave him to me," Broken Wing growled.

"It was his father," Wolf told the *Wihio* in English. "His *father!*"

The bluecoat wanted to flee, but he lacked the power of motion, even after Wolf Running and Stands Long Beside Him released their grip. Broken Wing flung the white man onto the ground, dropped a knee onto his chest, and began cutting away his clothing. Then the young man began cutting flesh.

"Don't watch," Wolf warned his youngest brother when Morning Hawk turned back. The boy nodded. They both shuddered when the *Wihio* let out a shrill, ear-piercing scream. It was the first of many. Wolf tried to ignore them.

Just ahead the *Oglalas* were chasing down the last three survivors of the attack. One fell fighting, but the other two surrendered. At first the *Oglalas* treated the white soldiers with respect, but when their *Suhtai* and *Tsis tsis tas* companions searched the wagons, they located other trophies from Sand Creek. Scalps, rings torn from fingers, men's and women's private parts . . . Some of the raiders identified relics of dead relatives. Others gazed into the terrified faces of the captives and read guilt. Those who fell fighting proved to be the fortunate ones that day. Everything that the bluecoats did to Black Kettle's people that horrible day at Sand Creek, the survivors then did to the bluecoats, alive and dead, at South Platte River. Even Big Horn, who had kept clear of the wagons until after Crazy Horse and Wolf had completed their charge, hid his eyes.

"No good will come of this," Stands Long whispered as he and Wolf walked to the river to remove their war paint.

"It tears at the harmony of the world," Wolf observed. "Still, I think seeing such a thing done to our people must have made our young men crazy. Perhaps in killing these dark hearts, they can put the pain behind them."

"Do you believe that?"

"No, but I can hope it will be true. Maybe we can take a sweat and heal ourselves."

"It will take more than steam and sweat to erase this thing from my memory," Stands Long insisted. "And your brothers? Broken Wing?"

"The young always heal faster."

"No one's going to forget this soon," Stands Long argued. "It was a sad day when *Heammawihio* first allowed the two-leggeds to rise above their fellow creatures. No wolf or bear ever preyed upon his own kind."

"We have the power to return to the sacred hoop, though," Wolf said, gazing hard at the icy stream. "The old ones who introduced me to the sacred path once explained that no matter how far a man strays, he can always turn back, restore harmony to his world. When this is finished, we'll wash ourselves and take a sweat. We'll speak the old *Suhtai* prayers, and their power will bring us back to ourselves."

"Will it?" Stands Long asked.

"It has to," Wolf replied. "It's all I know to do."

"Will it be enough this time, old friend? I'm far from certain."

Wolf sighed. If Stands Long had doubts, what about the others? What about himself?

That afternoon Big Horn and his little band remained at the river, celebrating what they saw as *their* victory and dividing the plunder. Wolf and Crazy Horse, whose bands had done most of the fighting and all of the killing, took only the *Wihio* ponies. They buried the retrieved pieces of the people killed at Sand Creek and hoped that would allow their ghosts to reach the other side.

"Did you take the hair of the bluecoat who killed your relatives?" Morning Hawk asked Broken Wing when Wolf led them away from the river.

"I cut the man's hair," Broken Wing admitted. "And other things, too. But when I looked at what I did, I remembered the others, those who were my father and my mother. I remember them enough. I left the man's hair behind."

"It's probably best," Morning Hawk observed. "My brother says we'll take a sweat. Maybe that will make us whole again."

"Maybe," Broken Wing said. He seemed unconvinced.

Morning Hawk then nudged his pony forward until he rode alongside Wolf Running.

"*Nah nih*, my friend's lost his way," the boy whispered. "Can you help him find it?"

"No one's ever so lost that he can't find his way back," Wolf declared. "I'll help, but only Broken Wing can restore the harmony of his world."

"You'll manage it," the boy insisted. "Your dreams will show you how."

Will they? Wolf wondered.

chapter
6

BROKEN WING WAS NOT THE only one who acted strangely following the fight with the Sand Creek murderers. Wolf Running saw the memory of that day etched into the foreheads of his brothers. As Wolf led the way northward toward the camp on Lodgepole Creek, he couldn't help noticing his brothers' brooding faces. No one spoke. When night fell, the raiders made a small camp on a snowy hillside overlooking the creek. Wolf listened to the stirrings of the young men that night, and he winced when he heard their voices cry out in the darkness.

"It's not only the sight of so many pieces of our people," Stands Long declared the following morning. "It's the killing we've done. The cutting! When have we ever stepped so far from the sacred hoop?"

"I never imagined it possible," Wolf said, shuddering.

"I'm not surprised when *Wihio* do things like that," Stands Long added. "But to see our own men cut and tear at bodies like that!"

"The world is changing," Wolf said, sighing. "Once these were good places to ride. The grandfathers made their winter camps on Lodgepole Creek and Platte River. They never knew half the trouble we've seen here this year."

"Long Dog was right," Stands Long observed. "We should have gone north."

"We're not old men," Wolf pointed out. "A warrior can't turn away as easily as an old man chief. You told me I was obligated to lead."

"Maybe I was wrong."

"Could we have left the young men to follow Big Horn? If we had gone north, they would have remained here anyway."

"It's true," Stands Long declared. "Once we always knew what was best. Now we're only confused."

"We'll build a sweat lodge and help Broken Wing and the other young men purify themselves. Maybe afterward we'll ride north and rejoin the *Suhtai.*"

"Yes," Stands Long agreed. "This is a road better put behind us."

The others seemed in agreement. After chewing some strips of dried buffalo meat, Wolf silently walked through the snow to his horse and prepared to renew the northward ride.

"He smells the end of his journey," Morning Hawk said when the horse began stomping its feet.

"Maybe he's only cold," Wolf said, drawing his youngest brother close. "He wears no elk hide."

"Yes," the boy admitted. "I'm cold, too."

"I have a warm buffalo robe you can wear."

"It's not that sort of cold," Morning Hawk explained. "It's not the wind or the snow that brings the chill. It's the remembering."

"Yes," Wolf said, clasping the boy's shoulders. "It's not a chill driven off by a fire, either. We'll make a sweat lodge soon, though. We'll ask *Heammawihio* to show us a path back to the sacred hoop."

"Is that what you did after the man who was our father began his long walk?"

"I've often taken a sweat when I became lost. Other times I've invited a dream."

"You'll allow me to go with you this time? And Broken Wing, too?"

"We'll do what's necessary," Wolf promised.

"It may take more than a sweat, *Nah nih*," Red Hawk remarked a short while later. "It wasn't only the young ones who spoke in their sleep."

"I know," Wolf said, staring out across the frozen landscape. "We can only do what we know, though. There's no cure for a whole world gone crazy."

And that, Wolf told himself, was exactly what had happened. How could Morning Hawk, a boy of fifteen summers, be expected to understand? Wolf didn't.

The raiders returned to their camp shortly after midday. The women and children raced out to greet their returning husbands, fathers, and brothers while pony boys took charge of the horses. Wolf lifted each of his sons in turn onto one shoulder and carried them around a bit. Then he turned them over to their uncles.

"What's wrong?" Sun Walker asked when they were alone. "I counted. All the brothers came back. You're unhurt?"

"It's difficult to explain," he said, accepting her hands.

"Tell me," she urged.

He hated darkening her world with the truth, but her eyes demanded an explanation. Afterward, he realized how eager he had been to purge himself of the memory.

"I see," she said when he finished. "Now I understand why the younger ones are so quiet. Once our men returned to camp shouting and singing brave heart songs. Now they return quietly, ashamed."

"I don't understand, either," Wolf confessed. "I intend to turn away from this dark road, though. We're going to build a sweat lodge. You'll help make the purifying prayers?"

"You'll perform the old *Suhtai* ritual then."

"I think that's best. My powers always come from the old ways, the old prayers and the old weapons. When I was little, the grandfathers told me that a man must seek renewal in his beginnings. He must go back to when the world was full of harmony. That's what we'll do.''

As Wolf and Sun Walker Woman prepared a section of earth near the river, Stands Long and the brothers split logs into firewood. Even in the midst of winter, the interior of the logs remained relatively dry. The outer, damper portions would dry in the flames and catch fire in turn.

Wolf began his portion of the ritual by clearing the snow from the chosen ground. He then located a number of heavy, solid rocks and placed them in a circle near where he would build a fire. Choosing the rocks was important. In that country of limestone and sandstone ridges, selecting a rock with inner air pockets could lead to tragedy. Once Wolf had come upon a *Wihio* trapper blinded by a fragment of exploding limestone rock.

''A man should know his business,'' one of the grandfathers had remarked. ''The earth punishes men who walk blindly.''

Wolf Running chose hard, solid rocks rounded by the passage of creek water. Next he traced a path a few paces away and marked a circle. He then erected short poles and draped a hide covering over them. Once the sweat lodge itself was formed, he devoted his efforts to building a fire outside. Finally, when everything was ready, he sent a pipe among the *Suhtai* and *Oglala* warriors. Although *Inipi*, the *Lakota* ritual, differed somewhat from the old *Suhtai* ceremony, several *Oglalas* joined their *Suhtai* hosts.

Wolf and Sun Walker Woman began by invoking *Heammawihio* and the four directions, Mother Earth and Father Sky. She sang the ancient prayers her people had spoken in the grandfathers' grandfathers' time. Only a few of the twenty men present understood any of the strange words' meaning, but they sat in reverent silence while Sun Walker chanted and shook her old healing rattles. Finally Wolf passed a pipe about, and each person touched his lips to the sacred smoke. Only then did they strip themselves and prepare to enter the sweat lodge.

By then the fire was crackling. Sun Walker rolled the

smooth stones onto the glowing logs and waited for them to heat. Wolf took over the chanting, and he warmed as the faces of his companions began to lose their hollow gaze. Even sitting there on the frozen earth, nearly naked, they were warmed by the feeling of the place and the glowing fire. Once the stones were sufficiently hot, Wolf rolled them down a narrow trench to the sweat lodge and formed them into a circle at the center of the lodge. He then carried a flask inside and sprinkled water over the sizzling stones. Steam clouds rose until they encircled his body. His bare chest stung from the heat, and he felt perspiration drip from his forehead and roll onto his cheeks. The salty droplets stung his eyes.

"We're ready," he announced as he stepped outside. Sun Walker brought him his pipe, and he stepped back inside. Stands Long followed. Each of the others came in turn.

Wolf and Stands Long spoke the initial prayers, but each newcomer added his own plea to be renewed. Some spoke old, remembered prayers. Others chose their own words.

"Give us back our hearts," Morning Hawk pleaded. "Carry off our bad thoughts and make the world whole again."

When Broken Wing's turn came, he remained silent a long time. Before, covered by buffalo and elk hides, the young man had appeared quietly respectful. As he reached his arms out toward the fire, Wolf realized what a thin, frail creature the fifteen-year-old was. Two jagged scars wove their way around his left side, and a third long scar traced its way from below his left knee to the ankle.

"*Heammawihio,* this one has suffered," Wolf whispered as he spattered water onto the rocks. The rising steam concealed the young newcomer for an instant. When he reappeared, tears appeared to be joining the sweat dripping down his cheeks.

"This is a place to forget," Stands Long whispered. "To release the pain."

"How can I?" Broken Wing asked, rubbing the scars on his side. "How can I forget what the bluecoats did to me, to my family? If I kill them all, I'll still remember."

"You must give up the ghosts," Wolf advised. "Your relations can't begin their long walk if you hold them here, on this side."

"I should have protected them," the young man muttered. "I had a bow. I ran. The bluecoats found me, and they cut me with their long knives. I lay there, bleeding, waiting for them to cut the life out of me, but they only laughed. Laughed! I was nothing! They didn't bother killing me."

"They were mistaken," Morning Hawk said, gripping his friend's wrist. "You proved that at Platte River."

"No, I only killed myself a second time," Broken Wing mumbled. "I see it all in my sleep. I'll never forget."

"Your shoulders are too small to carry such a burden," Wolf declared as he rose from his place in the circle of men and moved along to where Broken Wing sat, shuddering. "Men are ignorant. They understand nothing. Only *Heammawihio* determines the length of a man's path on the earth or what trouble he faces there. It's our task to walk like men, in the sacred manner. You can't do this when your heart is full of those other times. Stand up. Let the smoke take you."

Broken Wing rose, and Wolf eased the young man closer to the steam. Gradually the tense arms lost their iron feel. The boy's legs buckled, and his chin dropped onto his chest. The arms finally went limp, and if Wolf hadn't held him, Broken Wing would have collapsed.

"Now, listen," Wolf said, whispering the ancient words of a *Suhtai* song. "Say it."

The boy muttered each line after Wolf, and a new power seemed to flow into Broken Wing's arms. When they finished, Wolf repeated the old morning prayer he had spoken a thousand times.

> "Give us the struggles to make us strong,
>   *Heammawihio.*
> Brave up our hearts,
>   *Heammawihio.*

Show us the sacred path,
That we may walk within the harmony
Of the Hoop,
Heammawihio."

"What do I say now?" Broken Wing whispered as he slid out of Wolf's supporting grasp.

"Give up the ghosts," Wolf urged. "Remake yourself."

"*Heammawihio,* I feel your touch," Broken Wing cried. "Where I was dead, I feel alive again." Each of his companions had spoken those words, and the others nodded their agreement. Broken Wing remained beside the fire a moment longer, though. Then he added something more, something new.

"*Heammawihio,* we've lost our way. Once we walked the sacred path, knowing the right things to do, but now we're bewildered. The bluecoats cut down my family. They marked my flesh, and they cut away my father's hair, his ears, even his manhood. Each thing the bluecoats did, we've now done to them. It brought us no renewal, though. Only troubled dreams.

"*Heammawihio,* help us step away from this terrible thing. Give us a new, better path to walk. Give me my heart back, and let me return to the sacred hoop."

"It's a good prayer," Wolf observed, adding more water to the stones.

Broken Wing stared into the swirling steam and opened his mouth. The smoke rose and seemingly enveloped him. He closed his eyes a moment and then turned to Wolf Running.

"When I thought I was nothing," the boy whispered, "I believed that was a bad thing. Now I understand. It's all any of us are."

"It's true," Wolf admitted.

"*Heammawihio* will lead us away from the dark place," Broken Wing announced. "I feel it."

"Yes," Wolf said. "You've cast off the darkness and become whole again."

"You brought me back, *Nah nih,*" the young man said,

adopting the term for an older, wiser brother. "I'll follow where you lead."

"Yes," Stands Long agreed. "Many will."

"We all will," Morning Hawk declared.

"I'll try to find a path for us to walk," Wolf told his companions. "It's all a man can do."

"You'll find it," Broken Wing insisted. "*Heammawihio* showed it to me."

Wolf turned and gazed at the frail young man with surprise. Broken Wing appeared dazed, adrift like a man who had been drinking *Wihio* whiskey. Or, Wolf knew, like a man who had seen the truth in his dreams.

Wolf Running was not the only one to notice the change in Broken Wing.

"It was a good idea, the sweat lodge," Sun Walker Woman told Wolf that night when they sat together in their lodge. "It's mended tears we couldn't see."

"We saw the signs," Wolf argued. "How long will the healing last, though?"

"It might be a good time to go north," she said, resting her head against his shoulder. "The sun's been brighter lately. Maybe we'll see an early thaw."

"Winter stays late in the north country."

"We have fewer enemies there," she pointed out.

"Do you miss your relatives?"

"I have my family here," she said, nodding to the sleeping children.

"I have obligations here," Wolf said, lightly stroking her hair. "I accepted Crazy Horse's pipe."

"Yes," she admitted. "I've walked with the *Oglala* women. They're also growing weary of this raiding. Maybe we'll all leave soon."

"Maybe," he admitted.

"The air here's heavy with death, Wolf. You've been away from your sons too often. They worry about you. Game's become scarce here, and we're tired of chewing *Wihio* biscuits and eating the tasteless cow meat."

"I'll speak with my cousin," Wolf promised. "It would

be best to go north with the *Oglalas*. We're too few to do it alone."

"If we stay too long, we may be fewer," Sun Walker warned.

"I know," he whispered. "Broken Wing wasn't the only one reborn in the sweat lodge. We had some of our *Oglala* brothers there."

"Not your cousin," she noted.

"Crazy Horse has his own medicine ways. We're not unalike, we two. Each may seem strange to the other, but we're more different from other men than from each other."

"He's a troubled man, Wolf. It's not so different than with Broken Wing. There's an unspoken grief behind his eyes."

"He's a shirt wearer. He has many obligations."

"My husband also carries such a weight," she whispered. "Be careful."

"I'll try," he said, smiling. It was all he could offer.

The next morning Wolf located Crazy Horse at the creek. For the first time in many months they made the morning prayers together. Afterward Crazy Horse sat on the bank, watching clouds dance across the heavens. Wolf pointed to a large fluffy one and grinned.

"Perhaps Bull Buffalo's come to look at our camp," Wolf said, noting the similarity between the cloud and the animal.

"Maybe so," Crazy Horse replied. "The sweat did you good, Wolf. Your eyes are clear of the old pain."

"Which pain?" Wolf asked. "Platte River or some other fight?"

"All of them," Crazy Horse said, nodding solemnly. "I told my people we'll also make a sweat."

"It's a good idea."

"And afterward? Have you thought about what we'll do next?"

"Some say we should go north."

"What do *you* say?"

"Our camps are full of plunder, Horse. We have all the

ponies and cattle we can tend, and even the women are content with their many new possessions. If an enemy approaches, we'll have to leave much behind. Why take more?''

"Some other *Oglalas,* together with *Tsis tsis tas* and *Arapaho* allies, plan to raid the *Wihio* soldier fort near Julesburg.''

"We had little luck the last time," Wolf reminded his cousin. "The bluecoats will not be so eager to chase decoys this time.''

"If an attack's to be made, we should be there. The chiefs rely on us to steady the young men.''

"You're going?''

"I'm considering the matter. A band from the neighboring camp's going.''

"It's said that more bluecoats are coming out this way. Have the scouts seen anybody?''

"A few patrols. Some fire rifles at the scouts, but nobody's been hurt. You and I could run one of those patrols.''

"I'm weary of killing," Wolf confessed. "We fight again and again, but nothing changes.''

"Then maybe it's time to leave this place.''

"I think so, Cousin.''

"You know it's never as easy for me to make a decision," Crazy Horse said, frowning. "There are many among your people with light skin, so few say anything about it. The *Oglalas* consider it odd, though, and even now, a shirt wearer, I hear people whispering that I am *Wihio.* If I avoid this attack, the words will be spoken even louder.''

"Has nothing changed?" Wolf asked. "How long ago was it that you raced the Crows at Horse Creek, proving yourself against all those older, taller men? Boys whisper your name with respect. No one who's seen you fight could think you're afraid of battle.''

"I'll never belong, Wolf.''

"We're different, we two," Wolf admitted. "Our road is steep, and it's hard walking it. We see things, though.

We know what's best, and so we must speak louder than the shortsighted ones.''

''Will anyone listen?''

''Maybe they will this time,'' Wolf suggested. ''We have to convince them.''

''Are you so certain we should leave?''

''I wasn't before,'' Wolf confessed. ''Now I am. Your heart's not in attacking the bluecoats, either. I want to give the young ones like Broken Wing time to heal. Will you come with us?''

''We'll undertake *Inipi* first. Then we'll break down our lodges and start north. You and I will hang back, watching.''

''It's a good plan,'' Wolf agreed. ''I'll gladly do it.''

chapter
7

THE MOVE NORTH HAD ALREADY begun when the *Lakota* and *Tsis tsis tas* bands that were camped farther south launched their raid on Julesburg. Although Wolf Running kept his little band of warriors away from the fighting, news of the raid did reach the encampments. The raiders had emptied the Julesburg storehouses and burned some buildings. Decoys tried to lure the bluecoats out of their fort, but the wary white soldiers had refused to attack. Some other raiders captured wagons full of whiskey, and their drunken singing and irregular drumming drifted northward on the icy wind.

"It's as we feared," Crazy Horse declared as he rode alongside Wolf. Together with a handful of other men, they formed a rear guard for their northbound camp.

"Yes," Wolf agreed. "The raiders have won us nothing but new trouble."

That night the warriors met in council to discuss the problem. Earlier, scouts had reported seeing pillars of dust rising from the south. It was obvious that the larger camps were also moving. Hundreds of women and children were

fleeing South Platte River. Some effort to distract their
pursuers seemed necessary.

"It's impossible to hide so many people moving at one
time," Stands Long pointed out. "The bluecoats from the
fort may follow them."

"They're afraid to fight," Broken Wing insisted. The
young man rose to his feet, but when he saw the angry
stares of his elders, he swallowed his words.

"It's better to let the experienced voices make themselves heard," Wolf whispered to his young friend.

"So, what would you do, *Nah nih*?" Red Hawk asked.

"There are only a few of us here," Wolf said, gazing
around the circle until his eyes met those of his *Oglala*
cousin. "The *Lakotas* know this country best. Maybe
Crazy Horse has a plan."

"We're all brothers here," Crazy Horse replied. "If my
cousin has an idea, he should tell us about it."

"I'm not sure what we should do," Wolf confessed.
"The *Wihio* have many forts and soldiers on North Platte
River. The *Pawnees* are to the east. If the bluecoats at
Julesburg come north and these other ones come south, we
would face enemies on all sides."

"He sees danger everywhere," Big Horn complained.

"I'm surprised to see you here," Stands Long said, glar-
ing at Big Horn. "When I heard someone had captured
whiskey barrels, I was sure you would be there."

"I wasn't running away like some," Big Horn boasted.

"I never knew that you were a brave heart," an *Oglala*
named Pawnee Chaser said, laughing. "The last time I saw
you, the *Arapahos* were running you."

"No one of you came to my aid, either," Big Horn
grumbled. "We share the same blood, but you left me to
face my enemies alone."

"You made an enemy of those *Arapahos*," Crazy Horse
declared. "They were not our foe. You killed a friend over
whiskey! Some among us would deny you a seat in our
council. We're very few now, and it would be foolish to
drive anyone away. Be quiet, though. Spread no disharmony here."

"We were talking about the bluecoats," Stands Long reminded the council. "I see the danger, but what can we do?"

"It's cold," Pawnee Chaser observed. "Why would the bluecoats in the north leave the warmth of their fires?"

"They'll know about the move north," Wolf explained. "They can send messages on their wires and tell the other soldiers."

"How?" Broken Wing asked.

"I don't understand how," Wolf confessed, "but I know they can do it. I'm not certain the bluecoats will come south, but if they do, we're in danger from two directions."

"There are bluecoats close by, too," Crazy Horse said, sighing. "They have some people at Muddy Spring Creek, only a short ride north. They also have a wire there."

"Are the bluecoats always there?" Wolf asked.

"They've come to guard the ranch there and the wire," Pawnee Chaser explained. "I've traded with the ranchers who live there. Before, when times were better between us, we would swap them hides for powder and lead. I think the bluecoats are there to watch for us, too."

"There are a lot of soldiers at Fort Laramie," Crazy Horse said, staring off past the fire toward the north. "Too many for us to fight alone. We'd better keep the bluecoats at Muddy Spring Creek busy. That way we can move the helpless ones past them. If the others are there, too, we'll try to lead them away."

"We'll need help," Wolf said, frowning.

"I'll send riders to the other *Oglala* bands," Crazy Horse explained. "We'll have help. First we'll see how many bluecoats are at Muddy Spring Creek. I'll go there myself tomorrow. Who will follow?"

Twenty eager voices volunteered, but Wolf felt his cousin's eyes on him.

"I'll also come," Wolf declared. "Someone must watch the helpless ones, though."

"It's a brother's obligation," Red Hawk reluctantly noted.

"We'll do it," High Flyer agreed.

Crazy Horse assigned ten *Oglalas* to remain behind as well.

"You might also accept this obligation," he told Big Horn. It was a waste of words, though.

And so Wolf Running found himself riding out to battle once more. That morning he had made the required dawn prayers. He added an old *Suhtai* warrior chant. Then he painted his face red like the dying sun and took his shield in hand.

"You expect hard fighting," Stands Long noted when Morning Hawk brought out their horses. "I thought we were going to scout the enemy."

"Look," Wolf said, nodding to the twenty-five young *Oglalas* who had gathered around Crazy Horse. "We're too many to remain concealed, and they are too young to hang back."

"Pony boys have no place on a scout," Stands Long growled. When Morning Hawk mounted his pony, Stands Long nudged Wolf's elbow.

"I'll hunt Bull Buffalo this summer," the thirteen-year-old boasted. "Our brothers will look after the helpless ones. I should go along, *Nah nih*."

"We were no older the first time," Wolf told his brother-friend. "Hawk, stay close," Wolf warned. "The bluecoats are like coyotes, tricksters. They can surprise an unwary man."

Wolf Running was ill at ease from the beginning of the scout. Maybe it was the eerie haze that hung on the snowy hills beyond. Perhaps it was knowing his youngest brother was there. Wolf saw only uncertainty when he gazed around. He knew too few of the young *Oglalas,* and the country was a new and perilous world. He had ridden Platte River in summer, but he had never traveled that section in winter. The snow-clad hills and frozen streams transformed the rich prairie and low hills into a different world.

Up ahead somewhere lay a *Wihio* ranch. Bluecoats were known to camp there, but how many? No one knew. Did

they have good horses? Trudging through the snow,
Wolf's mount had grown weary. He would have trouble
eluding an enemy on a tired pony.

Suddenly Stands Long began singing.

> "It's good we're riding this morning.
> The enemy is strong, but we're *Tsis tsis tas.*
> "We'll run them, hah!"

The *Oglalas* responded with their own songs, and soon
the air lost some of its icy bite. Crazy Horse howled and
edged his horse to the left until he was alongside his
cousin.

"It's not far," he told Wolf. "I'm going ahead to have
a look. You'll come along?"

"Yes," Wolf agreed. He motioned his companions
back, but Stands Long, as always, rode on. Morning Hawk
started to follow, but Wolf insisted the boy remain with
the others.

"Don't worry, *See'was'sin mit,*" Wolf called. "Your
chance will come."

Wolf wasn't exactly sure what he had meant by that,
but the words worked. Morning Hawk did turn back. Crazy
Horse, Wolf Running, and Stands Long Beside Him continued to a small rise overlooking the frozen, meandering
stream known as Muddy Spring Creek.

"There," Crazy Horse said, pointing to a handful of
buildings half-hidden by snowdrifts.

Wolf studied the ranch a moment. The sun produced a
blinding glare on the glittering snow. Initially he had trouble making out anything beyond the actual buildings.
Eventually he detected a corral full of horses and mules,
the line of posts carrying the signal wire north and south,
and two clever trenches cut in the snow to protect the
buildings from raiders.

"They expect trouble," Crazy Horse observed. "Some
of their ponies have saddles on them."

Wolf hadn't noticed that, and he nodded gratefully to
his cousin.

"They've dug defenses," Wolf observed. "But they protect the ranch from the north."

"It's an old line then," Crazy Horse declared. "We can strike from the southwest, where they've got their horses."

"We?" Wolf asked. "Thirty men."

"Men?" Stands Long added. "Mostly pony boys."

"If we take their ponies, they can't harm the helpless ones," Crazy Horse argued. "There can't be many of them here. A large body of soldiers would have sentries."

"They could be well hidden," Wolf pointed out. "If we attack, they can send word on their wire. We should wait for the others before attacking."

"Maybe," Crazy Horse admitted. "But we're here, Wolf. When did we ever hang back? We can lure the blue-coats out of their trench and fight them. The last time we tried to decoy the enemy, the hot bloods spoiled our plan. Big Horn isn't here now. So, will you go down there with me?"

"Do the others know what to do?" Wolf asked.

"Yes," Crazy Horse said, grinning.

So, you planned this from the first, Wolf thought. He could only sigh, though. Stands Long muttered to himself. Both followed when Crazy Horse started toward the ranch.

Had the bluecoats been watchful, the three riders who approached the Muddy Spring Ranch might have been quickly dispatched. Instead Wolf followed cautiously as Crazy Horse circled the outbuildings and neared the corral. Wolf spotted a large herd of cattle to the north, but his cousin had little interest in those animals. His eyes were fixed on the corral.

"Go ahead," Wolf whispered. "Stands Long and I'll shield you."

Crazy Horse nodded. He edged his way to the corral, slipped quietly off his horse, and slid rails aside in order to open an exit to the corral. The horses quickly sensed something odd, and they began stomping around. Crazy Horse remounted his pony, and a moment later he led the first horse out of the corral. Two others followed. Stands Long circled around to the far side of the corral and began waving his hands. Only when he started shouting, though, did the horses run.

The shouts also startled the ranch people to life. A boy of perhaps sixteen summers was the first to rush out the door. He spied the raiders, paled, and retreated to safety. Two bluecoats next stepped out, rifles in hand, but they fired hurriedly. Their shots missed.

"Brother, don't wait too long!" Stands Long called as he waited for the last of the animals, a ragged-looking brown mule, to leave the corral.

"Go ahead," Wolf insisted. "I'll follow."

Wolf feigned a charge, throwing up a cloud of powdery white snow at the two riflemen in the doorway. Then he turned and followed the fleeing horses.

It had all been so simple. Almost too easy. The *Wihio* had barely noticed them, and even when they came out to fight, they were the frightened ones. Without horses, they couldn't pursue.

Wolf was still congratulating himself on the little raid's success when a rifle barked out from one of the outbuildings. He felt his horse stumble, and his right hand felt something warm and sticky.

Wolf tried to steady the animal, but the pony was in a bad way. A hidden bluecoat had shot the horse through its right side, and the horse managed only three more steps before collapsing into the snow. Wolf jumped free, landing hard. He lay in the snow, stunned, for a moment. When he caught his breath, he drew his shield close to his chest and searched for his bow.

"One of 'em's down, Billy!" a bluecoat shouted. "Get him!"

Rifles barked from the ranch, and two bullets struck the snow to Wolf's right. A third shot ended his horse's misery.

"It's as always," Wolf muttered as he strung his bow and drew an arrow from his quiver. "It's the unseen peril that kills you."

That appeared even truer when a door on a long building behind the main house swung open, and three men marched out leading horses. Wolf had not guessed that the ranchers would have both a corral and a stable. The three riders set off in pursuit of the raiders while five others began saddling ponies and preparing to follow. Wolf inched his way to a low rock wall beyond the corral and prepared to make a stand there. Five or six rifles concentrated their fire on him, and he winced as bullets tore fragments of stone from the wall. He had no target for his arrows.

Wolf knew better than to stay there. Sooner or later the ranchers or the bluecoats would circle around behind him. With their rifles, they had the advantage of range. He had to get away, but where could he go? For a hundred yards around the ground was open. If he reached the creek, he might get across. More likely the ice would break, and he would drown. If he didn't freeze first!

"Nothing lives long," Wolf whispered as he took a deep breath. "Only the earth and the mountains."

With a sudden, almost desperate lurch, he abandoned the shelter of the wall and charged blindly toward the creek. The snowdrifts grew deeper, and he fell three times. Two bluecoats tried to follow, but they also had a difficult time of it. By the time they reached the rock wall, Wolf managed to throw himself behind a pair of scrub oaks and avoid their shots.

The trees offered very little protection, but they did conceal Wolf's exact whereabouts. He was able to catch his breath and nock an arrow. Should the bluecoats make a charge, one of them at least would find it costly.

"He's in them trees!" one of the soldiers at the wall shouted. "Let's finish him!"

"Go ahead, Jubal," a second voice replied. "I got no interest in dyin' in the snow."

Apparently Jubal had not considered that possibility. He hesitated. The delay saved Wolf's life. That and Morning Hawk.

The boy had remained behind as instructed, but once the shooting began, he had ridden toward the ranch like lightning. He rode a Crow pony, one raised in the *Absaroka* country beyond the Big Horn Mountains, and that horse was accustomed to the chills of winter and the treachery of frozen landscape. Morning Hawk surged through the snowdrifts and galloped past Crazy Horse and Stands Long, searching for his brother.

"He's back there!" Stands Long had managed to shout. "Stay with the ponies, and I'll go back for him."

"It's a brother's obligation," Morning Hawk insisted. "The ponies are yours."

Stands Long had reluctantly allowed the boy to continue. Morning Hawk wove his way across the snowy hills and crossed Muddy Spring Creek. He instinctively headed for the trees when he noticed the *Wihio* shots striking the ground there.

"*Nah nih*, where are you hiding?" Morning Hawk called.

"Here!" Wolf called, stepping out from the trees and waving his bow. Morning Hawk slapped his horse into a gallop and charged the trees. He heard the bluecoat bullets whine past, but he never hesitated. He halted long enough for Wolf to climb up behind him. Then the two of them hurried away.

The handful of bluecoats who had ridden out after the stolen horses gave up the chase in favor of game closer at hand. Wolf counted five of them, and it took no particular talent to determine he and Morning Hawk had no chance of evading five men on fresh mounts.

"Can you get across the creek here?" Wolf asked his brother.

"I crossed upstream before," Morning Hawk replied. "I'm not sure."

"Try," Wolf urged. "We have a better chance with the creek between us and the *Wihio*."

Morning Hawk turned his pony and urged the animal toward the stream. The horse balked at making the crossing, though. Twice Hawk managed to get the horse into the shallows, but the pony shuddered and danced back to the snowy bank.

"It's no use," Wolf observed. "Try to reach those rocks just ahead. We'll make a stand there."

Actually Wolf intended to make that stand alone, but when he slid off the pony and ordered Morning Hawk to seek help, the boy refused to leave.

"I've heard you speak of it a hundred times, *Nah nih*. A warrior never leaves a man behind. He has an obligation to share the danger, to rescue the helpless ones."

"There's no need for both of us to die," Wolf argued.

"Maybe we won't," Morning Hawk said, jumping down and slapping his horse away. "I, too, have a bow."

For the first time since crossing Muddy Spring Creek, Wolf smiled. It warmed his heart to see his youngest brother so tall, so confident. He now understood the pride his father and uncle must have shared when Wolf had returned from his first hunt, his first raid on the Pawnee pony herd, his first fight.

"Try to conceal yourself," Wolf urged. "The bluecoats can't charge us, not here in these rocks. The snow will slow them, too. Take your time. Choose your target carefully."

"It's no different than when you first took me to hunt rabbits."

"It's quite different," Wolf insisted. "Rabbits don't shoot back. It's not so easy, killing another man, either."

"The *Wihio* have no trouble doing it, *Nah nih*," Morning Hawk argued.

"How can they disturb the harmony of their world? They've known no such thing. For us it's a very different thing."

Wolf wanted to say more, to explain some of it. There was no time, though. The *Wihio* riders arrived at that very moment, and they tore the sky with their shouts. They fired rifles and pistols at the boulders, but they failed to draw blood. Wolf drew back an arrow and launched it into the side of the first rider. He shot a second in the thigh. Morning Hawk hit a third, and the last two riders prudently withdrew.

"Ayyyy!" Morning Hawk shouted. Two of the

wounded men managed to ride away, but the other fell from his pony and stared up at the sky. Morning Hawk started to leap forward and count coup, but Wolf held his brother back.

"Others will soon be here," Wolf whispered. "We should leave."

chapter
8

WOLF WAS FAR FROM CERTAIN that he and Morning Hawk would get safely away. He wasted little time leading the way southward along the frozen creek. The sun had broken through the clouds, though, and the resulting warmth encouraged their frantic flight across the snowbound landscape.

"*Nah nih*, there's a good place to cross just ahead," Morning Hawk announced after they had gone a short distance. "I came this way."

Wolf examined the crossing and frowned. On horseback, a man could manage it easily enough. Wolf knew that after sloshing their way across the stream, the two of them would arrive on the far bank half-frozen.

"*Nah nih?*" Morning Hawk called.

"I'm not certain," Wolf admitted. "We're far from our camp."

For the first time Morning Hawk's face betrayed a trace of fear. The boy had always relied on his older brother, but now?

"Half a day's ride, I think," Morning Hawk declared. "A long walk."

"Too long with frozen feet," Wolf noted. "We won't easily make a warming fire on the other side of the stream, either."

"The smoke would show the *Wihio* where we are," Morning Hawk added. "But what else can we do? I don't know any other crossing."

"Crazy Horse didn't bring the ponies this way. There has to be another spot."

"We'll go on then?"

"Yes," Wolf said, clasping his brother's wrist with the old, accustomed firmness. "Don't worry. Help's sure to come."

"Is it?" Morning Hawk asked.

"The sun is overhead," Wolf pointed out. "You came. Is my brother the only brave heart riding this country?"

"They've grown accustomed to riding with Wolf Running. He does the rescuing."

"Not this time," Wolf said, grinning at his brother. "Someone else accepted that burden."

"He didn't do it well," Morning Hawk said, sighing.

"We're alive, *See'was'sin mit*. The other will come."

Wolf only half believed it, but he masked his uncertainty. Morning Hawk drew a deep breath and took a step southward. Wolf did likewise, and once they were in motion again, they had no energy for wondering. The snow was deeper, and a man made progress only by concentrating his every effort on each step.

In the end, the rescuers did arrive. Wolf had hoped Stands Long would come, but the stolen horses had drawn his brother-friend and cousin far to the south. Older, more experienced men would have waited, as instructed, for word, but there were few older men among the scouts that day. Most of the *Oglalas* had spotted the fleeing pony herd and followed their chief. Broken Wing and two other young men, Beaver Belt and Two Arrows, had started after Morning Hawk. The three boys collected five stray ponies, including Morning Hawk's, on their way north. Knowing their friend had found trouble, they continued along the river with a sense of urgency.

There was need. By the time they reached Wolf Running and Morning Hawk, the two warriors were stumbling through knee-deep snow, shivering from cold, and breathing in short gasps. Broken Wing spotted them first.

"Come," he called to his companions. He then slapped his pony into a sort of stumbling gallop. "Brothers, I'm coming!" he shouted toward the creek.

Wolf managed to raise his chin and eye the swirl of snow dust and phantom that was charging down a hill toward the stream.

"They've come," Morning Hawk whispered as he collapsed.

"Yes," Wolf said, helping his quivering brother rise. "We'll soon be warm again."

"Will we?" Morning Hawk muttered.

"Yes, *See'was'sin mit,*" Wolf assured him. "You've saved me after all."

Wolf had scant recollection later of what happened next. Broken Wing explained how they had collected the stray ponies, recognized Morning Hawk's mount, and begun their search. After locating the derelict raiders, the three young men brought them south to a shallow crossing, forded Muddy Spring Creek, and made a camp or sorts on the far bank.

"We built a warming fire and removed your frozen clothes," Wing told Wolf. "I'm afraid we had to cut the leggings. We kept you by the fire until the cold had lost its grip. Then we wrapped you in hides and brought you along to the camp."

Wolf had slept there all that day and half the next. When he awoke, his first thoughts were of his younger brother.

"What about me?" Sun Walker Woman scolded him as she replaced a warm elk hide over his chest. "I'm the one who's been tending you all this time."

"He's not dead?" Wolf asked, hoping her worried gaze wasn't hiding a terrible truth.

"Oh, he's young," she grumbled. "He's been sharing

the tale of his fight with the *Wihio* with the other young
men. Now he and the other brothers are hunting food.
We've camped here, and Crazy Horse thought fresh meat
would help you regain your strength.''

"We've camped?" Wolf asked. "We need to cross
North Platte River and continue north."

"That can wait," she declared. "The other camps are
close by now, and we'll go together. It's best," she added
somberly. "The bluecoats have ridden out of their forts.
We'll have to fight some of them."

Wolf frowned. He wanted to rise and assume his responsibilities, but his legs lacked the power to carry him
anywhere. He blamed himself for the delay in crossing.
The arrival of his three little sons drove ill-feeling from
his heart, though. He raised himself into a sitting position,
and the little ones threw themselves into his waiting arms.

"*Ne' hyo,* we were worried," Wind's Whisper confessed as he settled in under his father's arm. "Your skin
was blue."

"Blue," Winter Pup echoed.

"I was cold," Wolf told them, "but the memory of my
sons gave me strength."

"And me?" Sun Walker asked as she brought him a
bowl of warm broth.

"I only hoped some rescuer would bring me to you,"
he told her. "I knew my wife could restore life. She knows
the healing cures, you know."

"She sang the old songs," Whisper explained. "She
painted you with powder and fed you herbs in an awful
tea."

"We tasted it," Pup added, contorting his face.

"It brought me back to you," Wolf said, reaching up
and touching his wife's chin. "I'm thankful that the *Suhtai*
believe women can cure."

She discarded her scowl then, and as Wolf sipped the
broth, he warmed from the closeness of his family. He had
always found comfort in them, but there was something
new and unexpected as well. Before, he had been the giver,

the bringer of food, the protector. Now it was as if they had taken on all the burdens.

Wolf rested two additional days in the small camp near Muddy Spring Creek while the main body of *Lakota* and allied bands streamed north to the northern fork of Platte River. Crazy Horse and most of the other men had struck the ranchers across the creek again, but a hundred blue-coats had arrived from the forts farther west. The raiders managed to shoot some of the bluecoats' horses and mules, but there were too many *Wihio* there to drive away. They were well led, too.

"We can accomplish nothing there," Stands Long told Wolf afterward. "We can't get at the bluecoats, and more are coming. We keep them from troubling our camps, but we have to cross North Platte River soon, before the blue-coats block the fords."

"Yes," Wolf agreed. "You're not waiting on me, are you?"

"On the others," Stands Long insisted, grinning slightly. "Your cousin said that we should be the rear guard and protect the helpless ones. Don't you agree?"

"Naturally," Wolf said, matching his brother-friend's smile. "I'm strong enough to take my place among the warriors again, though. We should move the women and children across the river."

"That's welcome news," Stands Long noted. "I'll go and tell the others to begin preparations for the move. To-morrow we'll go north."

"Who knows? Maybe you'll find a wife among the *Lak-otas*. You didn't give all the stolen ponies away, did you?"

"Some strayed," Stands Long admitted. "I presented two each to the rescuers. I held back the best eight, though."

"Enough for a proper wife."

"Two taken from the enemy will be appropriate. One will take the place of the one you lost. As for the others, I thought you might need them for a giveaway."

"Yes," Wolf agreed. "My brother's carried a boy's name far too long."

"When we've crossed the river and driven off the bluecoats there, we'll call the Elks together."

"It will be good to see all our old friends."

"We won't see all of them," Wolf said, sighing. "Not
after Sand Creek."

"No," Wolf admitted. "Younger ones have grown tall,
though. They'll take their places."

Normally North Platte River was wide and deep. Even
at the low water crossings bands sometimes had to wait if
rains upriver swelled the stream. Wolf was pleased to discover that the river's surface remained frozen. Once the
scouts assured themselves that the ice was thick enough to
withstand the weight of horses and pony drags, the people
started across.

"It's a good thing that we've crossed so easily," Crazy
Horse told Wolf when the last of the pony drags was safely
on the north bank of the river.

"Why?" Wolf asked.

"The others are making a four night camp in the hills.
We can join them."

"We planned to," Wolf reminded his cousin. "What
aren't you telling me? Are there bluecoats on the river?"

"Nearby," Crazy Horse explained. "An eagle chief and
two hundred men. The scouts say that they plan to punish
us, but they'll be disappointed."

"We have time to get our people to safety?"

"Yes," Crazy Horse said, grinning. "This is our country now. *Paha Sapa* is close by."

Wolf nodded. He knew *Paha Sapa*, the Black Hills
country, too. There were numerous sheltered camping
spots for large and small camps. The *Wihio* had no roads
there, and they would have difficulty bringing their wagons. The *Lakotas* knew a hundred places where a hundred
good men could destroy two hundred bluecoats.

"Do you want to stay and watch for the bluecoats?"
Wolf asked.

"No, your brothers have sent out invitations to the Elks.
We'll smoke and talk. It's appropriate. Some young men
have counted coup and deserve recognition."

"My youngest brother has earned a man's name," Wolf explained.

"Yes, he showed he is your brother. You must teach him to keep his pony close, though. A mounted man has a better chance of getting away."

"He thought that he had come to die with me," Wolf said, sighing. "He's had no proper instruction as a warrior. My brothers and I have been too busy fighting to help him climb Man's Road."

"You'll do it now then. We've put a river between our enemies and the helpless ones. While we rest, they'll shiver in their *Wihio* blankets."

Wolf didn't reply. A thousand lodges had crossed that river. Two hundred soldiers were surely capable of doing the same. Now that the people had reunited in one place, though, his voice had little authority. The more numerous *Lakotas* would make any and all important decisions.

Actually, Wolf welcomed that. Always uneasy with the mantle of authority if not with the exercise of it, he was content to remain in the camp circle that he and his little band erected atop a bluff overlooking North Platte River. Crazy Horse's people had joined a larger *Oglala* camp nearby, but Crazy Horse and several others came over to join the Elk council Wolf convened. Long Dog and his sons were also there. Red Hawk and High Flyer had killed two winter elk, so there was plenty to eat. The celebration began at dusk and continued well into the night. The soldier chiefs summoned deserving young men to join their society, and Wolf nodded with approval when Morning Hawk was brought within their circle. Wolf then rose to speak.

"Brothers, this young man is also the son of my father," Wolf declared. "He has not walked Warrior's Road a long time, but he rides with the heart of an Elk warrior. Only a few days ago, when older men hung back, he rode to rescue me from the bluecoats at Muddy Spring Creek. He shared the danger and suffered the same cold as I did. It was a brave heart deed, his rescue, and it has earned him a place among us."

"Ayyyy!" the others howled. "He's an Elk!"

"When I was still a boy, my father climbed the hills to seek a dream," High Flyer said, rising. "He saw a hawk rising with the sun, and so he named his fourth son Morning Hawk."

"It's a name long carried by the boys of our family," Red Hawk added. "It's a boy's name, though, and our brother has no use for it anymore. We give it to the wind."

"He's earned a better name," Wolf said, stepping out from the circle and clasping his brother's hands. "From the grandfathers' grandfathers' time, brave hearts have carried it proudly. It's appropriate this nameless one should now take it."

"What should we call him?" Long Dog asked.

"Raven Heart," Wolf announced. "Our brother."

The others howled, and young Raven Heart turned to gaze on their excited faces. Stands Long then arrived leading four horses.

"It's long been a tradition among us to recognize brave heart deeds," Wolf continued. "In honor of our brother's courage, and to recognize his rebirth as Raven Heart, we present these ponies."

High Flyer and Red Hawk took charge of the horses. One at a time they led the animals around the outside of the council to where some deserving young man sat.

"In honor of Raven Heart, our brother, we give this pony," Wolf announced as his brothers gave away each horse. When they had completed the giveaway, Long Dog conducted the formal Elk initiation. Afterward the men danced and sang and celebrated.

It was a memorable evening, and Wolf hated to see it end. He was too weary to remain behind with his brothers after Long Dog dismissed the council, though. A full moon stood high in the heavens overhead, but that moon afforded little warmth. As with most clear winter nights, the air was numbing cold.

"Winter nights aren't kind to old men," Long Dog said after Wolf bid his brothers good night. "I'm glad you sent for us, though. We should share the perils winter brings."

"We should be safe in the northern country," Wolf noted. "The *Lakotas* know that area, and the bluecoats don't like fighting in the snow."

"I've heard others talk this way," Long Dog grumbled. "You've always been a cautious man, Wolf. Don't grow reckless now, with my grandchildren in your lodge. You say the bluecoats won't march in winter, but snow covered the bloody ground at Sand Creek. Black Kettle, our old friend, knew that country very well, but the *Wihio* struck him there."

"There's a difference," Wolf argued. "The Kettle trusted the bluecoats to keep the peace. I don't."

"It's a wise thing, being cautious," the old man observed. "Watch and listen. Expect trouble. Maybe you, too, will grow old enough to see your grandchildren."

"There aren't many grandfathers in our camps anymore," Wolf lamented. "My father did not live a long time, but he walked the sacred path. He was a man of the people, and his sons honor his memory. If mine walk the world as well, it would be enough."

"Sons require a father's guiding hand," Long Dog warned. "Not a child's faint recollection of a tall man carrying a painted shield."

"I can only walk my path. *Heammawihio* knows what tomorrow will bring. No one else."

Wolf left his wife's father and continued to his lodge alone. Sun Walker Woman was waiting for him, but the children were already asleep. He eased his way inside and quietly undressed.

"Are we poor in horses again?" she whispered.

"Poorer," he admitted. "But three of my brothers now walk Man's Road."

"It's a good thing," she observed. "You may need rescuing again."

"We'll soon be safely in the Black Hills," Wolf insisted. "Everyone's tired of fighting bluecoats and eager to rest."

"It would be good to enjoy some quiet days," Sun Walker Woman said, drawing Wolf close. "I hope you're right."

chapter
9

THE FOLLOWING DAY ALL HOPE of peace vanished. Shortly after midday, as Elks, still weary from the previous night, emerged from their lodges, criers hurried through the camp, altering the men to danger.

"Look, there on the ridge," Stands Long called as Wolf collected his wits.

A *Lakota* rider stood there, waving his robe in the air. It was the customary signal that enemies were in sight.

"It must be the bluecoats," Wolf muttered as he hurried to take his shield down from its stand. Wind's Whisper brought over a quiver of arrows.

"I'll bring the bow," the boy promised when Wolf accepted the arrows.

"Watch over your brothers," Wolf cautioned.

"I will, *Ne' hyo,*" Whisper promised. By the time he had returned with the bow, Red Hawk and High Flyer had collected several ponies. Raven Heart, who had danced and celebrated most of the morning, arrived last.

"We should hurry," Red Hawk urged. "Our *Oglala* friends are already mounted. We should join them."

"Not before we prepare ourselves," Wolf warned. "Be patient. The scout has given us time. We should make the appropriate prayers and paint ourselves."

Wolf knew that it vexed his brothers to perform the old rituals, but they trusted his judgment and voiced no objection. For his part, Wolf mixed paint while Stands Long kindled a small fire. As men from the neighboring camps scurried about, fetching weapons and gathering horses, Wolf performed the pipe ceremony. Then he offered up warrior prayers and began painting his brothers' faces.

It was daylight, and Wolf chose to color each face bright yellow. He then painted a black stripe from ear to ear across their eyes. Then High Flyer painted Wolf's face in a similar fashion. Finally Wolf tied the traditional elk horn charm behind his left ear. His brothers did the same. Even Stands Long, who relied on his own hailstone medicine paint, attached an elk horn charm.

"We're riding out together," Wolf sang when he had satisfied himself that everything had been done. "We brother Elks, ayyyy! We'll strike the enemy!"

His brothers began another song as Wolf climbed atop a buckskin mare. It was a different animal from the one he was accustomed to, but after all, he'd paid a price for the animals stolen at Muddy Spring Creek.

"Easy," Wolf whispered as he stroked the horse's neck. "We're one, you and I. I'll bring you no harm that I can avoid."

The mare remained skittish, though, and Wolf wished he could have tested it on the buffalo hunt before riding out against bluecoats. If they had brought their cannons along, the noise would startle this new horse and make it worthless in a fight.

"*Nah nih,* I've lost sight of the others," Raven Heart called from a stone's throw ahead. "Where should we go?"

Wolf gazed around at the swirls of snow dust thrown up by scattered parties of warriors. He was equally concerned about the confused stares of the women, children, and old people who remained behind.

"What should we do?" Stands Long asked.

"Ride out from the camps," Wolf declared. "Join the scouts."

"What about the others?" Red Hawk asked. "I saw some go north and others south."

"That's why we must be careful," Wolf explained. "We can't let the bluecoats get past us and attack the camps."

That notion chilled them all. At first glance it didn't seem possible that such a large string of encampments could be in any danger, but the *Wihio* had attacked such camps before, especially in winter. Many helpless persons had suffered in such raids.

"Do you want us to remain behind, guarding the camp?" Red Hawk asked.

Wolf read the faintly concealed disappointment in his brother's eyes and sighed.

"The enemy's there," Wolf declared, pointing across the ridge where the scout had issued his warning. "It's better to fight there, away from our women and children."

"Yes," Red Hawk agreed. "We can strike them a hard blow!"

"We'll be watchful, though," Wolf vowed. "We won't let the bluecoats get past us."

"No, we'll lead them away," Raven Heart boasted. "Our friends will also fight, and we'll run the *Wihio* from our country."

Ordinarily Wolf would have chided the young man for such boasting, but Raven Heart was no longer a boy. He had won a brave heart name, and he could no longer hang back. Sometimes, Wolf knew, boasting chased doubts from a youngster's heart.

"Wolf?" Stands Long asked.

"Follow me," Wolf replied. He then led the way toward the ridge.

It was an odd sight, the warriors riding out in groups of three or four that morning. It put Wolf in mind of a summer anthill stirred to life by a child's stick. It was only when he reached the crest of the ridge that he could get any clear notion of what was happening ahead. Even that provided few clues to what would transpire that afternoon.

The valley that opened up on both sides of North Platte River seemed alive with miniature figures that day. On the far side of the frozen river a line of white-topped wagons snaked along. Bluecoats rode ahead and behind and on both sides. Already the first parties of *Lakotas* and *Tsis tsis tas* were making their way across the treacherous ice. It was not an organized attack led by a skillful leader. No, it was more a case of individuals making their separate attacks.

Wolf, his brothers, and Stands Long descended the ridge and hurried toward the river. It was only a little way, but the snowdrifts slowed their progress. By the time they reached the north bank of the river, the air was full of shouting. Rifle shots whined and echoed. Across the river the bluecoats had made a circle of their wagons behind a slight rise. The *Wihio* soldiers hurried to scoop out snow and earth to offer some protection, but it was difficult to penetrate the frozen earth.

At that moment Wolf spotted Crazy Horse. The young *Oglalu* charged past a handful of bluecoats and tried to break through to the wagons, but riflemen drove him back. Nearby, Pawnee Chaser led a handful of younger men in support. A volley of rifle fire blunted their charge, and young Beaver Belt's horse went down.

"Ayyyy!" Wolf screamed as he slapped the mare into a trot. The horse had difficulty making any speed on the frozen surface, and Wolf expected some other rescuer to reach the boy first. Two Arrows tried, but he, too, had his horse shot down.

"*Nah nih,* wait!" Raven Heart called as Wolf turned the mare away from the outer line of bluecoats. "I'll go with you!"

"Ayyyy!" Wolf shouted. "I'm the rescuer today!"

Before, riding out from camp, Wolf had worried about the mare, but the animal barely flinched as it sloshed through the wet snow and surged past the surprised bluecoats. They shouted and fired their rifles, but Wolf paid them little heed. Their aim was poor, and he raced past like the wind.

"Look there!" Beaver Belt called as he helped free Two Arrows from his stricken horse. "Wolf Running's come to save us!"

Wolf warmed as he read the relief on the two young men's faces. He knew his own face must have carried that same look a few days before at Muddy Spring Creek.

"Here, climb up behind me," Wolf called, slowing the mare and halting a few feet from the youngsters.

"Go first," Beaver Belt said, helping his friend atop the mare. "I still have my bow."

"Belt?" Two Arrows called.

Wolf stroked the agitated mare as the young *Oglala* wrapped his arms around his rescuer's waist.

"You're ready?" Wolf asked.

"Hurry," Two Arrows urged. "You have to go back for Beaver Belt."

Wolf laughed and nudged the mare into motion. The horse sloshed its way through a drift and then jumped over a fallen cottonwood. It then sped along the frozen earth, past the bluecoat riflemen, and reached the safety of a nearby stand of trees.

"Lend me a horse and I'll go back for Belt," Two Arrows said when Wolf eased him off the tired mare's rump.

"You're weary," Wolf observed. "Today's my day to rescue *Oglalas*. Tomorrow you may have to save me once more."

Wolf turned the mare, but a pair of well-aimed rifle shots struck the beast in the right side. A third nicked Wolf's right elbow.

"It's no use," Stands Long declared as the horse collapsed onto its side.

Wolf managed to jump clear, but when he looked around for another horse to ride, Stands Long insisted it was a mistake.

"Look there," Stands Long said, pointing to where the bluecoats had managed to throw up a frail wall of earth and snow. They now extended their line on both sides of the narrow gap Wolf had used to make his rescue.

"We have to try," Two Arrows argued.

"Not on a horse," Stands Long insisted. "Together, going slow, we might be able to creep close enough to get through. A man on horseback's too good a target."

"He's probably right," Two Arrows muttered. "Wolf, did you see if the others got away? Your cousin . . ."

"It's hard to see anything," Wolf said, gazing through the mixture of snow dust and mist swirling up from the river.

"We'll follow you, *Nah nih*," Red Hawk then announced. "We five, Two Arrows, and more besides."

Wolf glanced behind him. His little party had grown to twenty men. Those still mounted rolled off their ponies and strung their bows. Wolf nodded somberly, slipped his shield onto his left arm, and examined the bluecoats' line. Rifles spit little tongues of yellow flame from the mist, but it was difficult to determine how many men were back there.

"Wolf?" a worried Two Arrows cried.

It doesn't matter how many there are, Wolf decided. *We have to try.*

Wolf, as was his habit, led the way. Two Arrows crept beside him. Stands Long followed, leading Wolf's three brothers. The others silently snaked their way along, being careful to heed every direction.

"The main thing," Wolf warned again and again, "is to keep low and avoid being spotted."

He didn't know how long it took the little band to creep past the bluecoats and approach Beaver Belt. As for the Belt, he was no longer alone. Three other would-be raiders had sought the shelter of the fallen horses, and they kept the riflemen firing from the wagons cautiously at a distance.

"Let me go ahead now," Two Arrows pleaded when they were a dozen paces away. "I can lead them back."

"It's for me to do," Wolf objected.

"You can punish the bluecoats," Two Arrows said, eyeing Wolf's bow. "I've got no weapon."

"No, but you carry a brave heart," Wolf replied. "Go. Call to them first. They might mistake you for an enemy."

"When Belt and I hunt rabbits, we make frog sounds," the young man explained. "I'll call to him, and he'll know it's me."

"Good," Wolf said, allowing the young *Oglala* to pass. "Be careful."

"As careful as you will be," Two Arrows said, grinning.

While Two Arrows crept toward his trapped friends, Wolf formed his companions into a line of sorts and led the way toward a slight rise. From there they could look down into the midst of the circled wagons. Even so, they still couldn't spy the bluecoats forming the outer line. Whenever a bluecoat moved about, though, one of the rescuers fired an arrow at him. The *Wihio* dodged the arrows, but they remained huddled behind their snow wall afterward.

"What do you plan to do?" Stands Long asked as Wolf studied the situation.

"See the trapped *Oglalas* get away," Wolf explained. "I don't think we can accomplish anything more. We can fire some arrows at these *Wihio,* but we probably won't hit anybody."

"We need to find higher ground," Stands Long observed. "Or charge."

"In this snow?" Wolf asked. "No, it's no use, as you said. We'll bother them some, though, and maybe they'll go back to their fort."

Wolf had largely given up hope of running the bluecoats from the river. Once Two Arrows led his companions to safety, Wolf motioned for the others to withdraw. They had scarcely returned to the trees when a fresh outburst of shooting erupted near the river. The *Lakotas,* Wolf quickly discovered, had slithered along the river and gotten close to the wagons. They had then opened a hot fire on the bluecoats.

Wolf could only imagine what was happening on the far side of the encircled wagons. He couldn't see farther than the nearby line of bluecoats. The firing continued, though, and men began racing along the outer line, shouting frantically. Only when a group of fifty or so bluecoats mounted their ponies and charged out of the corral did Wolf realize that the trapped *Wihio* soldier chief had decided to attack.

Beaver Belt was among the first to react. The young *Oglala* raced about in search of a spare pony, but he failed to locate one. Wolf had also lost his mare, but Raven Heart provided one of the extra ponies brought along for that purpose, and Wolf was atop the little buckskin in time to ride out to meet the charging bluecoats. The *Wihio* soldiers fired their pistols and used short rifles as clubs. They had no sabers that day. Wolf used his shield to deflect two bullets fired by a pistol-wielding bluecoat, and he finally killed the man with a single arrow through the side.

Beaver Belt made the bravest fight, though. Alone and afoot, he waited calmly as three bluecoats rode toward him. The seemingly helpless *Oglala* fired an arrow into the chest of the first man, hopped away from the second man, and was nocking an arrow to fire at the third when the *Wihio* fired a pistol into the boy's face. Beaver Belt fell back into the snow, and Wolf was certain the youngster was dead. The snow on both sides was spattered with blood, but once the surviving bluecoats departed, Beaver Belt rose to his knees.

"Ayyyy!" Two Arrows screamed. "Our brother lives!"

Wolf turned the buckskin and made his way through the powder smoke and snow mist to the two young *Oglalas*. Two Arrows had already washed most of the blood from his friend's face, and Wolf saw with relief that the bluecoat's shot had cut a deep groove in the boy's neck. There was a lot of blood, but no great harm.

A second group of bluecoats began their charge at that moment, and Wolf turned the buckskin to shield the *Oglalas'* flight. Pawnee Chaser had collected two *Wihio* ponies, and the boys quickly climbed atop the riderless animals. The *Wihio* charge broke through Wolf's hastily prepared line, but as other men rode over from here and there, they began driving the bluecoats back.

Other bluecoats charged the bands firing on the wagons. There was a hard fight there, too, but Wolf had little time to worry about it. A considerable number of bluecoats had cut their way out of the trap, and Wolf worried that they might bring help.

"We have to stop them!" he called to his companions. "Follow me!"

A similar shout came from a short distance away, and Crazy Horse rode out of the mist at the head of perhaps thirty well-armed *Oglalas*. Wolf's little band had shrunk to twelve riders by then, and he was content to attach himself to his cousin's party.

"Well, Cousin?" Crazy Horse called as he kicked his horse into a gallop. "Are we going to run them this time?"

"Yes!" Wolf howled.

The whole party seemed to share that sentiment, and they threw themselves with abandon on the fleeing bluecoats. The *Wihio* leader, a youngish man with a hairless face and surprisingly calm blue eyes, saw the charge and managed to turn his pony back toward the wagons. Less than half of his command followed. Most were past hearing orders, and as Crazy Horse's men overtook them, the bluecoats did their best to break away. They died in twos and threes, most of them. A few got away on foot, but Wolf doubted that they reached their wagons.

As many as fifteen bluecoats formed a line atop a snow-covered sand bank and bravely struggled for their lives. Wolf led the charge that broke their line, and he clubbed one man senseless and knocked a second from his horse. Others, mostly youngsters, fell on the helpless *Wihio* soldiers and cut out their lives. Wolf contented himself with counting coup. He had no heart for killing those bluecoats. They carried no scalps of slaughtered children.

Once the charges were broken and the bluecoats had returned to their wagons, the fighting grew quieter. Those warriors with good rifles exchanged shots with the wagon soldiers, and even some men with only bows crept close enough to get off a shot or two. By nightfall the fighting had died away, though. The air was growing cold, and the older men began breaking away.

Wolf himself thought of his camp, of Sun Walker Woman and the little children. He had brought nothing along to eat, and his belly reminded him of the fact.

"It's time we left," Stands Long finally declared. "We can accomplish nothing here. The *Oglalas* say that some of the bluecoats got away, and they may have reached help. We should go back and prepare the camps for the move north."

"He's right, *Nah nih,*" Raven Heart added. The young man's face was drawn, and sweat had painted black streaks of war paint across his cheeks. "I have no more arrows."

Wolf turned and gazed at the others. Most had empty quivers, and all were exhausted.

"Sun Walker Woman will have heard the shooting," Wolf told them. "She'll cook some buffalo meat for us to eat. We'll feel better tomorrow. Then we'll come back and finish the fight."

"If that's what you want to do," Stands Long said, "we'll do it. These *Wihio* are also tired, though. We killed some of them, so they'll no longer be hungry to fight us. We should take the helpless ones north and finish the fight when the grasses are green again."

"It's a good idea," Red Hawk declared. "We can hold another council in the Black Hills and recount our coups. We'll hunt fresh meat there, and you can tell your sons of the rescues and the fighting."

"Yes," Wolf agreed. "We're finished here. Let's go and eat something."

"Lead us, *Nah nih,*" High Flyer urged. "We'll follow."

chapter
10

WOLF RUNNING AND HIS COMPANIONS found little time to celebrate their clash with the bluecoats. Sun Walker Woman roasted buffalo meat and cooked fry bread, but the embers of the cooking fire were still glowing when she began the task of packing the family's belongings.

"The *Wihio* are too close," she told Wolf. "My father's people are moving north. We should join them."

If Wolf needed any encouragement, Crazy Horse's decision to take his band north settled the issue.

"Winter's too hard a time to fight," Wolf's cousin told him. "We'll wait for the ice to thaw. Then we'll hunt Bull Buffalo!"

Long Dog's dwindling band, together with a number of southern people, joined the *Lakotas* camped on Powder River that winter. It was good country, full of game and far from *Wihio* roads. The Crows sometimes hunted and raided there, but it was too far for the Pawnees to come. With so many allied camps, *Tsis tsis tas, Suhtai,* and *Lakota* alike felt safe.

Wolf passed that winter in the comfort of his lodge. He left the task of watching the ponies to his brothers. The *Lakotas* had taken up the habit of erecting log corrals to hold their best ponies, and he helped Stands Long build a similar structure. Mostly, though, Wolf sat by the fire with his growing sons and spoke of the old, half-remembered tales of his grandfathers.

It was a good time. For once *Heammawihio* kept death and sickness away. Winter was normally the season when the weak and the old began their long walk up Hanging Road, but perhaps the road was too crowded with the innocents slain at Sand Creek. Wolf expressed his gratitude each morning as he spoke the sunrise prayers. He hoped peace would last for a time. Soon, though, his dreams clouded with dark specters, and he warned his brothers to be vigilant.

"Trouble's coming," he declared. "We must be watchful."

The snow was still ankle deep along Powder River when the trees began to green. It was a welcome sight, a reminder of the renewal of the seasons, the continuity of life. Perhaps that was why he took his small sons with him to make the dawn prayers. And why, afterward, they joined the other men and boys in the shallows of the river for a chilling morning swim.

"The water's cold, *Ne' hyo*!" Winter Pup squealed.

"It's freezing!" Deer Foot added.

The little boys, shivering, huddled with Raven Heart and Broken Wing. Wind's Whisper, entering his seventh summer, bit his lip and refused to acknowledge the cold.

"Hardships make us strong," he told his brothers.

Wolf smiled with approval. The water had an icy bite, and little ones, thin from winter, had little to fend it off. Naked, they seemed even more vulnerable. The older boys, with lengthening bone and sinew and broadening shoulders, shook off the cold as they ran with their elders.

"I wanted my sons to share morning with their father," he explained as he led Wind's Whisper to the bank. Raven Heart followed, a nephew in each arm.

"It's a good thing, this sharing," Stands Long pronounced as he brought warming blankets to the children. "A stream washes away a man's weariness and restores his senses. It's unusual for boys so young to be invited. Your father honors you."

The younger boys made no reply. As Raven Heart rubbed warmth into their small limbs, they brightened. They remained quiet, though. Wind's Whisper, on the other hand, mimicked his father's actions. The boy dried himself and dressed slowly, carefully.

"Maybe we can go and shoot a deer later," he suggested. "You know I'm a good arrow maker. I can shoot, too. My uncles have taught me."

"He has the true aim," Raven Heart boasted. "Soon he'll need a bigger bow."

"Until he has one, maybe we should shoot rabbits," Wolf said, grinning at his son. "Deer and buffalo can wait."

"It won't be a long wait, though," Stands Long said, squeezing Whisper's shoulder. "The muscles are hard. Soon he'll be a young man."

It was true. Wind's Whisper had taken on a summer's glow. The boy's hair was dark, like his mother's, but his face had the lighter pigment that had brought Wolf and Crazy Horse so much trouble. Whisper was tall for his age, good with weapons, and fleet afoot. That was good. A light-skinned boy faced extra challenges.

Wolf and his oldest son shot two rabbits that morning and three more the next. They walked the far bank of the river together, examining their ponies. Later they crafted arrows, side by side.

Wolf would have preferred to pass more mornings in such a fashion, but it wasn't to be. Two days later Raven Heart came upon a bow and a quiver of arrows near the pony corrals.

"They're not *Lakota,*" Heart declared. "Not *Suhtai* or *Tsis tsis tas.* I know the Arapaho markings, too, but these are different."

"Crow," Wolf announced. "Our enemies are nearby."

Wolf and Raven Heart examined the odd impressions in the snow. There were several tracks left by horses. Then evidence that something had happened.

"A rider fell," Wolf said, pointing to the indentation left by a man's hand. "He rolled to one side. Now, look there. Footprints. A man staggered."

"He must have been hurt to leave his weapons behind," Raven Heart observed.

"What do these next tracks tell you?" Wolf asked.

Raven Heart studied the tracks. "Twelve ponies," he announced. "Only six had riders. Horse stealers!"

As word of the Crow arrows spread through the neighboring camps, men gathered to plan what to do. Crazy Horse, stripped and painted for battle, greeted his cousin with wary eyes.

"We must find these raiders quickly," he announced. "If they reach the Crow camps, they'll betray the location of our winter camps."

"Yes," Wolf agreed. "I'm nearly ready."

"Be careful," Crazy Horse added. "The Crows have far-firing rifles. They'll clever, these Crows. They've killed many of our relations."

"And we have killed many of theirs," Wolf added. "You should also be careful. You've become well known. The Crows would celebrate taking your scalp."

"No less than yours, Cousin. Ayyyy! Perhaps we'll be the ones to dance, though."

Wolf hoped so. As Stands Long arrived with the best ponies, Wolf began painting his face. He again used the dark stripe across the eyes, and he took special care in placing the elk charms behind his brothers' ears. In the end, eight men assembled. Broken Wing joined Stands Long, Red Hawk, High Flyer, and Raven Heart. Two young southerners, Standing Elk and Ringtail, completed the party.

"We're late starting," Ringtail grumbled after Wolf completed his prayers. "We'll never catch the others."

"The others don't need us," Wolf replied. "We're hunting raiders."

"And if we find them?" Standing Elk asked.

"Eight of us are enough to punish some Crows," Red Hawk boasted. "We're following my brother. He has far-seeing eyes. If the others haven't already run those raiders, we'll find them."

Actually following the tracks wasn't that difficult. In the beginning, the Crows left a clear path in the snow. Later, though, they concealed their trail by splashing into the river. The *Lakotas* followed a false trail left by one of the captured ponies. Standing Elk also wanted to go that way, but Wolf only laughed.

"Look at that pony's tracks," Wolf urged. "It carries no weight."

"Riderless," Broken Wing cried.

"Now study the stream," Wolf suggested. Up ahead several rocks glinted through the shallow water. Farther along, the water was muddy, and the bed betrayed the passage of ponies.

"Follow me," Stands Long shouted as he pointed to a patch of mutilated snow. Wolf nudged his pony into a trot, and the others followed. Eleven horses had left the river, but soon one fell behind.

"A poor leader, this Crow," Broken Wing muttered. "He's leaving the injured man."

Wolf sighed. It certainly appeared that was the case. After riding a bit farther, he confirmed his suspicions. Five stolen ponies stood near a tall cottonwood. A sixth pony, marked in the Crow fashion, wandered a stone's throw away.

"Careful," Wolf urged, waving his companions to the right and left. "He may have a rifle."

"No," Raven Heart declared, easing himself into the lead. "We found a bow, didn't we? Remember the hand. It was small. No, this one's just a pony boy."

"Probably a boy without brothers, perhaps even a father," Broken Wing added. "Somebody to take along and leave to the enemy."

"We would never do that," Wolf said, gazing deeply into Broken Wing's eyes.

"I've known few Crows to leave one of their own," Stands Long added. "We may kill them, but they're good fighters. This one, if he's still alive, won't be easy to kill."

Actually, Wolf suspected the young raider *was* dead. Stands Long had said it. Crows didn't leave boys behind for their enemies to kill. This time they had, though. Raven Heart pointed to the smallish figure sitting with his back to the cottonwood, skinning knife in hand. Hurt and abandoned, the boy nevertheless remained defiant. When Wolf approached, the Crow struggled to his feet and stumbled out, shouting and flashing the knife.

"This is no fight," Stands Long grumbled, turning away from the Crow. The boy's left shoulder dipped, and he limped badly.

"I'll end it then," Ringtail said, kicking his horse into a gallop. The young *Tsis tsis tas* raced toward the Crow, halted his pony, and jumped down into the snow. The Crow was only five arm lengths away when Ringtail nocked an arrow.

"Ayyyy!" the Crow screamed, lunging forward. Ringtail fired his arrow, striking the *Crow's* right hip. The young Crow stumbled. Ringtail's second arrow sliced through the boy's bare chest into his vitals. The Crow collapsed in the bloodstained snow and died.

"I'm first!" Ringtail shouted, touching his bow to the slain Crow's forehead. Standing Elk, who had followed his friend, jumped down and counted a second coup. The two southerners cut away their enemy's forelock and stripped the broken body. Before they cut the body itself, Wolf called them back.

"He was a brave heart!" Wolf shouted. "It's a bad thing, leaving such a boy behind to die alone. You've taken his life and his scalp. That's enough."

"The wolves will do it anyway," Ringtail argued.

"That's as it should be," Wolf insisted. "*Heammawihio,* who makes the sun rise and the rivers flow, has given the four-leggeds their tasks. Also the birds. It's not for us to mark such a man."

"They cut up my father!" Ringtail insisted as he drew out a knife. "My little brother!"

"This one didn't," Broken Wing said, riding closer to his young friends. "If you do this, you'll disturb the sacred hoop. This Crow will walk your dreams, and you'll remember only him!"

"He's right," Raven Heart added. "You heard him cry out this winter."

Ringtail hesitated. Standing Elk shuddered. Then both young men returned to their horses. Ringtail even discarded the scalp.

Wolf waved his companions along, and they soon located the fleeing Crows' trail. The remaining riders separated, though. Two turned north and three went east, toward a rocky ridge overlooking the river.

"Should we follow both?" Stands Long asked.

Wolf turned and eyed his companions. Red Hawk and High Flyer might manage on their own, but the others were too young. What if it was a trap, and all the Crows fell on one party or the other?

"No," Wolf announced. "We'll find these first three. The others can wait."

Wolf later regretted his decision. They never did locate the other two raiders. One was probably their leader, and he had chosen to sacrifice more of his party to aid his own escape. The Crows' ponies were grazing near the river. Footprints led into a hill of rocks and vanished.

"Up there," Stands Long said, pointing across the boulder-strewn ground.

"I've been in country like this before," Broken Wing said, sighing. "It's full of caves. There are a hundred places up there to hide. If we go up there, they'll find it easy to shoot us."

"We can't just let them stay there," Ringtail objected. "What will the others say?"

"You should have kept the scalp," Standing Elk grumbled. "That would have shown the others."

"We could take the ponies back to camp," Stands Long suggested. "Afoot, three Crows can't trouble anybody."

"It's true," Wolf said, studying the ridge. "A warrior doesn't turn his back on an enemy, though. I'm going up."

Red Hawk started to argue, but Stands Long simply laughed.

"You can as easily halt a buffalo stampede with a courting flute," Stands Long declared. "Spread out. Keep low."

Wolf intended to draw the Crows' fire, so he darted between the rocks, rising and diving away like a playful squirrel. The Crows remained patient—for a time. Then one finally fired his rifle. The ball whined past Wolf's ear, clipping a pine branch only a hair away.

"I see them!" High Flyer called. "Left of you and ahead."

Wolf noticed the faint powder smoke and took care to circle around it. A second rifle barked from a few feet farther away, but the ball was well wide.

The game continued for a bit. Wolf and his companions crept closer, and the Crows fired off their rifles defiantly. Gradually, though, the Crows fell back through a hollow notch into a rocky cavern. From their haven inside, the Crows screamed taunts in English and even in *Tsis tsis tas*!

"See what comes of our people trading at the forts," Stands Long complained. "Now they throw our own words at us!"

Wolf merely sighed.

"They can't kill us with words," he pointed out. "Soon they'll be no more trouble to anybody."

Wolf instructed Stands Long to watch the cavern while he circled around and spoke with the others. He had a relatively simple plan. They would build a fire and smoke the Crows out of their lair.

Broken Wing oversaw the gathering of dead wood, and Raven Heart struck the iron blade of his knife to flint in order to produce a spark. It caught a bit of tinder afire, and soon the old brittle wood ignited.

The Crows did their best to drive the fire off. They used the ramrods of their rifles to push the flaming twigs away, but Wolf and his companions countered by jabbing the branches with tree limbs. Wolf could hear the men inside coughing for a time, but they didn't come out.

"There must be another entrance," Stands Long declared. He continued on over a rocky hump and located a second mouth of the cavern. Wolf followed, and together they built a second fire. Once it burst into flame, the Crows became desperate. The heat and the smoke burned their lungs, and they screamed horribly. Finally they charged out through the burning brush, smoke-blackened, with hair and eyebrows singed, to fight a final time.

They never had a chance. In their blind fury, they stabbed empty air with lances. Red Hawk killed the first one with an arrow through both lungs. High Flyer jumped on the second Crow and bashed him senseless with a war club. The third Crow was even younger than the poor cripple left at the cottonwood. Coming through the flames, he had managed to catch his breechclout and leggings on fire. Screaming in agony, he ripped off the flaming garments and fell to his knees. His hands and feet were blistered black, and his tormented eyes pleaded for a merciful death.

"I can't," Raven Heart, who was closest, declared.

"Look at him," Broken Wing added. "He's too young to ride with the men."

"I'm no Crow lover," Ringtail said, marching toward the surviving Crow. By then the boy was on his back, hugging himself and whimpering a death chant.

"Kill me," the Crow pleaded, speaking English. "Quickly," he added. He repeated the plea, using *Lakota* words.

"I can't do it," Ringtail confessed, dropping his lance. The Crow boy was little more than a charred wretch below the waist and above the neck. The hair on the left side of his head was gone, as was one ear. Only his chest appeared human.

"He's suffered enough," Wolf called, waving to his companions. "Give him rest."

None of them stirred, so Wolf nocked an arrow and started toward the boy.

"No!" Broken Wing called, taking his lance and plunging it into the young Crow's chest.

"Wing?" Wolf asked, rushing to the young man's side. "I would have . . ."

"You have sons yourself," Broken Wing explained, tossing the lance away in disgust. "It was for me to do."

"There are always some who accept the difficult tasks," Stands Long said, allowing Broken Wing to collapse against his side. "My brother-friend has always been such a man. I believe that you, too, will be one."

"Perhaps," Raven Heart agreed, taking the discarded lance. "If his dreams don't choke him."

"We'll build another sweat lodge," Wolf declared. "We'll . . ."

"Yes," Broken Wing said, forcing a smile onto his lips. "We'll do it."

Ringtail and Standing Elk then stepped to the older Crows and cut away their hair. They also collected their knives. The lances and clothes were burned past saving, and the rifles inside the cave were useless. The heat had ignited powder and blown apart the barrels.

"Little to show for four men," Wolf observed. "Two scalps, some knives, and a few trinkets."

"I should have kept the other scalp," Ringtail grumbled.

"No," Broken Wing objected. "You should not have taken those two."

Broken Wing's eyes were full of fury, the same fury that had kept the scalping knives away from the burned Crow boy.

"We had to bring them back," Standing Elk said in a calm, thoughtful voice. "We need them for a scalp dance. We'll honor our courage and recount the story of the brave Crows. It will chase their ghosts to the other side."

"Maybe," Broken Wing muttered. His eyes reflected his doubts.

chapter
11

WHILE THE SOLDIER SOCIETIES CELEBRATED the defeat of the Crow raiders, Long Dog and many of the older men fretted over the two who got away. To make matters worse, the drumming and the singing of the scalp dancers drove the deer and small game from Powder River, and hunters had to venture ever farther away to bring fresh meat to the lodges.

"The noise which scares the animals will attract our enemies," Long Dog complained. "When will we learn to hold the young men in check?"

"Who can say?" Wolf replied. "Do you think we should break away, go south perhaps?"

"No," Long Dog muttered. "We're better off here, with our friends close."

Wolf knew that his father-in-law would once have led the *Suhtai* from Powder River, but then his words had held power. Now a feather held more sway.

"I've lived too long," Long Dog declared. "I'm ready to give over my burden to someone else."

"There are others who would take it," Wolf noted.

"They would only lead the people to their deaths. Have heart. Your grandson makes the morning prayers and swims the river with the men. Soon he'll hunt Bull Buffalo."

"I won't live to see that," Long Dog insisted. "You're not the only one who sees things in his dreams, Wolf. Dark times are coming."

But if they were, Wolf noticed few signs of it. The grasses began to green, and there was no sign of Crows or bluecoats along Powder River. The ponies grew fat, and the chiefs met to plan the summer hunting. It was time to invite Bull Buffalo to give up his sons so that the people could grow strong.

That summer the Crazy Dogs took charge of the hunt. They assigned men to guard the camps and directed the other soldier societies to scout here or there, seeking a herd. Wolf rode with the Elks, as was his custom, but for the first time he welcomed Raven Heart and Broken Wing to join the hunting.

"You've won a brave name," Wolf told his youngest brother. "Your days as a pony boy have passed. You'll ride with the scouts this year."

"Yes, *Nah nih*," Raven Heart said respectfully. "And when it's time to strike the buffalo?"

"You'll go first," Wolf said, smiling.

"You honor me," the young man said, dropping his gaze.

"You gave me back my life," Wolf reminded him. "This is my gift to you."

"Only one of many," Raven Heart whispered.

Perhaps it was the enthusiasm that Raven Heart and Broken Wing brought to the hunt that energized Wolf Running that summer. Certainly something did. Sun Walker Woman noticed it.

"You're at home again," she observed.

"What?" Wolf asked.

"Even since we learned of the killing of the southerners, you've been drifting away from us," she told him. "You sit with your sons beside the fire, but your eyes are distant.

It's as if you are dancing in the clouds, and we're back here, alone. No more.''

''I've had many concerns,'' he confessed. ''So much about our lives has changed. Now that we're gathered here, united and strong with our *Lakota* cousins, we can walk the sacred path again. The chiefs are making the proper preparations for the hunt. We've prayed and danced and planned. We'll enjoy success.''

Stands Long also saw the change.

''Last summer you would have spoken in the council,'' Wolf's brother-friend told him. ''You would have worried about the young men going and urged them to hold back. It's good to see Wolf Running's returned to us. We need bold leaders, good fighters.''

''We're only hunting,'' Wolf insisted.

''Today we ride out to locate Bull Buffalo. Tomorrow? You've heard the stories. The bluecoats have finished fighting the graycoats. More *Wihio* will bring their wagons to Platte River road. The forts will fill with our enemies.''

''Maybe not,'' Wolf said hopefully. ''The *Wihio* traders say it was a hard war and their chiefs want to rest.''

''No,'' Stands Long grumbled. ''Bluecoats are vultures. They're always hungry. They will soon grow hungry to kill our people, as they did at Sand Creek. They tried at Platte River. No, my friend, they'll be back.''

The words proved to be prophetic.

The summer buffalo hunting was as good as anyone could recall. Wolf's scouting party located one herd, the Bowstrings found a second, and the Crazy Dogs spotted a third. The camps split into three bodies, each trailing a herd. The hunters brought meat and hides enough to feed and clothe everyone. Soon the women were at work, roasting and smoking meat or scraping hides.

Wolf was especially pleased with his brothers. Red Hawk and High Flyer agreed to stand aside so that their younger companions could make the first kill. Raven Heart charged a great hairy bull and fired two arrows into its heart. Broken Wing, never far behind, made the second kill. Both recounted their coups in the Elk council, and

Long Dog tied an eagle feather in each youngster's hair.

"It's a good thing that the people have brave young men such as these," Long Dog told the council. "With so many enemies around us, we'll need them."

Wolf gave little weight to Long Dog's comments at the time. It was a moment for building up the young Elks, wasn't it? Later, though, after the chiefs met to discuss matters, Wolf learned that Stands Long had been right. The *Wihio* war in the East was over. The Platte River road was full of wagon people, and many soldier chiefs said it was time to strike a hard blow.

"If we wait for the bluecoat armies to arrive, it will be too late," Pawnee Chaser argued.

"Is there no chance of settling our disagreement?" Long Dog asked. "Our people have suffered most, but we used to be on good terms with the *Wihio.*"

"Black Kettle spoke of peace," Broken Wing said, sadly staring southward. "Then I had relations. She who was my mother and he who was my father. Brothers. Now they're on the other side because we listened to *Wihio* promises. When I die I will hold a lance in my hand!"

"It's appropriate," Long Dog noted. "You're an Elk. I have grandsons who are too small to hold lances. What of them?"

Broken Wing stared at his feet. He had no answer.

"I won't go to the *Wihio* chiefs like a whipped dog, begging for peace," Pawnee Chaser insisted. "I also have small sons, and I don't want them murdered like my cousins who were killed at Sand Creek. We can only treat with men who respect us. The bluecoats will only do so if they're afraid."

"Yes," others agreed. "We must run them."

"They fear us on South Platte River, at Julesburg and at the ranches there," Pawnee Chaser argued. "Now's the time to strike them on North Platte River. When they're frightened like little children, then we can talk."

Many *Lakotas* agreed with Pawnee Chaser, and Young Man Afraid of His Horses, a famous soldier chief, sent out a pipe. As the Bright Moon grew full, Young Man Afraid met with the other soldier chiefs. They decided to attack a group of Kansas bluecoats at an abandoned stagecoach station on North Platte River.

Wolf's instinct was to avoid the pipe and let Pawnee Chaser and his hot blood *Oglalas* fight the Kansans.

"We should continue hunting," he told Sun Walker. "I want to watch my sons grow this summer."

"It's a good notion," she agreed. Her eyes concealed an unspoken concern, though, and Wolf frowned.

"I expected you to be glad," he said, taking her hands in his own. "What's wrong?"

"My father is going," she explained. "He says that a chief can't hide on Powder River when there's fighting to be done."

"He's no lance carrier," Wolf objected. "He should stay behind and see to the safety of the helpless ones."

"He says that he's done that too often," she said, sighing. "It's because of my brothers. They're hot to fight, and he won't allow them to rush off with the other young men and be killed. He believes he can shield them from harm."

"Sometimes a father must give up the rein," Wolf observed. "It's no easy thing, though. Now that I have sons, I see how hard it would be. You want me to ride with the *Suhtai*?"

"You can't save him, Wolf," she admitted, "but having other good men there will lessen the danger."

"He'll probably be safe anyway," Wolf declared. "It will be as at Muddy Spring Creek. We'll take some horses. There are only a few bluecoats at this station, and they won't be eager to fight a large force."

"Maybe you'll both come back," she said hopefully. "If a bad thing happens, you won't let him die alone, though."

"I'm Wolf Running," he whispered in her right ear. "I'm famous for rescuing my brother Elks."

"Last time it was you that needed rescuing," Sun Walker Woman reminded him. "Keep Stands Long with you this time. You'll need men you can trust."

In all the years he had known his wife, she had never

spoken so openly before a fight. Wolf wanted to attribute
it to a daughter's concern, but he knew better. Sun Walker
also knew the medicine trail. She saw things in her dreams.
He could not dismiss her worried expression lightly.

Wolf set off to locate his brothers and explain his decision, but there was no need. High Flyer and Raven Heart
had already assembled the best ponies, and Red Hawk had
Wind's Whisper busy collecting arrows and filling quivers.

"We heard that Long Dog was going," Stands Long
explained. "When Sun Walker drew you aside, we suspected that the summer hunting was finished for us."

"Someone should stay and watch the little ones," Wolf
argued.

"There are plenty of men who will stay," Raven Heart
said, feeling the intensity of his oldest brother's gaze.
"I've counted coup on Bull Buffalo, *Nah nih.* I can't stay
behind this time."

"No one expects much trouble," Stands Long added.
"The women and children will be safe enough here."

"As our people were at Sand Creek?" Wolf asked.

"A thousand *Lakotas* are camped between them and the
Crows up north," Stands Long pointed out. "We'll be
between the camps and any prowling Pawnees. As for
bluecoats, there are few enough of them, and they'll soon
be busy."

"Yes," High Flyer agreed. "With us!"

So it was that Wolf Running again rode south to strike
at a bluecoat outpost. This time he wasn't with the band
that fought the Kansans. The two hundred *Lakota* and *Tsis
tsis tas* warriors who were there made a surround, ran off
twenty ponies, but failed to drive the bluecoats from their
log stockade. One bluecoat died trying to guard the horses,
and boasting *Lakotas* claimed some others were hurt, but
the raid achieved little other than to alert the bluecoats that
more trouble was at hand.

By mid-summer large bands of raiding *Lakota, Tsis tsis
tas,* and Arapaho warriors frequently struck coaches traveling the stage road. There was more chasing than fighting,
though. The bluecoats felt safe in their stockades or behind

circled wagons, and whenever they spotted a war party, they sought safety.

The largest and most dangerous band of bluecoats occupied a log stockade near a wooden bridge over North Platte River. Wagon parties, traders, and even mixed breed trappers and their families frequently crossed the bridge, and the bluecoats were there to protect the place. Young Man Afraid chose to attack the site, and he sent word to gather nearby. Before long three thousand warriors arrived. A few hundred *Tsis tsis tas* women and children also came.

After the soldier chiefs had planned the attack, individual warriors made their private preparations. In addition to preparing paint and offering charms to the young men, Wolf spoke the ancient *Suhtai* warrior prayers. Last of all he stripped the cover from his shield, allowing the sacred ornaments—elk teeth, bear claws, and two eagle feathers—to hang loose. He turned the shield four times toward the earth. Then he held it to the sky four times. Finally he spoke his personal medicine prayer.

> "Today we ride, *Heammawihio*,
> Remembering that we are only men.
> None of us last long,
> Only earth and mountain.
> Give us Bull Buffalo's heart, Eagle's sharp eye,
> Deer's fleet feet, and Badger's determination.
> The enemy's near, so we must fight.
> Ayyyy! We'll run them!"

It was a simple song compared to the long, loud boasting words preferred by many of his brother Elks. Wolf's medicine flowed from his modest manner, though. As was his habit, he wore only breechclout and war shirt into battle that day. He tied two feathers in his hair in place of the bonnet his many coups had earned him.

"What paint will we wear, *Nah nih*?" Raven Heart asked when Wolf began coloring his face.

"Red from the earth," Wolf explained as he mixed the dyes. "A yellow thunderbolt across the forehead."

"You'll do this and ride a pale horse, too?" young Broken Wing asked.

"A buckskin today," Wolf said, grinning at the youngster. "The white one doesn't like to hear rifles."

"It's good you leave it then," Pawnee Chaser said, joining them. "I'm leading the decoys. I need reliable men to follow. Are you willing?"

"Just us?" Wolf asked.

"Eight others," Pawnee Chaser explained. "No hot bloods."

"And what of the hot bloods we leave behind?" Wolf asked.

"The Crazy Dogs will guard the flanks," Pawnee Chaser explained. "The soldier chiefs and lance carriers will stand in front, preventing anyone from charging ahead. It won't be like before. We'll lure out the bluecoats, and the others will kill them."

The plan appeared sound, but Wolf knew how often good plans failed to bring the desired result. He nevertheless rode with his brothers and Stands Long when Pawnee Chaser led the decoys toward the stockade.

Nothing went as expected. The bluecoat sentries at the bridge fled to the stockade, and no one came out to fight. Worse, the bluecoats had a small howitzer, and they fired the gun at the decoys. Once, twice, three times the shells exploded in the sandy earth, throwing up sandy plumes and startling the ponies. Pawnee Chaser himself lost control of his mount, and three young *Lakotas* followed the chief into the nearby hills.

Most of the chiefs stood and watched, but Long Dog kicked his pony into a gallop, raced down to the decoys, and ordered them to leave.

"We've come too far to leave now!" an *Oglala* named Bear Claw growled. "I'm going ahead. Won't someone join me?"

A pair of *Oglalas* eagerly volunteered, but Long Dog silenced them.

"You'll only die that way," the chief barked. "If you insist on attacking, follow me."

Long Dog had frequently demonstrated his courage. That morning he wore a bonnet filled with eagle feathers. The younger men, noting that bonnet, yielded. The bonnet marked him as a worthy target, though, and rifles and howitzer concentrated on him. Long Dog ignored the peril. He nudged his horse along and out of view of the *Wihio* bridge. He then led the way across a shallow ford and resumed the attack on the far bank.

By then most of the other warriors had lost patience and turned back to camp. Long Dog's small party continued, though, and soon Pawnee Chaser and his three companions rejoined the fight. Altogether the decoy force numbered twenty riders. By odd chance they charged the fort at the very instant that a party of bluecoats approached the stockade from downriver. The decoys had the advantage of surprise, and they scattered the bluecoats in a single wild charge.

Briefly Wolf watched with approval as the bluecoats fled in panic. Three or four of them fell wounded. Then the gate of the stockade opened, and a mixed party of bluecoats and Snakes emerged on horseback. Wolf formed a line with his brothers, Stands Long, and Broken Wing. It could not withstand the power of the Snakes' charge, though. Wolf himself fell back to the river and tried to determine what to do. Pawnee Chaser was fighting a two-striped bluecoat, but Long Dog had simply vanished.

"There!" Stands Long shouted, pointing to a cluster of bluecoats near the river bank. A solitary old man was holding them off with a lance.

"We're Elks!" Wolf howled. "Ours is the difficult thing to do!"

He led the way, but his brothers followed. Together they escaped the Snakes and broke through the bluecoats encircling Long Dog. By then the old man was bleeding from three bullet wounds and two saber gashes.

"Wolf?" the weary chief called.

"Your grandsons will sing of this fight," Wolf said as he rolled off the buckskin and hurried to his father-in-law's side.

"They'll grow tall and strong," Long Dog declared, "but I won't see it."

Wolf started to argue, but there was no concealing the truth. The old man was dying.

"Where are the others?" Long Dog asked. "Are they charging? We decoyed the bluecoats out from their wall. Are they dying?"

"Yes," Wolf lied. "Your attack won the fight for us."

"It will be a remembered death then," Long Dog said, smiling faintly. "A man can expect little more. He walks a warrior's trail, and he doesn't live too long. You younger men must make the decisions now. I'm too tired."

Long Dog stared at the stockade, half-shrouded in powder smoke, and grinned. He couldn't see that the Snakes and the rescued bluecoats were riding through the gate. No, Long Dog saw other victories, other fights. Wolf hoped that when the old man closed his eyes on the final hour of a troubled life, he would find comfort on the other side.

chapter
12

LONG DOG'S THREE SONS, YOUNGER DOG, Spring Fox, and Rabbit, took charge of their father's body that evening. They had ridden away from Platte River with their companions, expecting Long Dog to bring the decoys along. They were not the only ones who were stunned to learn of the *Suhtai* chief's death. Word of the calamity spread through the camps, and angry voices urged a renewed attack on the Platte Bridge bluecoats.

"I have a son's obligation," Younger Dog told Wolf. "I'll send Spring Fox to bring our sister and the other women. We'll begin the mourning. I believe you should accept the burden of leading the decoys back to the bridge."

"Sun Walker Woman will expect me to be here," Wolf argued.

"She'll understand when I explain," Younger Dog insisted. "If I believed that enough of the others would follow, I would lead the decoys myself. They *will* ride with you."

"To what purpose?" Wolf asked. "The bluecoats are

too careful. They're guided by their Snake scouts. They won't come out, and we can't ride close to their log walls. Their long-firing guns will kill us.''

"Not all *Wihio* are cowards," Younger Dog insisted. "Some fought yesterday. If you bring only a few men, some bluecoats will attack you. They have to get water, and they need to chop wood for their cooking fires.''

"They can wait days before they have to fetch wood or water," Wolf observed. "Maybe some wagon people will come along, though. The bluecoats might fight to save travelers.''

"You'll lead the attack then?" Younger Dog asked.

"I'm an Elk," Wolf boasted. "The difficult tasks are mine to do.''

And so Wolf Running again called on his brothers and Stands Long Beside Him to join the decoy force.

"I thought you would join the mourners," Raven Heart said, frowning. "Sun Walker will expect it.''

"Her brothers asked me to lead the decoys," Wolf explained. "What can I do at the camp? Here I can be useful.''

"They don't want you to remind the others that they didn't follow their father," Stands Long complained.

"They couldn't know that he would lead an attack.''

"You never let your father ride out alone, Wolf. When a chief takes his camp north and leaves the young men to fight his enemies, people wonder why. What did he tell you? That he feared for his sons? Perhaps he was afraid they lacked the heart to fight.''

"Each man has his own path to walk," Wolf muttered. "If they lack a warrior's heart, it's better that I lead the decoys.''

Stands Long frowned, but he spoke no more of it. What was the use? Once Wolf set his feet upon a path, there was no turning him away from it.

Whatever his motives, Younger Dog had been correct about the willingness of others to follow Wolf Running. Even before Wolf could prepare a pipe, two hundred men assembled, armed and eager to strike the bluecoats at Platte

Bridge. Of the twenty or so decoy riders, half were from *Suhtai* or *Tsis tsis tas* bands. Broken Wing was there, riding as usual alongside Raven Heart. Wolf knew the others only slightly.

A large party of southerners under their war chief, Roman Nose, formed the ambush force. They broke into twos and threes and concealed themselves up and down North Platte River. *Lakotas* came, too. Wolf sensed a difference in the raiders this time. Instead of boasting fools like Big Horn, older, wiser men led each band. The younger men appeared content to follow famous fighters like Roman Nose.

It was still early when Wolf and the others arrived at the bridge. They dismounted briefly to make the appropriate prayers. Then they painted their faces and remounted their ponies. Finally Wolf alerted the others and rode warily toward the bridge.

"Remember," he urged. "Our task is not to run the enemy but to allow him to run us. We won't turn before our brothers strike. Be careful not to get too far ahead of the rest of us. When we turn, stay with me."

"Remember, too, that the bluecoats have good rifles," Stands Long shouted. "I don't like to think of you, brothers, with holes instead of noses."

The younger men laughed at the jest, but Wolf remained serious. One good man was already dead, and for what? Nothing. Before he'd see another such as Long Dog fall, he expected to punish the bluecoats.

The air was oddly still for a summer morning. The skies overhead were cloudless, and except for a ground squirrel scampering along the riverbank, nothing stirred. As Wolf and Stands Long moved across the wooden planks of the bridge, they sang.

> "It's good we're riding this morning.
>   The enemy is strong, but we're *Tsis tsis tas*.
>   We'll run them, hah!"

"First, though, they'll run us," Wolf said, laughing nervously.

The bluecoats appeared unconcerned by the approach of the decoys. Wolf heard no cry of alarm, and he saw no warning shots fired.

"Wolf?" Stands Long asked. "Have they gone away?"

"There's only one way to find out," Wolf replied. Waving the others back, he placed his shield on his left arm and held a lance in his right. Then, screaming, he charged the fort.

Wolf's charge quickly settled the question. Bluecoats appeared all along the stockade, and soon rifle balls were striking the earth all around him. Three struck the shield, but the heavy bull hide deflected each one. A fourth tore a slice in Wolf's left shoulder, and a fifth nicked his left hip.

"Ayyyy!" Stands Long shouted as he, too, made a run at the fort. The bluecoats shifted their fire to the new threat, and Wolf escaped. Red Hawk and High Flyer also charged the stockade. The *Wihio* continued to shoot erratically, and each brother returned unharmed.

"These bluecoats must have been sleeping," Stands Long observed. "I've never known any to be so poor at shooting guns."

"They're still dangerous," Wolf said as he bound his wounds. "We'll wait a moment. They may try to fire their big gun again."

Instead, the bluecoats sent a party of horsemen out from the stockade.

"Ah, here they come," Red Hawk said, pointing to a small band of horsemen approaching on gray mounts.

"All of you know our task," Wolf told his companions. "We're not here to count coup or strike these bluecoats. Our task is to draw them out to the others. Only then will we turn."

Wolf gazed into each man's eyes. No one objected, so Wolf turned his horse and led the way back toward the bridge. For an instant the bluecoats ignored their fleeing enemy. Then they increased their pace and started down the river in pursuit.

Wolf smiled approvingly as the ambushers remained hidden. They allowed the *Wihio* to cross the bridge unmolested and start down the river. Only when they were well past the crossing did a party of *Tsis tsis tas* ride out and charge the bluecoats. Instantly other parties charged from ahead and from each flank. The bluecoats made an effort to continue eastward, but as they saw the size of the ambushing force, they turned back toward the bridge.

Wolf and the other decoys finally halted and turned back on the bluecoats. Amid the powder smoke and a faint morning mist, the fighting quickly became confused. Two riderless cavalry horses raced past, and Wolf hoped that the bluecoats had dismounted to make a stand. That was a fatal tactic against so many enemies, though, and the bluecoat chief was too clever to make such a mistake. Instead he charged the line of men blocking the road to the bridge.

By the time Wolf arrived, most of the bluecoats were dead or in flight. The big *Wihio* gun was again booming out from the safety of the stockade, and Roman Nose had halted the pursuit.

Wolf gazed with surprise at the bluecoat chief. He remained atop his pony, but his eyes were vacant. An arrow protruded from his forehead, and he rode eerily along the road until a *Lakota* finally raced over and knocked him from his pony.

It seemed impossible to Wolf that any of the bluecoats could have escaped the trap, but most of them had. He counted only seven bodies besides the chief, although he supposed some others might have died after reaching their friends at the stockade.

Wolf had little chance to celebrate the victory. Watchers on the nearby hills waved blankets, signaling a new danger nearby.

"I'll go and see what it is," High Flyer volunteered. Raven Heart and Broken Wing followed. They soon returned with news that a larger body of soldiers was approaching from the east, escorting a line of wagons.

"How many are coming?" Wolf asked.

"I counted twenty in front," High Flyer answered. "There are more behind, with the wagons."

Wolf tried to locate some chief to pass on the news, but perhaps all the leaders had already started toward the wagons. Except for a few young men who had stayed behind to strip the dead bluecoats, the whole ambush force appeared to be on the move eastward.

"Someone should stay behind and watch the bridge," Stands Long pointed out.

"Maybe," Wolf admitted. "I don't think there are many bluecoats in that stockade who are ready to cause us trouble. This new force, though, is another matter."

"Besides, the bluecoats wouldn't guard empty wagons," Red Hawk argued. "There are probably some good things to take."

Wolf scowled. The chiefs likely thought the same way. Riding out in such a scattered and disorganized way offered little chance of victory, though. He wished the others would pause and plan their attack.

As it happened, the wagon chief acted just as foolishly. He was just a short distance from the bridge and the safety its stockade offered, but he halted. The wagon drivers formed their wagons into a circle, and men began freeing the mules from their harnesses.

"Wait just a little longer," Wolf whispered at the *Tsis tsis tas* and *Lakota* raiders hurrying on ahead. There must have been a chief up there, because the attack did pause. The wagon people led their animals down to the river, and the raiders caught them there. In the blink of an eye twenty young *Tsis tsis tas* captured the wagon mules and drove them on down the river. The startled drivers fled in panic to their wagons.

By then the raiders had their blood up, and several foolhardy young men charged the wagons. The teamsters and their escorts cut holes in the sides of the wagon boxes, though, and they fired their rifles coolly and effectively from relative safety. While arrows deflected harmlessly off the sides of the wagons, rifles tore brave hearts from the backs of their ponies.

It was a sad scene. Wolf gazed with dismay as ponies raced away, their backs smeared with the blood of their fallen riders.

"Someone must take these men in hand!" Wolf cried in anger. "Where are the older men? Where are the chiefs?"

Wolf was not the only voice calling for order. Roman Nose, too, was alarmed. He rode among the raiders, shouting at some and physically restraining others. Soon the rash charges stopped.

"We must kill these dogs!" Big Horn shouted, waving some of his young companions toward the wagons. Roman Nose made his way to the boaster and blocked the way.

"We'll take these wagon people's lives," Roman Nose insisted. "That isn't the way to do it, though, running in there and being killed."

Big Horn might have argued with someone else, but Roman Nose was more than a famous chief. He was a large man utterly fearless of anyone. Big Horn wore a bonnet of twenty coup feathers that morning, and Roman Nose snatched it from the younger man's head.

"I remember no twenty coups," the chief growled. "Look how you throw away the lives of your brothers! Go away from here before I take my quirt to your worthless back!"

Big Horn held his arms out for the bonnet, but an angry glance from Roman Nose answered him. Big Horn turned and rode away.

Roman Nose's plan was simple but effective. He organized the men with good rifles and sent them against the wagons. They crept ever closer, taking care to use the cover of fallen horses or small boulders to protect themselves from the *Wihio* shooters. In time Roman Nose's men began targeting individuals. Five or six shots tore through the thin wagon walls, and the gun behind grew silent.

Eventually the return fire slackened. Roman Nose

picked a few experienced men and charged the wagons. He took great care to dart in and out, but only a shot or two answered him. He waved his companions toward the wagons, and perhaps a hundred *Tsis tsis tas* shouted triumphantly as they broke through the wagon barrier and fell upon the surviving wagon people.

Wolf saw little more of that part of the fight. Powder smoke and dust obscured his view. He did spy three bluecoats fleeing the chaos.

"There!" Wolf shouted, pointing to the three frantic soldiers. Afoot, they had little chance of escape, but somehow they eluded the prowling raiders and reached the river. Wolf and Stands Long had ridden over that way, but by the time they arrived, the first bluecoat was already in the water.

"I'm going right!" Stands Long announced as he raised his lance.

"I'm going left!" Wolf answered.

The brother-friends then charged.

Wolf thought for a moment that he had caught the *Wihio* unawares. That was not the case. The bluecoat darted behind a cottonwood, escaping Wolf's lance. The *Wihio* then fired a shot that passed a hand's distance from Wolf's left ear.

"Ayyyy!" Wolf screamed, turning his horse in time to dodge a second shot. He next raced toward the cottonwood and jumped clear of his horse at the final moment. The surprised bluecoat fired two more shots, but they were wide of their target.

"Come on!" the soldier shouted, stepping out into the open. The pistol was empty, and he flung it away. Instead he drew his saber and started toward Wolf.

As for Wolf, he barely had time to catch his breath and gather his wits before the saber-wielding *Wihio* was an arm's length away.

"Well?" the bluecoat cried. "Think you can finish me?"

"I can," Wolf said, swinging his lance out to block his enemy's path. The bluecoat was surprised to hear English spoken to him. He paused a moment to study his opponent.

"Cheyenne, huh?" the bluecoat asked. "Good fighters. Well, you've got most of us. Won't be so easy finishing the job, though."

Wolf didn't reply. Instead he matched the *Wihio*'s movements and parried each thrust. Eventually the bluecoat made a lunge, and Wolf avoided the saber, hopped to the right, and clubbed the man senseless with the shaft of the lance.

"Uhhh," the bluecoat moaned as he dropped his saber. He gazed wearily up at Wolf and fumbled for the pistol he had already thrown away.

"Too late," Wolf said, touching the point of his lance to the *Wihio*'s chest. "I'm first."

"No!" the bluecoat screamed.

Wolf knelt beside the man and touched his open hand to the man's shoulder.

"See?" Wolf asked. "You're not so hard to kill."

The bluecoat's eyes widened. His eyes regained their earlier alertness. When Wolf set aside his lance, the *Wihio* made an effort to escape. Wolf drove a knee into the bluecoat's chest, though, driving him back to the ground. Wolf then drew a knife and sliced the buttons off the *Wihio*'s tunic. Once his bare chest was exposed, Wolf touched the man's throat with the point of the knife.

"Go ahead!" the bluecoat pleaded. "Get it over with. Lord, don't start cutting on me while I'm alive!"

"As your people did at Sand Creek?" Wolf whispered.

"That wasn't me," the bluecoat insisted. "I wasn't anywhere near that place. I've got a wife and children! Lord, we're not all animals!"

"Worse than animals," Wolf whispered. "Crazy, all of you."

As the *Wihio* started to reply, he saw something. The words froze on his tongue. Wolf instinctively turned, and the move saved his life. The second bluecoat had escaped Stands Long's charge and stood less than a stone's throw away, rifle in hand. The first shot struck the earth behind

Wolf's left hip. Had he not moved, it would have struck flesh.

"Ayyyy!" Wolf shouted as he rose to his feet. Without a second's hesitation he charged the bluecoat and drove his knife into the man's vitals. The *Wihio* coughed blood and fell in a heap at Wolf's feet. By that time, though, the first one had managed to crawl away.

"Not me!" he shouted as he stripped his shirt and kicked off his boots. Moments later he was splashing into the shallows, crying, "You didn't get me!"

Wolf was helpless to prevent the escape. The *Wihio* was already beyond the range of a lance. An *Oglala* with a rifle appeared, but Wolf motioned to let the white man go.

"His medicine was strong today," Wolf noted. "His friend gave up life to save him."

"It's good that two of them got back," Stands Long added later. "The bluecoats should know what we did to their wagons."

The fighting amid the wagons continued for a time, but Wolf had no heart for it. A few bluecoats made frantic final stands, but by then all were bleeding out their lives, and it was only a matter of finishing them. Afterward young men boasted of brave heart charges as they held high the bloody brown and yellow and red forelocks cut from those dying men. The older warriors were more concerned with rifling through the wagons in search of lead, powder, iron pots, and other loot.

Big Horn returned once the fighting was over. Wolf supposed he came to look for whiskey. A party of Arapahos was also there, and several of them remembered the earlier clash over the whiskey barrels. Big Horn again fled for his life.

Wolf and the other decoys found themselves ignored once the fighting was finished.

"We should have received a share of wagon goods," Red Hawk grumbled. "Some of the ponies, too. We undertook the greatest risk!"

"We didn't come here for rifle lead," Wolf reminded his companions. "Our task was to punish the bridge soldiers, and we did it. Our dead relative will find his path easier to walk on the other side. We should return and help him begin his climb up Hanging Road.''

"We should receive something, *Nah nih*" High Flyer argued.

"If any of you feel a need, I will happily give you what you want," Wolf told them. He offered his bow, a good hunting knife, and even his pony. The others hung their heads in shame.

"You're the one who's bleeding," Broken Wing said, touching Wolf's shoulder. "If you see no debt owed to you, who are we to ask for anything?"

The others howled with approval, and Wolf turned back from the river. He wished for nothing more than survival and a brief time of peace. He expected neither.

chapter
13

S O FAR AS WOLF RUNNING was concerned, the attack
on the Platte Bridge wagons and their escorting bluecoats accomplished nothing. While some of the raiders
rode away with captured ponies, *Wihio* rifles, bags of flour,
or others useful things, Wolf took only the reminder that
death never lurked far from his people. He joined Long
Dog's sad relatives as they mourned his passing over to
the other side. Younger Dog marked the occasion by presenting three good war ponies to deserving young men.
Wolf himself gave away two good horses—one to Broken
Wing and the other to Ringtail. Both young men were in
desperate need of better mounts.

Long Dog's sons placed the old man atop a scaffold not
far from Platte River. It was a good, high place, and Wolf
hoped it would ease the *Suhtai* chief's climb up Hanging
Road. For a time afterward peace settled over the Platte
Valley and the Powder River country. Wolf hunted several
days with his wife's brothers. Then, after consulting with
his brothers and Stands Long, he decided to seek out his
cousin once more.

"Will it will be hard, leaving your people behind?" Wolf asked Sun Walker Woman.

"We didn't camp with them last summer," she reminded him. "My people? You and my sons are my family now. My brothers are strangers, and he who was my father's gone. There are plenty of *Suhtai* women in the *Oglala* camps. I, too, have friends there."

So it was decided. Early the following morning Wolf broke down his lodge and began packing up the family's belongings. Stands Long, Red Hawk, High Flyer, and Raven Heart took down the rough shelter they used. Together they assembled their ponies.

Shortly before they left, Broken Wing joined them.

"You're going west?" he asked.

"To ride with the *Oglalas*," Wolf explained. "My cousins are there."

"I only have cousins with the southerners," Broken Wing explained. "They're strangers. I have my own name and a good pony. I'm no boy to run to an uncle."

"True," Wolf observed. "You have friends here. Come and go with us."

"I'll be no burden," Broken Wing vowed as he rode over beside Raven Heart. "I'm not yet tall, but I won't run from an enemy. I'm not hungry for killing friends or helpless *Wihio*. Not so long ago I followed Big Horn, but my eyes were clouded with hatred. I won't add to your burdens."

"You will help carry them," Wolf declared. "My brother knows you as a brother-friend. It's right you should come."

The young man smiled, and Raven Heart howled his agreement.

"It's settled," Wolf announced. "Now, let's begin. The *Oglalas* may not remain on Powder River forever."

They rode northward for two days, passing deeper into the heart of the Powder River Valley. Normally it was not a difficult journey. With his family along, though, Wolf set an easy pace. He also avoided the established trails. He recalled the Crow horse raiders, and he had learned that bluecoats were crossing that country on their way to dig gold from the streams farther north.

Wolf's caution allowed the party to escape trouble. They encountered no prowling Crows or wandering white people. Shortly after arriving on Powder River, Wolf picked up the trail of a dozen unshod ponies. Soon he was in the midst of several *Oglala* camps.

"We hoped that you would come," Beaver Belt exclaimed when he saw the newcomers.

"Hau!" Two Arrows added as he raced over to take charge of the ponies. "It's good to have our friends with us."

Crazy Horse was equally glad that they had rejoined his camp.

"I've dreamed of trouble," he told Wolf. "Did you see sign of Pawnees?"

"Pawnees?" Wolf asked. "In this country? Crows might strike us here, but Pawnees? No, they're brave enough in their own country, but they won't fight us here, in these hills."

"I can only tell you that I've seen them in my dreams," Crazy Horse explained. "You, too, see things, Cousin. Not all are clear, but there's no mistaking a Pawnee for a Crow!"

Wolf nodded. He, too, was now worried.

Trouble wasn't all that long in coming, either. The green grass moons of midsummer did not pass before word came from the *Lakotas* camped farther south that large numbers of bluecoats were marching north from Platte River. Others were moving westward farther to the north.

"It's as we feared," Wolf told Stands Long. "Now that the fighting among the *Wihio* in the east is finished, they're hungry to take more land from us."

Where before the *Wihio* arrived with presents and promises of new treaties, this time the soldiers came alone. They marched with the confidence of victorious warriors, and they came in their hundreds. Fighting so many bluecoats, armed as they were with long-firing rifles and cannons even, would prove to be a difficult thing. Wolf remembered Broken Wing's tale of the killing at Sand Creek.

"Do you think it's true?" he later asked his cousin.

"What?" Crazy Horse asked.

"That a thousand bluecoats will soon attack us," Wolf explained. "We should be enjoying the summer hunting, crafting arrows for our sons, or playing courting flutes. Not fighting bluecoats!"

"We will fight them, though," Crazy Horse insisted. "Red Cloud vows it."

"Already some of the chiefs are saying we must touch the *Wihio* pen and agree to a new treaty," Wolf noted. "We have little choice."

"We can die fighting," Crazy Horse argued. "I know it's a difficult thing for a man with sons to ponder, but I have no sons. I'll fight. Others will join me."

Wolf nodded soberly. It wasn't a comforting thought.

Only two days later a pair of young *Oglalas* arrived with word that a large force of bluecoats was camping on Powder River south of Crazy Woman Creek.

"Only a day's hard riding from our camp!" Crazy Horse cried. "Who will ride with me to run these enemies from our land?"

The *Oglala* shirt wearer quickly collected seventy warriors. He sent a pipe out to the nearby camps and enticed twenty-five others. Wolf Running's initial instinct was to remove his family from harm's way. When Raven Heart and Broken Wing rode into camp with news that they had spotted riders even closer, Wolf changed his mind.

"I can lead you back there, *Nah nih,*" Raven Heart declared. "You can see for yourself."

"We'll go," Stands Long declared. "First we have to tell the others."

While Stands Long set off to inform the *Oglala* chiefs, Wolf alerted his brothers. They, in turn, collected ponies and readied arms.

Wolf didn't expect to fight that afternoon. He expected to find a trail or perhaps even a handful of scouts. He let Raven Heart and Broken Wing lead the way. Wolf and Stands Long followed. Red Hawk and High Flyer remained in camp, watching over Sun Walker Woman and the little ones.

"It's not far," Raven Heart insisted after the four of them had gone a short distance. "Look, over there."

Wolf followed his brother's pointing finger to where the tracks of several ponies marked the sandy soil. Nearby, the shaft of a broken arrow rested in the crook of a cottonwood limb that had snagged it from a quiver.

"Not possible," Wolf muttered, examining the markings.

"Pawnee," Stands Long said, noting the distinctive notches. "Your cousin also has far-seeing eyes."

"The bluecoats employ Pawnee scouts," Broken Wing said, swallowing hard. "They must be looking for our camps."

"There are only a few of them," Wolf said. He counted twenty sets of hoofprints. It was little more than a strong scouting party, but if they had located the *Oglala* camps, then Sun Walker Woman was in peril. Before he had a chance to turn back, Stands Long called out.

"Riders," Stands Long announced, pointing out a column of seven horsemen approaching from the north. They rode in an easy style. Their leader called out, *"Hau,"* and Wolf dismissed them as *Lakotas*. As the two parties approached each other, Wolf grew concerned.

"Those aren't *Lakota* words," Stands Long said, stringing his bow.

The strangers took out rifles and began firing wildly. Then they charged. Any doubt that remained in Wolf's mind vanished. The screams, the shouts, and the war paint were all distinctly Pawnee.

"Ayyyy!" Stands Long screamed, rushing out to break the impact of the charge. Wolf followed. Their two young companions also advanced, but Stands Long took the brunt of the Pawnee assault. He deflected a war club with his shield, nocked an arrow, and killed a long-faced Pawnee with a solitary shot through the chest. Stands Long avoided two rifle balls, but a third struck his horse. Both animal and rider went down.

Before the Pawnees could close on their helpless enemy, Wolf arrived. He left his bow unstrung and wielded his lance instead. The fury of his charge drove two Pawnees away, but five of them remained. Wolf confronted one of them, a fat-faced man with yellow stripes drawn across his cheeks. The Pawnee lifted a shield and sang tauntingly. Wolf merely grinned.

"Come, Pawnee," Wolf called in English. "You Pawnees are good only for killing. Who have you fought? Naked children and helpless women!"

The Pawnee answered the insult in kind, and Wolf readied himself. Only three Pawnees charged, and by then Raven Heart and Broken Wing stood with Wolf. The Pawnee with the striped paint drew out a pistol, but he wasn't accustomed to fighting on horseback, and he had difficulty firing to any effect. Wolf made his own charge, slammed his shield against one Pawnee, and stunned the man.

"We're not children," Wolf said, plunging his lance into the Pawnee's side. "Nor women, either."

The remaining Pawnees made only a faint show of fighting. Once Wolf finished their leader, they fled. Wolf then hurried to Stands Long's side.

"Are you hurt, Brother?" Wolf asked.

"Only slightly," Stands Long said, wincing as he struggled to fee a trapped left leg from under the dead horse. He jerked free and tried to stand, but it wasn't possible.

Wolf jumped down and aided his brother-friend. Broken Wing joined them. Together they got Stands Long atop the dead Pawnee's horse and started back toward the *Oglala* camp. Wolf heard riders behind them, though, and turned back.

"Help him to our camp," Wolf told his young companions. "I'll decoy the Pawnees."

"One man can help Stands Long," Raven Heart said, offering the reins of the Pawnee pony to Broken Wing. "I'll go with you, *Nah nih.*"

"It's for me to do," Broken Wing insisted. He ignored the reins and kicked his horse into a gallop. Raven Heart reluctantly let him go.

Wolf did not intend to throw his life away. He planned to lead the Pawnees away and then return to his cousin's camp. Broken Wing's arrival complicated the plan. The youngster rode straight toward a tall Pawnee dressed in a bonnet of eagle feathers.

"No!" Wolf shouted as Broken Wing dodged a volley of hastily fired rifles. Balls tore his clothing, and one tore a notch in the side of his left calf. The young *Tsis tsis tas* nocked an arrow and fired from a mere five feet away. The Pawnee gasped as the arrow tore through his throat. As Wolf swept in from the right, the Pawnee chief was spitting blood and coughing out his life.

"It's time to leave," Wolf called.

Broken Wing jumped from his horse instead and snatched the war bonnet from the dead Pawnee's head. He took a moment longer to cut away the enemy's forelock. All the while the startled Pawnees stood, watching, as the reckless young man took their chief's hair.

"Woman-killers!" Broken Wing taunted as he remounted his horse. "Child-killers!"

"Yes," a new, deeper voice shouted from amid the handful of stunned Pawnees. "I'm here to kill you, boy!"

A stout, shortish Pawnee, with the hair on either side of his head cut away, glared at Broken Wing. The man wore no bonnet, and he displayed no trophies. He disdained honors. He held a lance in his right hand and appeared eager for battle.

"No, not him," Wolf called as he cut in front of Broken Wing. "It's for us to settle."

"Settle?" the Pawnee called. "Settle what? Our fight will be only the first. Later we're going to kill the rest of you."

"Boast afterward," Wolf said, grinning as he balanced his lance. "Now, come and kill me if you can!"

The Pawnee screamed and charged. Wolf waited a moment and then urged his horse forward. The two raced toward each other at breakneck speed. When they collided, Wolf blocked the Pawnee's lance with his shield. He then slipped his own lance under the braggart's shield and jabbed his ribs. The Pawnee gazed down in surprise at the blood running across his belly. Wolf then plunged the lance downward so that it opened a great tear in the Pawnee's right thigh. Wolf feared for a moment that the Pawnee would run, but instead the man began singing. Wolf thrust his lance through his enemy's chest, striking the heart and dealing the man a final, instantly fatal blow.

The Pawnees shouted and cursed, but when Wolf edged his way toward the others, they backed away.

"*Heammawihio,* all that we've done this day flows from you," Wolf cried. "We're only dirt in the wind, Man Above. Nothing."

"Take his hair," Broken Wing urged.

"Why?" Wolf asked. "So that I can boast of killing a Pawnee? I've done nothing, and neither have you, Wing. We enjoyed *Heammawihio*'s favor. That's all."

"All?" Broken Wing asked, disappointed that his friend failed to recognize his deed.

"The important things remain ahead of us," Wolf insisted. "We must protect our camp."

chapter
14

WOLF RETURNED TO FIND THE *Oglala* camps astir. Small parties of young men assembled ponies while the older men organized scouting parties. Each soldier society had its own plan of action, and the chiefs began quarreling over who held authority in the camps and who should decide what was the best thing to do. Among the *Oglalas,* Red Cloud stood highest in the eyes of the people. In the end, he was the one who did the deciding.

"He knows what needs to be done," Crazy Horse told Wolf when they visited Stands Long that afternoon. "This is our country. The treaty papers promise us that the *Wihio* will stay out of it. Now they come, bringing our old enemies, the Pawnees, to fight us. We'll fight back."

Actually Wolf considered such talk foolish. Naturally the bluecoats were coming. Since Sand Creek no *Tsis tsis tas* or *Lakota* gave treaty papers much thought. There could be only fighting so long as bluecoats rode down to attack peaceful bands.

The bluecoats, as was their custom, examined the matter from a different viewpoint. Even if they had attacked

Black Kettle's peaceful *Tsis tsis tas* village and Left Hand's equally tranquil Arapaho camp, that provided no justification for the raids on the stage stations and wagon parties along Platte River.

"They come to punish us," Crazy Horse told the young *Oglalas*. "For what? We are only walking the earth as our grandfathers did. We were here before the *Wihio* saw his first buffalo. Why should we leave so that he can make roads through our last good hunting country?"

Many of the chiefs and most of the warriors felt the same way. The great buffalo herds that had once grazed along Platte River were growing smaller each summer. The Powder River Valley and the Big Horn Mountains beyond were the last truly good hunting lands remaining to the people. *Wihio* roads only brought more wagon people, more disease, and more death. A man might as well die with a lance in his hand as cough out his life from the some spotted fever or starve when the Hard Face Moon painted the land icy white.

It didn't surprise Wolf to hear young men vowing to fight. He nodded approvingly to the arrowmakers. And when hunters brought word that a party of bluecoats followed by heavy wagons was less than a day's ride from that very camp, Wolf painted his face and readied his pony.

Before leaving, though, he spoke with Stands Long.

"Brother, don't go," Stands Long urged. "I'm hurt, and a man shouldn't fight bluecoats without a brother-friend there, ready to do the hard things."

"I still have brothers in this camp," Wolf pointed out. "Cousins, too. You won't be there, but Red Hawk and High Flyer will. Raven Heart and Broken Wing are growing taller. I'll have rescuers nearby."

"It's true," Stands Long admitted. "But when they rush into harm's way, you'll go to help. It won't be enough, one man fighting so many."

"The *Lakotas*—"

"Are good fighters, but will they give up their lives to save you?"

Wolf frowned. How could anyone know that? In the end, he clasped Stands Long's hand firmly and left to join his brothers. Sun Walker Woman tried to draw him aside, but he only shrugged.

"What is there to say?" he asked. "Hold the little ones tightly. I won't be gone such a long time."

She scowled, and Wolf regretted his words. He had spoken similar words too many times before.

Wolf merged his little party with that of his cousin. Crazy Horse led a band of young *Oglalas* in the vanguard of Red Cloud's war party. The scouts remained in advance of them all, and only when Crazy Horse's column approached the actual river did Wolf spy the bluecoats.

"There," Broken Wing said, pointing to where two lines of *Wihio* horsemen were riding on either flank of a snakelike line of wagons.

"They'll fight us," High Flyer pointed out.

"Then they'll die," Red Hawk insisted. "They only have a few men, and we enjoy every advantage."

"Not all," Broken Wing argued. "They're equipped with good rifles, and they have plenty of shots!"

"We follow Wolf Running, though," Flyer pointed out. "He's a shield bearer. His charms will keep us safe."

"They won't be needed today," Wolf announced as he unstrung his bow. "Look there. The chiefs will parlay."

It was true. Several bluecoats moved ahead of their wagons and aproached the *Tsis tsis tas* and *Lakota* line with white cloths attached to long sticks. There was some talking. Then the bluecoat commander, an eagle chief, insisted on treating with Red Cloud.

"We should have told the bluecoats that Red Cloud was elsewhere," Crazy Horse grumbled as he invited Wolf to the parlay. "There's no use in talking. We should fight them here while we enjoy an advantage."

"We may have to do it anyway," Wolf added.

"No, I know my chiefs," Crazy Horse muttered. "They must make an effort to avoid fighting. The old men believe there are too many white men for a successful fight, but—"

"I know," Wolf grumbled. "We *will* fight."

That day it appeared that the chiefs might reach a reasonable agreement. The *Lakotas* remained opposed to the passage of the wagons through their best hunting country, but the eagle chief wished no fight. Because the chiefs did not understand one another's language very well, Wolf and two others translated. Red Cloud insisted that the bluecoats turn back. The chief forbid the building of roads or forts along Powder River. The others eventually persuaded him to accept a wagon full of goods as payment for the *Wihio* passage.

"You can go on," Red Cloud finally decided, "but you must leave the game alone. Don't send your young men into the hills, and leave our camps untroubled."

The eagle chief agreed to do it, and Red Cloud summoned a pipe. It seemed to Wolf that the pipe smoke still hung in the air when scouts later brought word that bluecoats were shooting deer along Powder River.

"Nothing changes," Crazy Horse growled. "The *Wihio* have broken another agreement."

"We should go down and remind them," Wolf suggested.

"We should punish them," Crazy Horse argued. "Hurt them. Kill them."

"And if the eagle chief doesn't know that these bluecoats break his word?"

"He should enforce his will," Crazy Horse declared. "They expect us to heed a chief, even a man with little power. The eagle chief should be more watchful."

Crazy Horse remained unsatisfied, but the cousins rode down together to speak with the bluecoats. The *Wihio* in charge, a man with strips of a silver cloth on his shoulders, produced a pistol and fired at the two intruders.

It was the worst possible reaction. Wolf and Crazy Horse turned away, and shortly thereafter twenty young *Oglalas* charged the bluecoat hunters, disarmed them, and ran them back to the wagon camp.

"They're fortunate men," Crazy Horse said as he stood on a ridge overlooking the wagons. "We might have killed all of them."

"We still may have to fight them," Wolf declared. "Nothing's settled anymore."

That proved to be true. In the days that followed, there were frequent clashes along Powder River. Some of the *Lakotas* who had not received presents fired on the bluecoat wagon people. Two other parties of bluecoats and their Pawnee scouts raided isolated *Tsis tsis tas* and *Lakota* camps, achieving little, but stirring up even more anger among the plains peoples. Those particular bluecoats, perhaps emboldened by the repeated successes of the scouts, saved their heaviest blow for the Arapahos.

Wolf Running learned of the attack by accident. He, Raven Heart, and Broken Wing had ridden off into the nearby hills in search of game. Instead of deer and elk, they found two Arapaho girls cowering near a small spring.

"You aren't rabbits," Broken Wing said, sliding down off his pony and grinning at the girls. "You shouldn't fear my bow."

The oldest girl, a thin-faced child of perhaps eight summers, stared up with solemn eyes. She said nothing. The smaller girl hugged her sister's side and wept.

"They don't understand our words," Wolf observed. "Why are you here?" he asked, using a mixture of Arapaho words and signs. "Where is your camp, your mother?"

When the children failed to respond, Wolf also dismounted. He left his pony with Broken Wing and went ahead, studying the small footprints left by the Arapaho girls. He quickly located a third set, strung his bow, and started toward a slight rise ten paces away.

"Who's there?" Wolf called. A shadowy figure darted away, and Wolf charged after it. Pursuit was difficult in the thick brush, and Wolf winced as briers tore at his knees and elbows. He finally spied the quarry, though.

"Why do you run?" Wolf asked a boy of perhaps twelve summers.

The youngster was as mute as the others. Wolf stepped

closer, but when he touched the boy's bare right shoulder, he ducked away.

"I'm *Tsis tsis tas,*" Wolf said, making the Arapaho sign for that allied tribe. "Friend. Your people will have heard of me. Wolf Running. I ride with the Elk soldiers."

The boy dropped to his knees and covered his face. Softly, he sang a death chant. Wolf studied the youngster. He wore only a breechclout. His feet were bare and bloody. A gash under his left arm and a jagged tear on his left thigh also bled.

"Who's done this to you?" Wolf asked. When he touched the boy a second time, the youngster screamed.

"No," the older girl pleaded as she raced past Wolf to the boy. "He's our brother. Don't kill him!"

Wolf was more perplexed than upset.

"Wolf?" Broken Wing called as he and Raven Heart escorted the smallest girl. "What did she say? I don't understand Arapaho words."

"He's her brother," Wolf explained, pointing to the boy. "He's hurt. Not shot, though."

"Bluecoats?" Broken Wing asked, adding signs to clarify the meaning of his words. The girl shook her head. The boy made a sign for Pawnees.

"Nearby?" Wolf asked, tensing considerably.

"Near," the boy agreed. He began to lose his anxiety a hair when Wolf turned his attention in the opposite direction.

"They came to our camp," the older girl added. "Thirty of them. Then the white men. Mother, father, my uncle . . ."

"Dead?" Wolf asked.

The children dropped their gaze, and Wolf frowned.

"They're still close," he observed. "I can smell them."

"We should leave, *Nah nih,*" Raven Heart declared.

"No, I'll remain," Wolf insisted. "Go and get our brothers, *See'was'sin mit.* Others, if they're willing to come. There may be other Arapahos in these hills. We'll save them."

"There are others," the boy said, taking Wolf's hand.

"Mostly women and little ones. A few boys like me. If we had our bows, those Pawnees would bleed!"

"It's for you to look after your sisters," Wolf argued. "We older men will tend to the Pawnees."

Wolf waved Raven Heart toward the *Oglala* camps and left Broken Wing to look after the children. He went ahead alone, but he didn't remain so. Every few feet another Arapaho emerged from his or her hiding place. Soon more than thirty stood together on the hillside. Below, the remains of their camp burned.

"*Wihio,*" Wolf muttered as he studied a young officer who was directing the roundup of Arapaho ponies. The bodies of a dozen men and women littered the ground. Wolf was surprised to see a large group of captives. The Pawnees actually appeared reluctant to kill the helpless ones. One Pawnee warrior pleaded with the bluecoats to allow the captives to go free.

"Too far to take them," he told the young bluecoat chief. "Leave them."

"Alive?" the officer cried. "We'll only have to fight them again."

"There's no honor in murdering them," the Pawnee insisted. The others agreed, and when his curses failed to stir the scouts to action, the bluecoat spit at the captives and left them to go their own way. Most fled into the nearby hills.

The Arapaho ponies were another matter. The bluecoats and the Pawnees agreed to drive the pony herd, all six hundred animals, back to their own camp. Wolf merely grinned. The bluecoats could never control such a large herd. The Pawnees would simply select the best mounts for their own use and ignore the rest. A few determined men might retrieve a considerable portion of the Arapaho pony herd.

Such men were soon at hand. Raven Heart returned with Red Hawk, High Flyer, and twelve *Oglalas*. They brought ten spare ponies. Several Arapahos volunteered to go along on the raid, and Wolf assigned Red Hawk the task of selecting the ten best fit for the task. Wolf then did what he could to calm the fearful Arapaho survivors.

"They're still afraid," Broken Wing declared when Wolf decided it was time to begin the pursuit. "We should forget the ponies. We're needed here."

"What will these people do without ponies?" Wolf countered. "How will they hunt Bull Buffalo? Without hides, how can they remake their lodges? Without meat, how will they survive the freezing time? We can stay and speak kind words or we can give them what they need to survive. Which is the greatest gift?"

"You don't understand," Broken Wing declared. "I remember how it was when the bluecoats attacked us at Sand Creek. These little ones are too frightened to think. They need protecting."

"Their own people will do that," Wolf insisted. "There were only a few killed down there. Most of the helpless ones will have relatives wandering these hills. Everyone will do what he can. We must bring back some of the ponies."

"I know," Broken Wing said, frowning. "It's only that I was . . ."

"Remembering?" Wolf asked. "It's hard to forget such a thing, but a man must walk his path in the light of today's sun. He can't drown in yesterday's shadows."

Broken Wing didn't reply. Instead he mounted his pony and joined the raiders.

Wolf didn't know the Powder River country half as well as many of his companions, and after a time he allowed River Rock, an Arapaho, to take the lead. River Rock halted the party long enough to consider what to do. He then broke off the pursuit in favor of a different tactic.

"We know the *Wihio*," River Rock explained. "They'll stop near the river to pass the night. We can strike the herd best by coming at them from the far side."

The Arapaho went on to explain how they could cross the river upstream and circle in behind the unsuspecting bluecoats.

"And the Pawnees?" Raven Heart asked.

"They'll be more watchful, but they won't stand and

die to protect bluecoat horses,'' River Rock declared. ''They've grown too fat and cautious to fight thirty good men.''

Wolf counted only twenty-five raiders. Two *Oglalas* had already turned back because of tired horses. Moreover, half the Arapahos were little more than pony boys. It was hardly the sort of force to chill Pawnees who had already destroyed an entire Arapaho camp!

''Are you worried, *Nah nih*?'' Red Hawk asked.

''Cautious,'' Wolf replied. ''It's not a bad habit to be careful in enemy country.''

''This is *our* country!'' an *Oglala* named Bull Head complained. ''After we run these Arapaho ponies back to their camp, we'll smoke and plan how to chase the *Wihio* back to their forts.''

Wolf couldn't help smiling. Bull Head had only recently plucked his first chin whiskers. Even so, the boy understood the task ahead.

It was nearly dusk when River Rock led his weary companions along the far bank of Powder River to where the bluecoats and their Pawnee scouts had made camp. The enormous pony herd spread out on the opposite bank. Only a few boys kept watch there. Most of the Pawnees celebrated their coups around a council fire. The bluecoats were better organized, but they were more concerned about their pack animals and wagons than captured ponies.

''We'll wait for dark,'' Wolf said, studying the eager eyes of his companions. ''That will give us cover, and our ponies can rest some. Once we start running the horses, we can't stop. The Pawnees will be after us.''

''Then we'll run them, too,'' Bull Head boasted.

''That won't be easy,'' Wolf argued. ''Don't grow reckless or they'll kill you. Just because they spared some helpless children and a few women, don't forget that they're our old enemy.''

''It's not easy to forget,'' an Arapaho named Stone Knife said, lifting his shirt to reveal an ugly scar that ran down his left side from nipple to hip.

''Remember,'' Wolf urged as he dismounted. The others

followed his example. They painted their faces, spoke their individual medicine prayers, and waited for the sun to drop into the western horizon.

With dusk shrouding their movements, Wolf led his companions to their ponies. River Rock insisted on leading the charge with his Arapahos. Wolf deemed it a poor plan, striking first with the weakest band, but he refused to argue. Disharmony might prove fatal. Once River Rock started, the *Oglalas* followed. Wolf had hoped to use them in a flanking move across the river, but that chance slipped away. Frustrated, he waved for his brothers and Broken Wing to follow. Wolf would flank the herd himself.

Everything went well in the beginning. River Rock's Arapahos charged with a fury that drove the bluecoat pickets from the river. Two Pawnee pony boys made a brief stand, but they had only boys' bows, and Bull Head had a good pistol. He shot both Pawnees.

Those shots started the trouble. The celebrating Pawnees halted their scalp dance and began gathering their horses. A bluecoat started blowing his bugle, and the entire enemy force came alive. A volley of rifle fire killed two *Oglalas,* and Wolf felt a rifle ball whine past only inches from his ear.

"There!" Red Hawk shouted as he turned his horse toward three onrushing riders.

Wolf also turned back, but Broken Wing was the first to strike a blow. The young man fired an arrow into the neck of a charging Pawnee. With their leader dead, the other Pawnees hesitated. It was a fatal error for one of them. Red Hawk came in from the flank and drove a lance through the Pawnee's side.

Wolf found himself facing the remaining Pawnee. In the dim light, it was difficult to see much more than shadows. The Pawnee appeared reluctant to close the distance, and for a moment Wolf thought the fight was finished. Instead the Pawnee howled and charged anew. Wolf dodged a lance thrust and used his unstrung bow to club the Pawnee. The dazed enemy rolled off his pony. Wolf strung his bow and notched an arrow.

"*Nah nih!*" High Flyer called. "More are coming!"

Wolf started to release the arrow, but the recollection of the merciful Pawnee in the Arapaho camp flooded his mind. He fired the arrow into the earth beside the Pawnee and rode on.

The remaining Pawnees lost heart. The bluecoats never managed more than a few volleys and some wild firing. Wolf and his raiding party drove two hundred ponies, a third of the whole herd, back to the Arapahos.

It was many days later, after the Arapahos had completed a buffalo hunt, when River Rock invited Wolf and his brothers to a makeshift camp a half day's ride downriver. The women roasted buffalo strips and fried bread for the feast. Their sons and husbands spoke glowingly of their generous allies. After eating, Wolf and Sun Walker Woman joined in the dancing. The children played with their Arapaho hosts. Red Hawk and High Flyer walked the river trail with two Arapaho sisters, Gull Maiden and Chokecherry Maiden. They were River Rock's cousins, and he stressed their fine qualities to Wolf later when the two men sat beside a warming fire.

"My people are in need of good hunters, strong young men who would take their place in the council," River Rock added. "I know you perhaps wish your brothers to take *Lakota* wives, but my cousins are better choices. I'll ask only a few ponies, and Arapaho women are not quarrelsome or selfish."

"It must be my brothers' decision," Wolf replied.

"They've followed you many moons, though. If you oppose the matches, they won't agree."

"I wouldn't enjoy seeing them leave my side, but it's the way things happen. We share a father's blood, but no two men walk the same path."

Wolf said much the same thing when Red Hawk and High Flyer drew him aside the following day.

"It's hard to know what's best sometimes," Wolf added. "You once told me to trust my heart, and I took Sun Walker Woman as my wife. You were right. Warrior's road is a cold path to walk alone."

"We might remain with the *Oglalas*," Red Hawk said.

"You must go with your wife's people," Wolf argued. "These Arapahos need you. When our peoples visit, our sons will run and swim and hunt. Ayyyy! That will be a day to remember."

And so Red Hawk and High Flyer took wives. Wolf provided the four horses necessary for the giveaway, while Raven Heart and Broken Wing helped with the feasting.

"We've become fewer," Raven Heart said when he and Wolf returned to the *Oglala* camp after the marriage celebration concluded.

"Stands Long will soon be healed," Wolf noted. "We have good friends nearby and brothers among the Arapahos. It's good that my sons will have cousins. You, too, will soon take up a courting flute."

"Yes," the young man said, grinning. "Flyer gave me his."

"Ah, and I thought I would have another one to make."

"You can make one if Flyer's fails me. Who could refuse a handsome young man like me, though?"

"Especially when his brother offers four ponies," Wolf whispered.

"Four?"

"Five maybe," Wolf added. "You're not so handsome as you think."

chapter
15

D URING THOSE NEXT FEW WEEKS, Wolf had little time to think about courting flutes or younger brothers. The bluecoats and their Pawnee scouts remained in the Powder River country, spawning fresh concerns and frequent fighting. Parties of *Tsis tsis tas* and *Lakota* warriors often rode out to harass *Wihio* wagon drivers. Less fortunate white men met up with vengeful Arapahos.

As the Plum Moon marked the passing of yet another summer, some of Roman Nose's scouts brought word that bluecoats were again camped along Powder River a half day's ride from Crazy Horse's *Oglala* camp.

"I never knew *Wihio* could be so foolish," Stands Long grumbled when Broken Wing shared the news.

"Roman Nose is making his preparations," Broken Wing explained. "He'll take only experienced fighters. Raven Heart and I want to go, but we're young. If you lead us, Wolf, Roman Nose will welcome all of us."

"My brother-friend's wounds have not healed," Wolf pointed out. "Roman Nose has enough fighters."

"He's a good man to follow, and many are eager to go

with him," Broken Wing noted. "It doesn't mean that we'll enjoy success, though. One man's not enough to hold the hot bloods back. You could help."

"*We* can help," Stands Long declared. "I'm fit enough to ride."

"You can hardly sit a horse," Wolf argued. "We have the autumn buffalo hunting to do soon. You should rest."

"Someone has to go," Stands Long insisted. "We've always accepted the obligation. We should do it this time, too, Wolf."

"Tell Roman Nose that we'll come," Wolf said, staring at his toes. "My brother-friend's decided we must do it. I won't lead, though. We'll hang back and watch the younger men."

As the other warriors set about making medicine and preparing for the coming fight, Wolf continued to insist that he would not take a major part in it. His companions remained unconvinced, though. They were not alone.

"When did you ever hang back?" Sun Walker Woman asked. "When the fighting starts, you'll rush to the front."

"A man has obligations," Wolf pointed out.

"Yes," she agreed. "We all do. Not all of yours ride with the Elks. You have sons who need you."

"I'll be careful," he promised. "I know we have the autumn hunting to do. We'll need heavier coats for the children."

"Others might provide such things," she observed. "Not a father's guiding hand."

"Don't worry," Wolf said, lifting her chin. "No owls visit my dreams. Snow Wolf's brought me no dark warning. I'll come back."

She nodded soberly, and he sighed. Wolf rarely rode to battle without a sense of loss, knowing some good man was likely to die whenever the Elks fought such well-armed enemies as Pawnees or bluecoats. This time, though, he felt no foreboding. After days passed idly along Powder River, he was riding out to punish the murderers of the Arapaho innocents. He was striking a blow against the lying *Wihio*.

"You've seen nothing in your dreams?" Sun Walker Woman whispered.

"Nothing to trouble us," he explained. "Bull Buffalo bringing his sons to feed the people. Nothing else."

"Yes, hunting," she muttered. "Don't forget that in this country, we're not the only ones hunting."

"I won't forget the Arapaho children," he vowed. "Nor my own."

Wolf didn't, either. As he, Stands Long, Raven Heart, and Broken Wing stood together on a hillside, making their warrior prayers, they spoke briefly about the coming fight.

"Not so long ago the bluecoats would never have come into this country," Stands Long noted. "Then, we and our relations were strong. Any horse-stealing Pawnee who ventured into this country would ride with a death chant upon his lips."

"Now the bluecoats have killed my family," Broken Wing said, biting his lip until blood ran down his chin. "They killed the Arapahos next. Soon they'll strike our camp, too."

"No, we'll run them first," Wolf vowed.

The others agreed, and Wolf produced a gourd filled with whitish powder made from chalk rock and pounded buffalo horn. With it he painted a great white moon on his chest and those of his companions. He also painted his face a ghostly white. Stands Long dotted his face with painted hailstones. Raven Heart and Broken Wing chose the yellow paint of the rising sun.

Otherwise Wolf dressed modestly. Even his younger brother wore a coup feather in his hair. Wolf wore none. Compared to chiefs like Red Cloud or Roman Nose, both famous for their splendid medicine bonnets of eagle feathers, Wolf seemed naked.

"It's a habit we share," Crazy Horse announced when Wolf and his companions joined a growing body of *Tsis tsis tas* and *Lakota* riders.

"You should have the medicine chiefs craft you a suitable bonnet," Swift Hare, a young *Oglala*, urged.

"Yes," Big Horn agreed, laughing. "How will the bluecoats know that they've killed anybody worth their powder when they shoot you?''

"You wear many feathers, Horn," Broken Wing said, studying the young man's bonnet. "I didn't know a warrior could count coups inflicted on whiskey bottles."

Some of the others laughed, and Big Horn lifted his lance. Wolf nudged his pony between the two younger men.

"Bonnets are nothing," Wolf said, shaking his head. "Men are nothing. Only the earth and the mountains last, and even the wind and the rain eat away at them. We have enemies enough to fight today without striking each other. Come, let's follow Roman Nose. He's made strong medicine."

At that very moment Roman Nose was riding among his followers, braving them for the coming fight. Wolf deemed the raiding party too small and far too young to run a well-disciplined party of bluecoats, but then most of the bluecoats that came to Powder River were weary from the many summers they'd spent fighting the graycoats. The officers were too boastful to be prudent, and except for the clever fort chief at Platte Bridge, few had fought very well against a well-led war party.

"Ayyyy!" Roman Nose called. "Brave up! We have enemies to fight this day!"

Others also shouted to their companions. Men sang old warrior songs, mixing *Suhtai* and *Tsis tsis tas* words with *Lakota* and Arapaho phrases. Finally Roman Nose divided the band into smaller parties. He led the first toward the river.

It was always remembered as Roman Nose's fight. That was appropriate. Roman Nose, after all, sent the pipe out to assemble the war party. It was also Roman Nose who made the first charge, and the two afterward that caused the *Wihio* to lose heart. Even Wolf, who had both made and witnessed many charges, admitted afterward that it was a remembered thing. Twenty summers after Roman Nose was dust young men sang of it around council fires.

Wolf knew from the beginning that something unusual

was about to happen. The hot bloods, who so often had raced ahead to spoil a plan, remained back with the others. Roman Nose, who was known for his lengthy preparations, took a long time donning his bonnet. It was a wondrous headdress, finely crafted of eagle feathers by Ice, the *Tsis tsis tas* medicine prophet, whose bullet-proofing medicine had failed the people at Red Shield River almost ten snows before. Roman Nose trusted the bonnet to shield him from the cavalrymen's bullets that day. He vowed to empty the *Wihio* rifles.

After so many disappointments, many of the older men dismissed the medicine of Roman Nose's bonnet, but the youngsters believed. They waited for the chief to make his charge. Their faith was absolute, and it stilled their impatience.

Wolf remembered the hard fighting at Red Shield River. He recalled the good men who had died there. He didn't trust Ice's visions, but he recognized the power of Roman Nose's words. After all, the chief had shown his power at Platte River.

"Do you want to remain behind?" Raven Heart asked when the others began forming a ragged line opposite the bluecoats' wagon camp.

"We'll be careful," Wolf replied. "If the others break, we'll organize a line of men to shield our camps. If the others charge or the bluecoats run, we'll charge, too."

"Agreed," Stands Long declared.

"Yes, *Nah nih*," Raven Heart added.

Roman Nose then kicked his pony into a gallop. Howling defiantly and raising his lance in a gesture of contempt, the chief charged one end of the wagon camp and then the other. Rifles and carbines spit yellow flame at their tormentor. Lead pellets whined under, over, ahead, and behind Roman Nose. None struck. Finally satisfied that he had broken the spirit of the enemy, Roman Nose beckoned his companions to the attack. A handful rushed forward, followed by the entire line. It appeared as if the raiding party might overwhelm the defenders for a moment.

The *Wihios* were far from beaten, though. If they

couldn't kill Roman Nose, they could certainly hit his followers. Some of the cavalrymen carried new, fast-firing
guns, and those weapons brought forth a maelstrom of
lead. Horses fell everywhere, but miraculously no man was
killed. Only when the bluecoat soldier chief ordered his
cannon to begin firing did the attackers suffer the loss of
a man. One cannonball landed on an elderly *Lakota,* sitting
on a hillside well beyond the river. The poor man exploded
into pieces.

Wolf remained at the river, rallying the fleeing young
men and helping the wounded mount spare ponies. Roman
Nose was also still there, taunting the bluecoats and trying
to organize a fresh attack. The people had lost heart,
though. Later all they would recall were the brave heart
charges of a charmed chief. Wolf only noted it as another
failed effort to drive the bluecoats back to Platte River.

The bluecoats did not remain at the river to celebrate
their triumph. Even as the *Tsis tsis tas* and *Lakota* chiefs
were reorganizing their broken line in the nearby hills, the
Wihio hitched their horses to their wagons and continued
on their way. Days later the night wind brought the first
breath of winter to Powder River. The heartless cold did
what charges could not. Those next two days half the bluecoat animals died. Much of their equipment had to be
abandoned, and soon the *Wihios* were struggling to escape
with their lives.

Although a small party of *Lakotas* remained behind to
observe the suffering, they did little to add to the *Wihio*'s
torments. The cruel cold nights and scarcity of rations left
the bluecoats in a pitiful state. If not for help from their
Pawnee allies, half the whites might have perished. Some
did anyway.

Wolf did not remain behind to watch the bluecoats' or-
deal. He could taste winter's approach. It was time to hunt,
and he turned his attention to Bull Buffalo. As a man of
the people, he placed the welfare of the helpless ones fore-
most. He knew only too well how winter could bring the
ache of hunger to a starving child. There were not enough
heavy robes and far too little dried meat to last until spring.

As always when some great undertaking was at hand, Wolf sought guidance. Stands Long, who remained weak, suggested that Wolf should invite Raven Heart and Broken Wing to go along as watchers. The three of them rode out from camp alone into the hills overlooking Powder River.

For Wolf, such journeys were commonplace. Not so for his young companions. Raven Heart tried to strike up a conversation, but Wolf remained mute. After a time the three of them rode on in silence. Only when Wolf located an appropriate spot high on the bare side of a hill recently swept by a rock slide did he explain what he required of watchers.

"I have a difficult task," Wolf explained. "I must seek a dream. To gain *Heammawihio*'s favor, I have to starve myself. I must sing and dance and suffer. If Man Above hears me, He'll send a vision. I will fall into a deep sleep, and that's when I'll see what I must do. I'll struggle and cry out, but you must not wake me. If the night is cold, you should build up the fire and cover me with a warm robe. Only after I'm asleep, though. So long as I'm awake, I must feel the cold. It will hurry the fever."

"Fever?" Broken Wing asked. "You will invite a fever?"

"It's necessary," Wolf explained. "A man dreams best when he's lost in such a fever. Only then can he see what's true."

The young men didn't understand, but Wolf assured them that he did.

"It's not always necessary to understand a thing," he said, drawing them close. "Remember how Roman Nose rode before the rifles? Have you ever seen such a thing? A man should have been killed, but he wasn't. There's no explaining the power of a man's medicine. Roman Nose couldn't tell you. Still, he knew that morning that the bullets couldn't find him. They didn't.

"More than once I've seen strange things in my dreams. They made no sense. I trusted those dreams, though, and they've often kept me from peril. It's no different this time. A dreamer can't worry about anything but the dream. He

requires watchers. You will keep me safe from prowling
Pawnees or Crows. You will prevent curious boys from
approaching our camp. And when I receive the vision,
you'll have meat ready to help me regain the strength I
have given to the dream. So, in a way, it's your dream as
well. I could not carry it home without your help."

Of course, Wolf couldn't be certain that the dream
would come. Sometimes they didn't. That summer the people's needs were great, though. *Heammawihio* would not
fail them.

Wolf made his preparations as he always did—slowly
and carefully. First he removed his clothing. Then he kindled a small fire. As the flames flickered, he drew out a
pipe and performed the sacred pipe ritual. He beckoned his
young companions over, and they, too, touched their lips
to the pipe. Wolf next painted his chest an unearthly white
and began making small cuts in the flesh. The blood that
began to flow seemed all the brighter against the ivory-
colored flesh.

Once the bleeding had commenced, Wolf started singing. He began with old *Suhtai* warrior songs. The words
mystified Broken Wing and Raven Heart, but they nodded
respectfully. Later, when Wolf sang the more familiar
hunter songs, they joined in.

Wolf first began to feel dizzy when the sun dropped into
the western hills. He disdained food. Pain and hunger hurried a fever, and he sank to his knees.

"Is there something we should do?" Broken Wing
called.

Wolf ignored the youngster's worried gaze. Raven Heart
added logs to the embers of the fire.

All that night Wolf continued to sing and suffer. He cut
the flesh of his arms and thighs. He danced for a time,
hoping the exertion would invite sleep. It was almost
dawn, though, when he finally collapsed. The dream came
much later.

It began with a white sea of snow. At first Wolf seemed
to be resting there. Later he realized that it was a cloud,
and he was actually floating above it. Gradually the cloud

began to thin, and he was able to glance below at the earth rushing past.

"Where are you, Bull Buffalo?" Wolf whispered. Broad rivers cut their way through lush green valleys. Beyond, mountains stretched their snowy peaks skyward. But there were no buffalo, no antelope, and no horses. Wolf grew cold as he also realized there were no camp circles of *Tsis tsis tas* or *Lakota* lodges.

What sort of world was this? No animals? No people?

He drifted toward the ground and stood atop a slight rise overlooking a river. It was the sort of place where boys might swim away a summer afternoon. It would have made a good place for hunters to camp. A small band might have made its home there. Graceful cottonwoods provided shade, and there was plenty of fresh water and ample firewood.

Wolf felt strangely lost. He knew he had been in that place before—perhaps as a boy. Yes, that was it. When the plains peoples had gathered to speak with the *Wihio* treaty chiefs, Wolf and his cousins had swum that river. Young Curly had beaten the Crows in a horse race. It was a better day, a time when a young *Tsis tsis tas* boy might save a white boy from drowning, as indeed Wolf had done.

Who would have imagined then that the power of the great tribes would fade so quickly? Only a few hundred bluecoats had camped at Horse Creek that summer. No *Tsis tsis tas* boy could have foreseen the armies that *Wihio* chiefs like Sumner and Chivington brought out to break the power of the people.

The vision seemed to fade a moment, but then Wolf heard a low growl. It came from the cottonwoods. He turned and looked upon the snow-white beast that had so often visited his dreams.

"Snow Wolf, why have you brought me here?" Wolf called. "Where is Bull Buffalo?"

Snow Wolf crept slowly across the hillside and then raced out across Horse Creek. He seemed to dance along the water and run across the valley. Wolf ran after the beast, and for a time it seemed as though the two were one. They crossed Platte River and flew across hill and stream, mountain and valley. Only then did Wolf spy game. Bull Buffalo was there, as were elk and antelope.

Wolf recognized the valleys and streams that lay between Powder River and the Black Hills. Yes, that was the place to hunt, to make winter camps safe from the intruding bluecoats and their Pawnee scouts.

The vision began to cloud over, and Wolf saw nothing more. A great weariness overwhelmed him, and he drifted off into a deep sleep. He didn't awake until another day had passed. Even then he was barely conscious.

"*Nah nih?*" Raven Heart asked.

"Wolf?" Broken Wing added.

"The dream came," Wolf explained. "Build up the fire. Bring me something to eat."

"What did you see?" Raven Heart asked as he added logs to the fire. Broken Wing draped an elk robe over Wolf's bare shoulders.

"Nothing that's easily understood," Wolf explained, shivering from a sudden sensation of cold.

"You'll tell us?" Raven Heart asked.

"Later," Wolf said, accepting dried strips of buffalo meat from his brother. "First I'll rest."

The youngsters scowled. Their eyes betrayed that mixture of impatience and disappointment that came with being young. Wolf had no answers to give them just then, though. Perhaps when he had rested, he could discover the dream's meaning. Perhaps . . .

chapter

16

T HEY REMAINED ON THE HILLSIDE another day. Wolf
rested, accepted food and water, but said very little.
Raven Heart and Broken Wing saw to his needs. Their
eyes betrayed their disappointment.

"*Ne' hyo,* are the people in danger?" Raven Heart finally whispered.

"Are the bluecoats coming?" Broken Wing added later.
"Is that what you saw? More killing?"

Wolf remained mute. It was not so much that he didn't
want to share the dream. But how could a man explain
something he didn't understand himself?

Even when they returned to camp, Wolf remained silent.
His friends and family noticed the change, but they were
accustomed to such odd ways. Once an old medicine man
might have drawn Wolf aside. The old ones who understood such things had climbed Hanging Road, though.
Who remained? Only younger, uncertain men like Wolf
Running.

In the end, it was Sun Walker Woman who took him
aside.

"You're lost," she said as they walked along a shallow creek. "You rode out to find a path to walk, and you've come back more confused than before."

"I know," he confessed. "The world itself's misted over, and I can't find a trail to follow."

"The dream showed you what to do," she declared. "It's for you to see it."

"Maybe," he admitted. "But I can't make sense of it."

"Sometimes it's difficult for a man to understand what's clear to others," she said, gripping his hands. "Tell me what you saw. I, too, know the medicine trail. I can help you see."

Wolf frowned. He hated adding to her burdens. What else could he do, though? He shared the dream.

"Soon you must begin the fall hunting," she declared. "We'll find Bull Buffalo farther north, in the Black Hills country."

"I understood that much," he grumbled. "What of the othcr part? What did it mean? I haven't camped on Horse Creek since I was a boy."

"I think it was a warning," she said, sighing. "All the game gone. No people. It's what will happen if we continue to fight the *Wihio*."

"Or *unless* we fight them, drive them off," Wolf argued. "We signed a treaty paper at Horse Creek. It was the beginning of our troubles."

"That's not the story I remember your brothers and cousins telling about that time," she said, forcing a smile onto her face. "Crazy Horse won a horse race there, remember?"

"Yes," Wolf said, nodding. "He beat the Crows."

"You did something, too. Remember?"

"Yes," he admitted. "We were swimming in the creek, and a *Wihio* caught his foot in a log. I swam out and freed him."

"Your first rescue, Wolf."

"It was a *Wihio*," he muttered. "An enemy."

"I know him," she said, gazing southward. "We share a name, after all. He, too, is called Walker. He's the trader

Logan's son. Now he's a trader himself. The *Suhtai* buy rifles and powder from him. They trade their hides and get fair value from him. Whenever his own people grumble about it, he tells them he owes his life to us. It isn't us, though, Wolf. It's you."

"That was before, when he was younger," Wolf insisted. "I haven't seen him since the world's turned upside down. For all I know, he rode with the bluecoats who killed our relatives at Sand Creek."

"Not him," Sun Walker objected. "I looked into his eyes and read his heart. He's one *Wihio* you can always trust."

"Even if he was, he may no longer trade at Fort Laramie."

"Why would the dream have directed your thoughts there if he was gone?"

"Who can say?" Wolf asked, staring at his feet.

"I can," she told him. "Wolf, I have eyes and ears. I know that some have said your skin's too light to be a true *Tsis tsis tas*. One of my brothers argued against our marriage, saying you were too friendly with the traders' sons. You might be one yourself. *Lakotas* accused Crazy Horse of the same thing. It's made you both strange. You've suffered, yes, but that can make a man stronger. If our people are to survive this time, it will be because men like you can find a way to quiet the *Wihio* anger, to show them we can establish peace in this country without one of us dying."

"I'm not sure it's possible."

"If it's not, the dark vision in your dream will come to be," she said, sighing. "Bull Buffalo will be gone. So will I. So will you. So will the children."

The darkness of her gaze struck him hard, and he pulled away from her grasp.

"I won't let that happen!" he vowed. "I'll . . ."

"What, fight them?" she asked. "That's no answer. If you want to see our children grow tall, you must go and talk with the *Wihio*."

"I must hunt," he argued. "We'll need meat this winter."

"You'll hunt," she agreed. "Then you'll go and speak with the trader."

Wolf sighed. He had no desire to journey to that place, to walk among the bluecoats. They would gladly kill him. Worse, they might put him in one of their iron cages. It had happened to some of the *Sicangu* chiefs. Wolf accepted the risk of death, as any warrior did, but the thought of giving up the sun and the sky? That was more than a man could bear!

"Make the preparations for the hunting," Sun Walker whispered. "There will be time to decide about the other thing later."

"It's already decided," he told her. "I may not understand the dream, but I trust your advice. I'll go to the fort."

"Good," she said, resting her head against his chest. "My husband's a man of the people. He'll listen to the *Wihio* and speak with the chiefs. Maybe we'll restore harmony to this land."

Wolf did not share her optimism. Nevertheless, he set aside his doubts and began making preparations for the autumn buffalo hunt. He met with some of the *Oglala* chiefs and helped organize the Elk soldiers. When the hunters met, Wolf performed the ancient *Suhtai* prayers. Later he led one band of scouts northward into the Black Hills. That country remained free of *Wihio* intrusion, and the hunting went well. Wolf exhibited a brother's pride when Raven Heart made the first kill, and he himself shot three bulls. Afterward he devoted his energies to overseeing the safety of the younger hunters. He also saw that meat was fairly apportioned among the lodges, especially those with newly adopted children or older men and women.

By the time the first snowflakes of winter were falling, Wolf had led a handful of *Suhtai* and *Tsis tsis tas* families southward into the foothills. Winters were not mild there, but Wolf knew the country. He feared that winter might be the last time they would be able to camp safely away from their *Lakota* relations. It would similarly provide Wolf with an easy route to Fort Laramie and his promised reunion with Walker Logan.

It was not a ride Wolf was eager to make, and he delayed his departure.

"The snows will only grow deeper," Sun Walker Woman scolded. "If you don't leave soon, you may not return before first thaw."

"I should stay then," he suggested. "I spotted some Pawnees a day's ride from here. It's not wise to leave you with enemies so close by."

"Wolf, it's foolish to ignore a dream," she warned. "Stands Long will be here, watching over us. We're not a camp of women. There are good men here to protect us from Pawnees."

"We're too few already," he argued. "No, I'll go later, when the hard cold has passed."

That winter proved to be a strange time. Red Cloud and other chiefs remained in the Powder River country, bothering the bluecoats who had built a small fort at the southern end of the valley. Up north *Wihio* treaty makers had signed all sorts of new agreements with minor chiefs. In the midst of a blinding snowstorm, one party of treaty people rode into Wolf Running's camp, offering presents if he would touch the treaty pen.

"Come, warm yourself," Wolf told the group's *Lakota* guides. "What kind of crazy white men have you brought here? Don't they know that I'm no chief?"

"Ah, they don't know one chief from another," a *Sicangu* named Hairy Robe explained. "They don't know Pawnees from Snakes. They carry good things, though. Heavy blankets. Flour. Tobacco. Touch their pen, and they'll give you anything you want."

"I only want to be left alone," Wolf grumbled.

"That's the one thing they won't agree to," Hairy Robe explained. "They're going to build an iron road along Platte River. They'll steal all the country they need. You might as well have something in return."

There were other treaty makers at Fort Laramie. They

also sent messengers among the scattered *Lakota* and *Tsis tsis tas* camps, calling the headmen to a great council. Each time a messenger arrived, Sun Walker Woman urged Wolf to return to the fort with him.

"It's still winter," Wolf insisted. "I'll leave when the rivers begin to thaw."

Later he chose other excuses.

"It's a difficult journey to make alone," he declared.

"Take Raven Heart," Sun Walker suggested. "And Broken Wing."

"Boys," he grumbled.

"They carry men's names," she reminded him. "They won't worry the bluecoats, either."

"There are too many bluecoats there now," he complained. "I'll go later, when some of our people have come south."

"You won't help anyone then," she objected. "You should go now, while you can offer advice to the chiefs."

"I'm no one to gain a chief's ear," he argued. "I'll go later."

Actually Wolf was reconsidering whether he should go at all. From travelers he learned that bluecoats continued to travel the thieves' road through the Powder River country. More and more bluecoats rode west along Platte River, and a band of Arapahos claimed that armies of wagon people planned to travel that road when summer arrived.

Wolf worried about the signs of continuing trouble. He doubted he could do anything to avert more fighting—and dying. He began to suspect that he would never ride into the fort to speak with Walker Logan. The next day, though, Raven Heart and Broken Wing arrived with word that the very same Logan was riding toward their camp.

"It's not possible," Wolf declared. "Not even a crazy *Wihio* would ride out here when Hoop and Stick Moon's still filling the midnight sky."

"He says he comes to find you, Wolf," Raven Heart explained. "He says to ask you if you still have the silver eagle he gave you at Horse Creek. He says he still has what you gave him."

Wolf grinned. He tried not to, but it wasn't possible. He reached under his heavy elk robe and touched the small charm he still wore round his neck.

"What did you give the trader?" Broken Wing asked.

"His life." Raven Heart explained. "I told you the story."

"Ah, the *Wihio* that almost drowned," Wing said, nodding. "I never heard about the charm. Maybe it wasn't as foolish a thing as I'd thought, saving a white man."

"No, not *that* white man," Wolf admitted as he spied riding closer a slender, hairy-faced man bundled in heavy buffalo hides. "To be truthful, though, he isn't a very good *Wihio*. He doesn't carry any of our scalps, and he doesn't cheat anyone."

"No, that's hardly a *Wihio* at all," Broken Wing agreed.

It had been some time since the two old friends had met, and Wolf watched with interest the way Walker Logan stripped the saddle from his pony and removed bundles from two pack animals. He took his first steps toward Wolf only after providing oats and water for the weary horses.

"You haven't forgotten everything," Wolf observed as he clasped the trader's hand.

"I've forgotten nothing," Logan replied, speaking first in English and then using the *Tsis tsis tas* words he had learned as a boy. "I hoped that I would find you well. Hairy Robe said that you were camped here."

"I'm glad he didn't tell the bluecoats," Wolf said, scowling. "They enjoy riding into our winter camps, leaving our children dead in the snow."

"I know about Sand Creek," Logan said, sighing. "It's remembered in the East, too. Not all whites approve of murder. If the people deciding what to do knew the truth, they wouldn't allow that sort of thing to happen again. It's why I came here."

"Yes?" Wolf asked.

"To talk about establishing peace in this country. You and I know it's possible to live together."

"It is?"

"Of course," Logan insisted. "It's too cold to talk about such things here, though. Can't we find a fire somewhere?"

"Yes," Wolf said, laughing. "My lodge is full of children, but there's a good fire there, and Sun Walker Woman can make us something to eat."

"Good," Logan said, grinning. "I've brought presents. Tobacco. Coffee and sugar, too," he added, pointing to the packs resting in the snow near the horses.

"I'll bring them, *Nah nih*," Raven Heart volunteered. "Wing can take charge of the horses."

"I'll do it," Broken Wing announced.

"You'll stay with us for a time?" Wolf asked. "Rest. Eat."

"Yes," Logan agreed. "We'll talk, too."

Wolf led the way to his lodge, and the children scurried to one corner in order to make room near the fire for their elders.

"My sons," Wolf explained, pointing to the three boys. He introduced them to their visitor, but only Wind's Whisper responded.

"You have a hairy face," the boy said, grinning.

"Yes," Logan confessed. "Helps shield my *Wihio* skin against the bite of the wind."

"A man ought to know better than to ride out here in winter," Sun Walker scolded as she offered Logan a cup of steaming sassafras tea.

"There's more than a few such fools riding about this year," Logan replied as he accepted the tea. He sipped it, then took a deep breath. "I don't know how much Hairy Robe told you, but the government sent peace commissioners up the Missouri River a while back. They got all sorts of signatures on their treaties."

"Not mine," Wolf growled. "None of the chiefs agreed to anything."

"The commissioners now know that," Logan said, shaking his head. "They're coming back to meet with the chiefs. They've sent word to Red Cloud, Spotted Tail, and some of the others. Truth is, though, no one's sure anybody's coming in. These men will listen, Wolf. They can make a fair agreement. If none of the chiefs come to Fort Laramie and share their grievances, the treaty makers will get whomever they can to sign. The army will attack the hostiles.''

"The bluecoats will listen to the treaty makers?''

"They'll have to,'' Logan insisted. "My people are weary of war. We've just finished fighting the Southerners, Wolf. You can't imagine how many have died. I've never seen more than a few thousand people gathered together in one place, but in some of those battles in the East thousands were killed in a single day. You've fought, Wolf. You've killed. You know the darkness that comes with war. My people want to cast off that darkness, not start a new war with the plains tribes.''

"You say it well,'' Wolf said, filling a pipe with tobacco. "I understand your words, and I see that you believe them. But if that's true, why did the bluecoats ride into Powder River Valley? Why do they put up forts along the road they've stolen from us there?''

"It's been a mistake,'' Logan argued. "The treaty commissioners will make it right.''

"Every time we meet with treaty men, they ask us to give up something,'' Wolf said, staring into the fire. "They ask for a road along Platte River, and we give it up. Now Bull Buffalo doesn't come here anymore. They ask for forts to protect the gold diggers, and then their armies attack our children! When I was little, I held no hatred in my heart for anybody. I remember you, Walker Logan,'' Wolf said, pulling the silver charm from under his shirt. "When the bad hearts talk of attacking the ranches or wagon people, I say we should fight soldiers and leave the helpless ones alone.''

Broken Wing and Raven Heart entered the lodge then, and Wolf motioned Wing closer.

"This young man now rides with my brother,'' Wolf explained. "He should follow a father. He should chase brothers through the rivers next summer. He can't. He has none.''

"Sand Creek?" Logan whispered.

"*Wihio*," Wolf muttered. "Do you know the meaning of that word, Walker?"

"It's the word your people use for mine," Logan replied.

"It doesn't mean white, though," Wolf explained. "It means oddly sick, out of harmony with the sacred hoop. *Wihio* will never make true peace with us. It's not possible for a man who doesn't know harmony to treat honestly with others. He'll lie and steal because he only knows hunger. He fills his belly, but that doesn't satisfy him. He wants your food and mine. If he has twenty horses, he wants thirty.

"You say your people fight each other, killing thousands! Why not? It's your way, isn't it? In the grandfathers' time, a warrior would ride out to fight his enemy. Two men might fight, but each was content to count coup on the other, to show he was better. They didn't kill, because to do so only disturbed the harmony of the sacred hoop. It kindled anger that drove other men to fight. Instead of raids, we have battles now. Instead of coups, we count scalps. The killing never stops."

"This treaty—"

"Means nothing," Wolf grumbled. "You can't bring peace with paper. It flows from men's hearts, and there's no honor in our enemies anymore."

"You've met too many soldiers," Logan argued. "We're not all butchers."

"I know," Wolf said, lighting the pipe. "The problem is that too many of your people don't understand that we, too, should not be judged by the worst among us. Wing, would you ride to the fort at Horse Creek and speak with these *Wihio* treaty makers?"

"Will they be bluecoats?" Broken Wing asked.

"Some will be," Logan admitted.

"These are the men who cut little children into pieces," Broken Wing said, shuddering. "I won't treat with them."

"He's young," Logan said, turning to Broken Wing. "He can afford to hate. We're older, Wolf. We have to think of our children, of the future. If courage and honor could win this fight, you would stand a good chance. It won't. There are too many bluecoats. They'll win if it comes to a fight.''

''I've seen what will happen if they win,'' Wolf said, sighing. He paused and whispered the old *Suhtai* words to the pipe ritual. He offered tobacco to earth and sky, to the cardinal directions, and then touched his lips to the pipe. ''We will eat and smoke today as friends,'' Wolf declared as he passed the pipe to his guest. ''Your heart's good, and you come here to help, but it doesn't matter. Unless these treaty makers take their soldiers out of our country and leave us to live untroubled, we'll fight.''

''And die?'' Logan asked, studying the pipe.

''Nothing lasts long,'' Broken Wing declared.

''Only the earth and he mountains,'' Logan said, smiling at the surprise etched across the young *Tsis tsis tas*'s face. ''I won't smoke in honor of a vow to fight,'' he added. ''I'm not prepared to celebrate a world without Wolf Running and his people, without Bull Buffalo and Antelope, Deer and Elk. I'll keep trying, Wolf, as long as I see hope of encouraging peace.''

''I know,'' Wolf said, lifting the pipe to his old friend's lips. ''Smoke to that, Walker Logan. Smoke to understanding between old friends. It's all we'll manage, I'm afraid.''

''Perhaps,'' Logan agreed. He smoked, then passed the pipe to Broken Wing. ''Will you at least come to the fort and hear what the commissioners have to say?''

''I'll come when the snows thaw,'' Wolf promised. ''We'll trade, and your sons may swim Platte River with mine.''

''My sons have gone east with their mother,'' Logan said, frowning. ''They left after the Julesburg raids.''

''Maybe you, too, should go,'' Wolf whispered.

''I can't,'' Logan explained. ''I still owe a debt.''

''You may find it an expensive one to pay,'' Wolf replied.

''Perhaps, Wolf, but a man has to walk his own path.''

''Yes,'' Wolf agreed. ''He does.''

chapter
17

B Y THE TIME THE SNOWS began melting and the rivers started to thaw, Walker Logan had long since departed. Wolf busied himself hunting deer in the nearby thickets and gathering his ponies from the nearby hills where they had scattered during the winter.

"What do you plan to do, *Nah nih*?" Raven Heart asked when they brought in the last of the horses.

"Move west," Wolf replied. "The grass will green earlier there, and we should rejoin our *Oglala* relations."

"You're not going to the fort?" Raven Heart asked. "I thought . . ."

"I'm going to talk with our cousin," Wolf explained. "We don't know what's happened since we left."

"Don't you trust the trader?"

"I do, but who knows what's happened since he was here? I remember other times when our people have gone to forts, believing they would be safe there."

"Yes," Raven Heart agreed. "It's best to find out first."

And so the little band made its way westward toward Powder River. The nights were still cold, and twice fresh snow fell on them. Wolf watched the little ones shiver and the old people suffer, but none of them complained. They all knew waiting for winter to pass meant traveling when the bluecoats might be riding north again.

Wolf's little band snaked its way along half-frozen streams almost a week before meeting up with a party of *Sicangu Lakotas* near Pumpkin Butte. They were part of Spotted Tail's band, and they were headed to Fort Laramie. Hairy Robe led them, and he greeted Wolf warmly.

"I've saved your people a hard journey," Hairy Robe declared. "The tribes are meeting at the fort to receive presents and hear the words of the treaty makers."

"All of them?" Wolf asked. "Even Red Cloud?"

"The *Oglalas* are fighting bluecoats at Powder River," the Robe muttered. "They insist on staying. It's a foolish thing. Some will die there, and for what purpose? The treaty makers will order the bluecoats south."

"Is that what the agreement says?" Wolf asked. "You've heard the words read?"

"No," Hairy Robe confessed. "Look at this new rifle the *Wihio* gave me. Would they give us guns to fight them with? No, they mean to make peace."

Wolf studied the rifle. It was a new, unfamiliar type. Hairy Robe drew it out of its saddle scabbard and showed Wolf how it worked. The rifle could rapidly fire many times.

There was no need to reload between shots as with the old guns provided by the traders. Hairy Robe was right. It wasn't the sort of weapon even a crazy man would give to an enemy.

"Come with us," Hairy Robe urged. "The others will follow. Look at us. We've not even got good cooking pots, and we're out of powder. We need to trade."

"You rely too much on *Wihio* pots and *Wihio* powder," Wolf grumbled.

"Why shouldn't we accept the good things they can provide?" a young *Sicangu* named Snipe asked. "They've taken what they could from us."

"It's true," Wolf agreed. "Now they take our old ways,

too. Soon our young men won't remember how to craft arrows, and our women will forget how their mothers made clay pots."

"There's no arguing with this one," Hairy Robe explained. "He's like his cousin, the strange *Oglala*."

"Crazy Horse?" Snipe asked. The Robe nodded, and Snipe grinned. "You're the rescuer, then, the one called Wolf Running."

"Yes," Wolf admitted. "It's difficult to rescue people sometimes, though. Their ears won't hear my words."

"We have too many needs," Snipe explained. "If the *Wihio* are lying, I'll return. Some of us aren't yet afraid of fighting."

"It's good to know the *Lakotas* aren't forgetting everything," Wolf said, grinning. "How far away are the *Oglalas*?"

"Not far," Snipe said, dismounting. He drew a map in the snow, showing Wolf where Red Cloud and Crazy Horse's bands were camped. He then slid his foot across the snow, erasing it from view.

"I'm continuing west," Wolf declared as the *Sicangus* broke away. "The *Oglalas* are only three days away."

"Why aren't we going with Hairy Robe?" Sun Walker Woman asked.

"I'll speak with my cousin first," Wolf explained. "Then I'll decide what's best."

She frowned. Her eyes betrayed her disappointment, but Sun Walker wasn't a woman to quarrel with her husband when others were nearby. Instead, she followed as he turned westward. Half the band chose to go south with the *Sicangus,* though.

"You can't blame them," Sun Walker told Wolf that night. "What will we find on Powder River? More bluecoats? Hunger?"

"I *don't* blame them," Wolf replied. "Winter's never an easy time, and I understand why those old people would hurry to a fort where *Wihio* treaty makers are promising presents."

"It's not just the presents," Sun Walker argued. "It's the hope of peace."

"It's natural to hope, I suppose," Wolf said, frowning. "Black Kettle wanted peace, and the bluecoats gave him bullets instead. After Sand Creek I thought our people would be wiser."

"The old ones are tired, Wolf."

"And the younger people?"

"Most have little ones."

"We have children, too," Wolf pointed out. "It's because of them that I won't trust *Wihio* promises."

"Instead, you'll lead them to Powder River, to the same valley where the bluecoats killed the Arapahos!"

"We have friends here," Wolf said soberly. "Men I trust."

"You don't trust the trader?"

"I do, but he's not seen the darkness in the bluecoats' eyes. He doesn't want us to come to harm, but he can't really stop that from happening."

"What about your dream?"

"It directed me to Logan," Wolf admitted. "We spoke. He believes I may help the treaty makers understand, but my words hold no weight with *Wihio* chiefs. They will speak with Red Cloud, if he decides to come to the fort."

"So, you'll speak with the *Oglalas,* tell them about the treaty makers?"

"I'll share what I know. Then perhaps we can decide what to do."

"You'll tell them about your dream, too?"

"I'll share everything," he vowed. "I'll also consider your feelings."

"My hair's still short, Wolf. It hasn't been very long since I cut it to mourn the death of another good man. We're too few already."

"Yes," he agreed. *But not so few as I fear we will become.*

Wolf's spirits began to rise once he approached Powder River itself. He and Stands Long rode ahead of the others, warily scanning the countryside for signs of peril. Twice

Wolf heard the sounds of gunfire from the west, but the shooting was too far away to pose any immediate danger to his little band.

"Do you want to ride on ahead?" Stands Long asked. "We could climb the hills and look down on the river."

"I'll go," Wolf replied. "You ride back and warn the others."

"You're not going alone," Stands Long insisted. "We'll ride together or warn the others together."

The two brother-friends eyed each other with a mixture of impatience and curiosity. Wolf couldn't recall a time when Stands Long had questioned a decision.

"I'm no longer lame," Stands Long whispered. "I don't need protecting."

"I do?"

"Yes," Stands Long declared. "Since the trader came to your camp, you haven't been yourself. You're unsure what to do. A man who doubts himself can get killed."

"It's hard to be sure anymore," Wolf confessed.

"That's why it's good to have a man you can trust close by."

Wolf nodded somberly and turned his horse back toward the others. There was no need to ride back there, though. The wind had carried the sound of the shooting more than a mile. Raven Heart and Broken Wing were racing their ponies toward Wolf that very moment.

"Ayyyy!" Wing shouted as he slowed his pony. "Are there bluecoats ahead?"

"I don't know," Wolf confessed. "Stands Long and I are going to have a look. Wing, ride back and warn the others to be watchful."

"*Nah nih,* what should I do?" Raven Heart asked.

"Come along," Wolf explained. "You can ride back with our news."

"I could do it," Broken Wing suggested.

"I know," Wolf said, nodding respectfully to his young friend. "Raven Heart has a swifter pony, though. If there's trouble, the others need to know quickly."

Broken Wing frowned, but he accepted the decision. He

turned his horse and galloped back to the main party. Wolf then started for the nearby hills.

Powder River was unfamiliar country, and Wolf moved cautiously. He was well south of the spots where he'd camped with the *Oglalas*. He could no longer hear rifles, but that only meant no *Wihio* was firing. Only a few *Lakotas* carried rifles, and they would have shot their bullets away early.

Once on the far side of the hilly ridge, Wolf spied the river itself. Beyond it was a detail of woodcutters. Several bluecoats kept watch in pairs while their companions chopped cottonwoods into firewood.

"Look there, in the shallows," Stands Long whispered.

"It's a body," Raven Heart said. "There's another at the edge of the trees."

"Bluecoats," Wolf declared. "The *Oglalas* probably attacked them."

"They didn't stay long," Stands Long complained. "Thirty men cutting wood. You and I could run them, Wolf."

"Our friends weren't after the woodcutters," Wolf argued. "Look down there. Do you see any ponies? No. The *Oglalas* took the horses."

"They haven't left, either," Raven Heart said, pointing to movement in the underbrush. An arrow flew out of the trees, and an axman fell. Other arrows flew, and two other bluecoats toppled to the ground. The remaining choppers discarded their axes, grabbed their rifles, and fled into the woods. Some shots and a scream followed. Later a handful of *Oglalas* emerged from the brush.

"There's our cousin," Raven Heart said, pointing to where Crazy Horse and his brother-friend, Hump, stood.

"Yes," Wolf said, nodding. "Stands Long and I will ride down and talk with him. You should ride back and tell the others to bring the pony drags to Powder River. We'll camp with the *Oglalas* tonight."

"We haven't found the camps," Stands Long observed.

"No, but Crazy Horse can direct us," Wolf said as he nudged his pony forward. "I'll speak to him about it."

Before the sun set, Wolf had spoken with his cousin about many things. First, Wolf learned that the *Oglalas* and some other bands had passed the winter harassing the bluecoats at their little fort on Powder River. Sometimes there was a minor fight, but most of the time the *Wihio* soldiers turned and ran.

"The bluecoats are only part of the trouble," Crazy Horse added. "Small parties of wagon people come through our country on the stolen road."

"Have you heard about the treaty council?" Wolf asked.

"Yes," Crazy Horse grumbled. "The *Wihio* always want to make a new treaty when they decide not to keep the last one. When I was still a boy, some of us gathered at Bear Butte, where Sweet Medicine brought *Mahuts,* the sacred arrows, to the *Tsis tsis tas.* We said we would never agree to give up another piece of our ground to the whites. I don't break my vows, Wolf. I'll treat with no *Wihio.*"

"Is that how Red Cloud feels?" Wolf asked.

"He has his own path to walk," Crazy Horse insisted. "He doesn't share his intentions with me."

"Will you continue to fight if the bluecoats leave Powder River?"

"Who will there be to fight? I'm not a man who hungers for war. I fight because my enemies come into my country."

Wolf nodded. He then shared his dream and the talks he had with Walker Logan.

"You see things, Wolf, and you must find the truth in the dream. I, too, dream, and I see only dead bluecoats. No matter how many councils meet, I know more fighting's coming."

Wolf was less certain. As winter gave way to spring, a stream of messengers from other bands visited the *Oglala* camps. Hairy Robe came three times, but it wasn't until a party of *Sicangus* arrived with word that Spotted Tail had agreed to treat with the peace commissioners that Red Cloud responded.

"A chief can't always walk his own path," Wolf told

Crazy Horse after Red Cloud announced his intention to visit the fort. "When important matters are discussed, he should be there to listen."

Wolf himself decided to leave Powder River when he learned that Morning Star and several other leaders of the northern *Tsis tsis tas* were now camped near Fort Laramie.

"I know the *Wihio* words," Wolf told his cousin. "I can listen and give their true sense to the chiefs. Perhaps that's the meaning of my dream."

"Maybe," Crazy Horse admitted. "But when you tire of *Wihio* words and *Wihio* promises, come back here where you belong."

Actually, Wolf thought it best if the women and children remained in the Powder River camps. A small band of *Oglala* chiefs could ride swiftly to the fort, discover the treaty makers' intentions, and return. Red Cloud disagreed, saying it would be a bad sign for warriors to ride alone to the fort. Bringing the helpless ones showed peaceful intentions.

"The women wouldn't stay behind anyway," Sun Walker told Wolf as they broke down their lodge. "We want to trade with the *Wihio*. We have good robes to barter. The messengers say the *Wihio* will make a great giveaway, too. Why should we not accept presents?"

Wolf soon found that he was no longer the leader of an independent band. Instead, he was their captive as they hurried southeast toward Fort Laramie. As the grasses began to green and the sun burned away winter's chill, a thousand *Lakota* and *Tsis tsis tas* people rode along Platte River toward the fort.

"I'm glad you came," Walker Logan announced when Wolf and Sun Walker led the children through the door of the trader's store. "You look fatter."

"I shot an antelope yesterday," Wolf explained. "Sun Walker's too good a cook."

She grinned shyly, and Logan nodded.

"The children also look well," Logan said, touching Wind's Whisper's forehead. "I miss mine. Maybe when the new treaty's signed, they can return."

"You believe a new treaty will be signed?" Wolf asked.

"Now that the major chiefs are here, I can't see why not," the trader replied. "As I told you last winter, the people in the East are tired of fighting. The soldiers you've got penned up at the Powder River fort are mostly paroled Confederates, prisoners released on a vow to serve on the frontier. Their hearts aren't in this fight, and half the garrison here at Fort Laramie are just waiting for papers so they can go home. There's been enough fighting."

"What about the thieves' road?" Wolf asked.

"Oh, we can come to terms on that easily enough."

"Can we?" Wolf asked. "Will you give up the road?"

"Are your chiefs willing to die for it?"

"I know one who is," Wolf declared. "There are others who remember what happened to the buffalo when we agreed to give you a road on Platte River. Powder River and the Big Horn country is our last good hunting ground. To give it up is to give up our soul."

"Feeling's that strong?" Logan asked.

"Stronger," Wolf assured his old friend. "What can you promise us in return? Presents? Promises that you'll change when it suits you? No one believes *Wihio* pledges anymore."

"Then it will be difficult," Logan observed. "You and I have to do what we can to kindle trust and understanding. That's what you saw in your dream, wasn't it? You'll try?"

"I'll do what I can," Wolf promised. He didn't believe it would be enough.

The major obstacle to holding peace talks was the absence of the treaty makers. Despite all manner of assurances, the summer moons were in the sky before the commissioners arrived. At one point Red Cloud threatened to leave, but the bluecoat colonel in charge of the fort offered to send Red Cloud's personal invitation to the commissioners over the telegraph, the magical "singing wire" that had long mystified the plains peoples. The rapid reply, a promise to arrive soon, placated Red Cloud and provided him with a wonderful story to share with the other chiefs.

When the commissioners did arrive, Wolf found himself invited to the discussions.

"We're being asked to translate the chiefs' words," Logan explained. "You and me. It's your dream coming to life."

Wolf found little cause for celebrating, though. Chiefs and commissioners made long speeches that had little to do with reaching agreement. When one commissioner mentioned the "long history of peaceful relations between us and the plains peoples," Wolf had difficulty repeating the words. Two of the *Tsis tsis tas* representatives had vivid memories of Sand Creek.

When the treaty makers had finished speaking that day, Red Cloud surprised everyone by asking for a week's delay in the negotiations. The *Oglala* chief explained that he had received word from other *Lakota* chiefs that they, too, were coming.

"No agreement can mean anything if they're not here," Red Cloud declared.

The commissioners conferred. A few minutes later they agreed to the postponement. In the meantime, the trading and celebrating could continue.

"Red Cloud's a wise man," Logan told Wolf when the council broke up. "He knows everyone will be in a better mood to compromise after we trade and feast and get to know each other."

Wolf frowned.

"He meant what he said," Wolf explained. "Other chiefs are coming. If you expect Red Cloud to give away Powder River, you'll be disappointed."

chapter

18

A S IT TURNED OUT, IT wasn't the chiefs who hindered the treaty makers. The very day the peace commissioners prepared to resume discussions, several *Sicangu* scouts rode to the fort with news that a large army of bluecoats was marching westward along Platte River.

"Is it true?" Wolf asked Walker Logan.

"Probably just replacements for the garrison," Logan suggested.

Wolf studied his old friend's eyes. Logan knew more than he was telling.

"The scouts counted hundreds," Wolf continued. "Standing Elk, who favors touching the pen and reaching agreement, says they've come to build a road along Powder River for the gold diggers."

"That's not decided," Logan insisted.

But you knew, didn't you? Wolf asked silently. Logan looked away.

"Don't the treaty men understand anything?" Wolf grumbled. "There are children in our camps scarred by the long knives and bullets of bluecoats. I see them every day.

No agreement's possible without trust. How do you trust a man who makes promises while his army's marching toward your lodges?''

Red Cloud was similarly upset when the treaty commissioners introduced the eagle chief of the bluecoats, Carrington. Not one of the two thousand *Tsis tsis tas* and *Lakota* people camped near Fort Laramie remained ignorant of the bluecoats' arrival. Even after Man Afraid of His Horses vowed to fight the bluecoats if they marched toward Powder River, the bluecoat continued to argue that he was only trying to protect the miners traveling the stolen road.

Finally Red Cloud lost patience. His eyes were full of fire, and he glared at Carrington in particular. His words, which Wolf translated for the *Wihio,* were harsh. There remained no room for misunderstanding.

"You treat us like children!" the *Oglala* chief growled. "It's always the same. Each time we come and meet with you, you ask us to give up something. Once we rode through this whole country. Now we have only a piece of it, and you want that, too. You kill the game! You bring your sicknesses here to kill the children!

"We gather here to make peace. You say you want no more killing, but while we set aside our weapons, your soldiers remain in our country. Now you send bluecoats to take the road while we're not watching!''

The *Lakotas* grew angrier each moment, and the commissioners eyed each other nervously. Even Carrington, who had brought armed men along, backed away. Finally the treaty makers decided that it would be best to stop the discussions and let everyone calm down.

"It's useless," Red Cloud told his companions. He then marched straight toward Carrington, forcing the bluecoat chief to step back. Red Cloud continued on. He didn't even acknowledge the *Wihio* soldier's presence.

"We'll meet again tomorrow," the chief commissioner, Taylor, declared.

The *Oglalas* ignored him. Logan led Wolf aside.

"Red Cloud seemed angry," the trader observed. "Is there something we can do?"

"We?" Wolf asked. "Do you mean you and me? Or do you mean the treaty makers?"

"I meant the commissioners," Logan said, swallowing hard. "You understand, Wolf. It's in everyone's interest to stop the fighting."

"It's easily done," Wolf insisted. "Tell the bluecoats to go home. Abandon the fort on Powder River. Leave us to hunt and camp as our fathers did. Stop killing us!"

The last words, spoken angrily and in English, drew alarming stares from Carrington, the commissioners, and several armed soldiers. When two bluecoats started toward Wolf, Logan waved them away.

"You want things to be as they were," Logan whispered. "Nothing's ever the same, though. The soldiers will protect the road because gold has more value than promises made to Indians. It's a *Wihio* truth, old friend. It's hard to understand, I know, but it's the truth just the same. I wish I could change somebody's mind. I admire your people, and I value our friendship."

"Tell them," Wolf pleaded, pointing to the commissioners.

"I speak with a small voice, Wolf. They won't listen. No one will."

"Then there will be no peace," Wolf said, sighing. "Red Cloud will be gone by morning. I'm sick of war, of fighting and killing, but I'll ride with him. I'm tired of watching the women cut their hair and the children starve. That's what my people will find on Powder River, death and starvation."

"What will my people find?" Logan asked.

"The same," Wolf vowed. "If they come, we'll fight them."

"There are too many to kill," Logan observed. "In the end, you'll be the one to die."

"We'll kill many," Wolf explained. "Already I've seen the days of the *Tsis tsis tas* pass. Now I camp with the

Oglalas. If they, too, must begin the long climb up Hanging Road, then I'll go with them.''

"And your children?"

"No one lives long, Walker Logan. In my family, few men ever see their hair grow white. My sons," he began. Emotion choked him, though, and he halted.

"Should know a better time," Logan added.

"If a man gives up what he is, he's nothing," Wolf argued. "We have so little, and the *Wihio* has so much. The buzzards who pick a man's flesh from his bones wait for him to die. Must you eat us while we're still walking?"

"It's not me," Logan cried.

"Go east and walk the world with your sons," Wolf urged. "You won't like the world you say is coming here. Your heart's not cold enough."

"I know," Logan admitted. "Maybe you're right. Perhaps I should leave. But I figure that as long as I'm here, there's at least one person who knows . . ."

"Knows what?" Wolf asked.

"That once there was a man among the *Tsis tsis tas,* a shield carrier who always placed the welfare of his people above his own."

"Such a man should be remembered," Wolf agreed.

"He will be," Logan promised. "By me if by no one else."

Wolf nodded respectfully. Then he drew the silver charm from his neck and passed it into his old friend's hands.

"Give it to your son," Wolf suggested. "To one with ears to hear the story and understand how once *Tsis tsis tas* and *Wihio* became brothers."

"Wolf, I . . ."

"It's the only way you can pay the debt you owe. You won't see me again."

"But . . ."

"By sunrise tomorrow the *Oglalas* will be gone," Wolf said, forcing a somber grin onto his face. "We don't craft our own path, Walker Logan. We only walk it. If there are too many bluecoats to defeat, then we'll fail. There are plenty to kill, and enough to kill me. I've never stood in the shadows, old friend. I'm Wolf Running, a shield carrier. My place is in the front!"

"I know," Logan said, sighing. "I'll find my path more difficult now. Before, I always knew Wolf Running was out there."

"Be careful which waters you choose to swim," Wolf warned. "Next time there will be no rescuer."

"It's true," Logan agreed, clasping Wolf's wrists. "For either of us."

By midafternoon long streams of pony drags were leaving the scattered *Lakota* and *Tsis tsis tas* camps. Although some of the chiefs argued that it was better to stay and treat with the bluecoats, most chose to follow Red Cloud and the *Oglalas* into the Powder River country. To Wolf's dismay, many of his winter companions remained with Morning Star's band of northern *Tsis tsis tas*. Only Stands Long and Broken Wing accompanied Wolf's own family as they snaked their way north and west.

As for the wisdom of the decision, Sun Walker Woman had doubts.

"Our relatives will receive good blankets, powder for their rifles, and flour for bread making," she told Wolf. "If you join your cousin and the other *Oglalas,* who will hunt Bull Buffalo? Who will provide the food your children eat?"

"I will," he replied. "When have I ever let anyone starve? There's plenty of game in the hills around Powder River."

"And who will do it when the bluecoats shoot you?" she asked. "While you're fighting them, who will guard our camps? You have only a young brother with you now. He's eager to walk man's road. He won't remain behind."

"We'll talk and decide how best to protect the helpless ones," Wolf argued. "Whoever remains to guard our camp won't have to worry about the bluecoat army camped at Fort Laramie. Our friends who stay, waiting for presents, are in peril. They trust the same promises that the bluecoats made before attacking Black Kettle's people at Sand Creek.''

Actually the people who stayed at the fort saw little of Carrington's army. The bluecoats hardly paused at the fort before continuing northward up their stolen road toward the Montana gold fields. Wolf, on the other hand, saw Carrington's column almost daily. After persuading Raven Heart and Broken Wing to escort Sun Walker and the boys north of the *Wihio* fort, Wolf led Stands Long and a handful of *Oglalas* toward the dust raised by Carrington's wagons.

"It's not difficult tracking such men," Stands Long observed as they rode. "Only a blind man could fail to notice so much dust!''

"Standing Elk was right,'' Wolf said, frowning. "This is no scouting party. These bluecoats have come to build forts to guard their stolen road.''

Wolf hoped that somehow he was mistaken, but once he came within sight of the bluecoats, he knew the truth. From a hillside he watched as two hundred wagons churned deep ruts in the summer sod. Worse, Wolf, spied wagons heavily laden with strange machines, window frames, chairs, trunks, and even horns for musicians. Other wagons carried cases of rifles and barrels of powder. There was flour and meat enough to supply Walker Logan's store for ten summers!

The most disheartening sights of all were the women and children who accompanied the bluecoats. Bringing families into the heart of enemy country was the ultimate insult. The *Wihio* showed they had no fear of Red Cloud or anyone else.

"I've known the Crows to show contempt,'' Stands Long growled. "No Crow would ever bring his women to Powder River!''

"Perhaps it's only ignorance,'' Wolf said, fighting back the urge to charge the wagons and prove Carrington's mistake. "Maybe we can run these bluecoats.''

"So many?'' Stands Long asked.

"If we don't, we've lost this country forever,'' Wolf

declared. "Look at them. They bring their houses along, their women and children. These bluecoats come to stay."

"Yes, we'll run them," Stands Long declared angrily. "You and I can't be lazy hang-around-the-forts. We're shield carriers."

"Yes," Wolf agreed. "If we allow these bluecoats to stay, we'll have to put our shields away. Our bows and lances, too. There will be no more Elks, no more men."

"I would rather feel the sting of *Wihio* bullets again than see that day."

"I know. There are others that feel the same way, too. This *Wihio* Carrington won't find an easy path before his feet."

Thereafter Wolf and Stands Long were never far from Carrington's army. Sometimes they would creep along the line of wagons at night, taking a few horses from the pony herd. Other times they would leave an arrow in the cap of some sleeping bluecoat or startle the pickets into spreading an alarm. The brother-friends weren't the only ones to bother the bluecoats, but no one was better at it. Soon the *Oglala* camps were full of stories about their little raids.

The green grass moon of early summer stood high in the midnight sky when Carrington finally reached the *Wihio* fort on Powder River. They called the place Fort Reno after a dead bluecoat chief, but it was little more than a box made by a wall of logs with pitiful rough cabins inside. The men who had passed the winter there were little better than rabbits trapped in their holes. *Oglalas* had kept watch over the place, and anyone venturing more than a stone's throw from those walls came to a bad end.

Wolf stood on the far side of the river, watching, when the filthy survivors of the garrison came out to greet their rescuers. He expected the heavily bearded wretches to raise a cheer or fire off their rifles, but they merely stumbled around as if drunk. Carrington and the other bluecoat chiefs barked angry orders and soon had their men racing about furiously.

"An army of crazy men," Stands Long called them.

"When have white men been anything else?" Wolf asked.

Within a few days the old garrison collected its few possessions and marched away from Powder River. Carrington, too, left, heading north toward the gold camps. A fourth of his bluecoats remained at Fort Reno, guarding the southern section of the stolen road. These bluecoats drew Wolf's attention.

He made his preparations carefully. First he rode to the nearby *Oglala* camp where Sun Walker Woman and his sons rested in their lodge. He brought a freshly killed deer with him to provide for their needs. Stands Long led six ponies taken from the bluecoats.

"You can trade these for what you need," Wolf told Wind's Whisper. As the eldest male, the boy bore a heavy burden.

"*Ne' hyo,* won't my uncle see to our needs?" Whisper asked.

"His place is with the warriors now," Wolf explained. "We face a difficult fight, and we need all our men."

"I'll grow fast then," Whisper said, taking his father's hand. "Soon I'll be tall enough to go along and hold your horses."

"That will be a good day for our people," Wolf declared. "It's a fine thing for a man to ride to battle with his sons."

Sun Walker interrupted them then. Wolf recognized the dark glare in her eyes and tried to avoid the words that were certain to follow. It wasn't possible.

"How easy it is for you to tell a boy of eight summers that he'll soon walk Man's Road," she complained.

"It's not easy," he insisted.

"You leave us a deer and think you've provided everything. Who will show Wind's Whisper how to stalk deer? Who will make the new bow he'll need to hunt game? It's a great thing for men to ride off and fight, but who will cut wood to keep our lodge warm? Who will work the hides into clothing? Who will—"

"You will," Wolf said, taking her hand. "I know who carries the heaviest burden."

"And what if you don't come back to us?"

"If that day comes, I hope your sons will be tall, and your hair long white. If not, I hope you will invite another, better man into your lodge. It's not right that my sons should climb Man's Road alone. They'll need a man's guidance."

"Yours."

"It's what I hope will happen, Sun Walker, but only *Heammawihio* knows what will be. We can only walk our paths and do our best."

"Yes," she agreed. "Now you'll ride to the fort with Stands Long and those children. Watch over them, Wolf. They have no mother to mourn them."

"Perhaps not," he said, lifting her chin. "They know one woman who will cut her hair, though."

"Yes," she said, smiling faintly.

Wolf sent Raven Heart through the camp with a pipe, and soon ten men gathered near Wolf's lodge. Wolf, Stands Long, Raven Heart, and Broken Wing were there. Two young *Suhtai* cousins and four *Oglalas* completed the party. The *Suhtais,* Falcon and Weasel Foot, were also Sun Walker Woman's nephews. The *Oglalas* included Bucktail and Crooked Horn, who had counted coups during the winter fighting. Stone Arrow and Mountain Panther were marking their fourteenth summers by embarking on their first raid.

"Follow Bucktail," Wolf advised the boys. "Be careful. Nothing the bluecoats have is worth your life."

Wolf led his little party to Powder River. There, on a slope overlooking the fort, he made the warrior prayers and painted his face. He then tied elk tooth charms behind the youngsters' ears and explained what he intended to do.

"They send men out to cut wood," Wolf explained. "We'll follow such a party. When they stop to cut wood, Bucktail, Stone Arrow, and Mountain Panther will run their horses. Then Stands Long and I will charge. You others will follow us. We'll make only one charge. The bluecoats can either stand and be killed or run.''

"They usually run," Bucktail observed. "My brother and I ran some of them all the way to the fort last winter."

"These are different men," Wolf warned. "Their bellies are full, and they don't respect us."

"Yes," Bucktail agreed. "We've seen their women. It's an insult!"

"They don't regard us very highly," Raven Heart muttered.

"They'll change their minds," Broken Wing growled.

So it was that the raiders struck furiously when they spied woodcutters that afternoon. Only six men sawed logs while four kept watch. The guards called out in alarm when Bucktail's band swept in and raced off with the ponies. When Wolf screamed out and charged toward the cutters, the bluecoats cast their saws aside and fled.

Stands Long was the first raider to count coup. He clubbed a fat *Wihio* across the forehead, jumped down, and took his scalp. Falcon shot one of the guards through both lungs, killing him. Another guard turned to fire at Weasel Foot, but Wolf shot the bluecoat in the chest.

With two guards dead and no help in sight, the bluecoats either dashed for the cover of a nearby thicket or tried to defend themselves. A third bluecoat died running, but the others managed to escape.

"What now?" Stands Long asked as he stripped his dead bluecoat of a rifle and cartridge belt.

"Wait for the next wood party," Wolf suggested.

As if reading his mind, another party emerged from the fort that instant. This time they drove two wagons. A disappointed Wolf decided it would be too difficult to free the wagon horses from their harness. Bucktail shook his head and waved his lance at the wagon. The *Oglalas* charged.

The fight that ensued was a confused affair. Mostly it consisted of mounted raiders chasing bluecoats through a stand of cottonwoods and down a path to their fort. Wolf joined the chase, but somehow he became separated from the others. He slowed his pony and tried to determine where the fleeing bluecoats might be. At that instant he heard a twig snap to his left.

Wolf drew his lance and leapt off his horse. Three quick steps brought him out of the trees. Just ahead three young *Wihio* boys stood shivering in the shallows of the river.

"You're not soldiers," Wolf said, eyeing the three. The oldest was about Falcon's age and size. He took a nervous step in front of the others and fixed Wolf with a hard stare.

"Go ahead!" he shouted. "Kill me. All I ask is that you make it quick."

"Yes," a younger boy agreed. "Don't go cuttin' us up, neither. My ma's up that hill, and she's not a well woman."

Wolf studied the boys, unsure what to do with them. They were probably miners' sons. They had a hardness to their faces, and their bodies showed the scars of rough work and rougher handling.

"Why have you come here?" Wolf asked. "This is our land."

"You're welcome to it, mister," the third boy said, sidling toward the bank. "Just let me get my trousers, and I'll be glad to leave you to it."

Wolf laughed. He tried to maintain an angry gaze, but it wasn't possible. They were only children, and he could no more make war on them than on his own sons. He waved them to the bank, then ran the tip of his lance along their bare chests until a droplet or two of blood appeared on each.

"Remember this day when you see the scars," Wolf said as touched each boy's chin in turn. "Tell your fathers to go away and leave us alone. If they stay, many will die here."

The oldest boy muttered an incoherent reply. Then he grabbed his clothes and raced away. A second boy followed, but the youngest remained, frozen in fear.

"Why?" the boy whimpered. "Pa said . . ."

"Look here," Wolf said, opening his shirt to show his bare chest. "My skin's not white. I have no *Wihio* heart. We don't kill children. You're safe."

"Thanks," the boy said, touching the shaft of Wolf's lance. "I'll tell Pa, too."

The stupefied boy managed to step into his britches. Then he turned back and forced a grin onto his weary face.

Wolf matched it. As the boy raced off to join his companions, Wolf wondered what sort of madness let a warrior chase swimming boys from Powder River. In a week he might well find himself striking down their fathers.

Wolf's actions didn't please his companions, either.

"They're older than the brothers I lost at Sand Creek," Broken Wing grumbled.

"They'll soon be soldiers themselves," Mountain Panther added.

"I'll kill them then," Wolf insisted.

"I told you he was a strange one, like his cousin," Bucktail told Stone Arrow. "He's a good man to follow, though. He brings his band many horses, and he never leaves a man behind."

"Let's take more ponies next time, though," the Arrow suggested. "You can't ride a saw."

chapter
19

WHILE WOLF'S LITTLE PARTY AND others harassed the bluecoats at Fort Reno, Carrington continued north, alarming the *Lakota* camps located there. Hundreds of warriors began stalking the bluecoats, driving off ponies and attacking wood and hunting parties. Finally Carrington made camp at the junction of Big Piney and Little Piney creeks. There, in the heart of the best hunting country left to the *Lakotas,* the bluecoats constructed a second fort to guard the thieves' road.

Messengers rode from one encampment to the next, spreading word of Carrington's new fort.

"The bluecoats will soon own Powder River as surely as they possess the Platte!" Storm Eagle exclaimed. "We have to stop this *Wihio* chief!"

While small bands of *Oglalas* broke away and rode north to join Red Cloud's main war party, Wolf remained in the south. That northern country was unknown to him, and he believed his family would be safer in the south, away from the bulk of Carrington's army.

That summer Wolf and Stands Long passed most mornings hunting deer in the thickets near Powder River. On one such occasion, two horsemen appeared at the river. Wolf strung his bow and prepared to fire an arrow, but a familiar voice quieted his fears. It was only the *Oglala* brother-friends, Two Arrows and Beaver Belt. The youngsters had been up north with Crazy Horse, and Wolf was glad to see them.

"Have you run out of bluecoats to run?" Wolf called. "We have a few left here."

"No, we have plenty of fighting to do at Big Piney Creek," Two Arrows explained. He dismounted and took a beautiful beaver pelt from where it had been tied on the back of his pony. "We've come from your cousin. He sends you this."

Two Arrows presented the beaver pelt. Inside was a long red-bowled pipe. Two hawk feathers were attached, as was an old elk tooth charm that Wolf himself had made.

"Have the *Oglalas* grown too few to fight Carrington?" Stands Long asked, joining the discussion. "We have trouble enough here."

"I can only bring you the pipe," Two Arrows said, studying the river. "You know what's required."

"We make our own fight," Stands Long declared.

"The new fort's too strong for us," Beaver Belt said, dismounting. "We must discover what the *Wihio* plan to do. Red Cloud's asked some of the treaty signers to visit Carrington, but he needs a man who can understand the bluecoats' words. Too often we've misunderstood. Each time we've suffered."

"Red Cloud intends to treat with the bluecoats?" Wolf asked.

"Someone will talk with them," Two Arrows said, smiling. "We'll not give away our heart, but it's good to know an enemy's intentions. Crazy Horse knows that. It's why he sent the pipe to you."

"A man who rescues foolish boys can be relied upon," Beaver Belt added.

"Perhaps," Wolf admitted.

"It's a long journey, though," Stands Long argued.

"Summer's coming to an end, and we should hunt."

"You can winter with our band," Two Arrows suggested. "Your wife has friends there, and it's safer."

"How?" Wolf asked. "You're closer to Carrington's army, and the Crows make their winter camps a day's ride farther north."

"Yes, but there are enough of us to keep watchers in camp," Two Arrows pointed out. "Besides, we'll soon be killing the bluecoats. Crazy Horse has vowed it."

"Has he seen something in his dreams?" Wolf asked.

"Who can say?" Beaver Belt replied. "He's a strange man. He says little about what he sees, but we know the power he holds. If he says the bluecoats will die, I believe they will."

Wolf was less certain. Still, Crazy Horse would not have sent the elk tooth unless there was need of him. The cousins had exchanged charms as boys, and there was power in that sort of bond.

"We're going?" Stands Long said, reading his brother-friend's eyes.

"Twice my cousin has asked me for help. Twice, in all his life," Wolf explained. "These boys are right. Crazy Horse sees things. I have to go, but you could stay here and watch Sun Walker Woman and the little ones."

"When did one brother-friend ride to battle without the other?" Stands Long asked. "I stayed behind when I was hurt, but my flesh is whole again. We'll ride together."

"Then I have preparations to make," Wolf told the visitors. "We'll leave tomorrow."

Two Arrows nodded. The young men then remounted their ponies and continued their journey. Wolf gazed silently at the stone points of his arrows.

"It's the only thing that's not changed," Wolf noted. "And even that's changed for most of our people. Boys now use points molded from melted down *Wihio* cooking pots."

"Such arrows never carry the power yours do," Stands Long observed. "It's sad to see how many of the young men ignore the ceremonies. They forget who they are, and so they're lost even if they're not yet dead.''

That notion rested heavily on Wolf's mind that afternoon when he explained to his little sons why they were
traveling north once more. He had already heard Sun
Walker's objections, and he feared the boys, too, would be
reluctant to leave such rich country and journey to a for-
eign place.

''*Ne' hyo*, we have to fight these bluecoat devils,''
Wind's Whisper declared. ''Everyone says so. We've seen
Broken Wing's scars. When our people last trusted the
bluecoat chiefs, soldiers killed his brothers.''

Wolf grinned at the boy. Whisper tried to hide his trembling fingers and steady the quiver in his voice. It wasn't
entirely possible, but Wolf was proud of the effort.

''We'll soon be old enough to go with you,'' Winter
Pup added.

''You'll be a young man before long,'' Wolf told the
six-year-old. ''By then I hope we have run these bluecoats
from Powder River.''

''Yes,'' Wind's Whisper added. ''You'll do it, *Ne' hyo*.
There will be others, though.''

Wolf frowned. The boy was right, of course, but it was
a hard thing for a father to realize. Even a man who prayed
that *Heammawihio* would send his sons the challenges that
would make them strong could still hope their path might
be gentler than his own.

When Wolf reached the junction of the Piney creeks, he
was surprised to find the bulk of the northern *Tsis tsis tas*
tribe there as well. Two Moon and Black Horse had their
entire bands there. So did Morning Star, whom the *Wihio*
insisted on calling Dull Knife. The Star had touched his
pen to the treaty, and the other chiefs chided him for doing
so.

''It's one of the reasons you're needed here,'' Crazy
Horse told Wolf. ''Morning Star was told the paper said
nothing about giving up our land. It was only an agreement
to accept presents.''

Wolf thought that unlikely, but he didn't doubt that the

Star had been deceived. The chief was genuinely angry, and he wasn't known as a man easily riled.

At any rate, the three *Tsis tsis tas* chiefs approached the fort builders calmly, claiming they only wished to talk. Carrington, perhaps because he recalled Red Cloud's angry words in the treaty council or the large number of *Lakotas* camped nearby, agreed to speak with the visitors. He had two well-known guides with him at the Pineys—the black scout Medicine Calf Beckwith and the famous pathfinder Jim Bridger, the Blanket. Both men knew much of the tribal languages. They also had eyes known for spying truth.

"They're suspicious," Stands Long whispered to Wolf.

"They should be," Wolf replied. "They camp with the bluecoats, so they share the trouble."

It was an odd meeting. Carrington and his hotheaded cavalry chief, Fetterman, were ill at ease with each other. Fetterman insisted that he, too, be called an eagle chief, and he resented his commander. He had only contempt for all Indians, and he never considered that one of the visitors might understand English.

"Give me half a day and my old regiment and I'll put an end to this business," he growled to a companion. Such arrogance could prove useful, Wolf told himself.

Carrington, on the other hand, was cautious. He shepherded the chiefs around his command, taking care to reveal only the best trained and equipped of the soldiers. Later he brought out one of the four big cannons he had brought north. When the thunder gun fired, a second explosion on a nearby hillside startled Wolf and frightened some of the younger men who had never seen such a gun before.

"He shoots it twice," Black Horse declared. "*Wihio* fires once, and *Heammawihio* answers."

The scouts turned Horse's mocking words into something approaching reverence, and Wolf hid a smile. Carrington seemed convinced that the chiefs were impressed, and he announced that he would happily give any war party approaching his camp a second demonstration of his power. He then handed out pieces of paper stating that those people had agreed to a lasting peace with the white men.

"Another *Wihio* trick," Morning Star muttered as the chiefs left the bluecoat encampment. Wolf gave his own paper to the wind. He hoped that it might carry back to the fort, demonstrating the weight such empty words possessed in the Powder River country.

Wolf walked a short distance with the chiefs. When they mounted their horses and rode to a nearby hill to confer with Red Cloud, Man Afraid of His Horses, and other *Lakota* leaders, Wolf returned to his own lodge. He had barely spoken to Sun Walker Woman when Two Arrows appeared.

"Another pipe?" Wolf asked.

"You never smoked the other one," Two Arrows said, grinning. "Your cousin says that it's time."

"I guess Red Cloud isn't running from the thunder guns."

"Red Cloud has his own thunder," Two Arrows explained. "Soon the bluecoats will know it."

Indeed, Red Cloud wasted no time. Once the chiefs finished their discussions, raiding parties rode out to attack miners and freighters using the stolen road. Wood and water details made up of small numbers of bluecoats soon found themselves under fire. Red Cloud himself carried out the most punishing raid. The following morning the *Oglalas* struck the bluecoat pony herd, driving off almost two hundred horses and mules.

Wolf watched the raiders' escape from a low ridge. He, Crazy Horse, and a handful of others had volunteered to serve as decoys to draw any pursuing bluecoats into an ambush.

"It's an old trick," Wolf objected when his cousin suggested the ploy. "Some hot blood usually spoils the plan."

"The men we'll take will follow you and me," Crazy Horse insisted.

"Even if that's true, we've used the trick too often. Remember how the *Wihio* stayed in their forts at Julesburg and at Platte Bridge? They know they're safe behind the thunder guns.''

"You don't remember the hot blood eagle chief," Crazy Horse argued. "He boasted that he'll run us. Let him try."

Wolf thought it unlikely. The eagle chief, Fetterman, was quick to boast, but he had fought battles before. No, he wouldn't be easily trapped.

Fetterman was not leading the pursuing bluecoats. A younger, less experienced man led fifteen horsemen after the raiders. Wolf and Crazy Horse allowed the horses and their captors to gallop by. The decoys then charged the pursuing bluecoats.

"Ayyyy!" Wolf shouted as he rode past two startled bluecoats. He slapped one across the forehead with a lance and touched the other on the back. Both times Wolf cried, "I was first!" In that way he counted the first two coups of the battle. Once the bluecoats recovered their wits, they struck back.

"Follow me," Crazy Horse cried, turning away. Wolf and Stands Long urged their younger companions to flee. Then they also turned away.

For once there were no hot bloods to spoil a plan. Moreover, Crazy Horse had instructed several *Oglalas* in the clever manufacture of dust. By swinging a rope tied with pine limbs behind their horses, a few riders could appear to be hundreds. The bluecoats mistook the decoys' dust for the raiding party and followed the wrong trail.

Wolf rode furiously through the dust, spitting it out of his mouth as he blinked it from his eyes. He could taste dust. He felt it cling to his flesh. When he spied the first concealed warriors lurking in the trees to the right and left of the trail, he gratefully slowed his pace. The fifteen *Wihio* horsemen continued on. Only when Wolf turned and waited, lance in hand, did the youngish *Wihio* soldier chief realize he had made a mistake.

"Halt!" he shouted. "Bugler, blow 'recall.' ''

A rider drew out a horn, but his parched lips could not manage the correct notes. It was already too late anyway. Dozens of *Oglalas* and *Sicangus* raced out. An ocean of vengeful humanity swarmed across the trail and enveloped the bluecoats.

Three died quickly. Two others were hurt, but their ponies carried them back to the camp. The young chief fought bravely, killing an *Oglala* named Yellow Bow with a saber and freeing a companion from the attention of three enemies.

"Wolf?" Crazy Horse called.

The *Wihio* chief also turned to Wolf. He drew out a pistol and fired three shots rapidly. Wolf scarcely had time enough to raise his shield. Snow Wolf took the force on two bullets, but although they penetrated the outer cover, neither penetrated the horsehair and bull-neck hide. Thwarted, the remaining bluecoats turned and ran.

"No!" Wolf shouted when Two Arrows started to give chase. "They have the advantage back there."

Broken Wing and Raven Heart, who had only just discarded the pine drag, were clearly disappointed.

"We hurt them enough," Crazy Horse said, riding from man to man. "We took their animals. We killed their men. If they choose to come up into these hills, we'll kill the rest of them."

"Ayyyy!" the youngsters howled. "We'll kill them!"

The raiders and even most of the decoys rode along to their scattered camps. Wolf chose to ride to Little Piney Creek instead. He stripped himself and plunged into the chilly stream. The soothing water alleviated his thirst and washed away both the dust and the weariness.

"You're bleeding, *Nah nih*," Raven Heart observed as he joined Wolf in the stream.

"It's nothing," Wolf said, noticing a bloody notch torn in his left arm by a bullet. "I didn't even feel it."

"You should leave the bleeding to us," Broken Wing complained.

"You have enough scars," Wolf told the young man. "I've bled more from cuts I made to hurry a dream."

Wolf then lay back in the stream and floated to where a large boulder rested in the creek, diverting its path. Stands Long swam over, and the brother-friends stood there, watching the water pour past on both sides of the rock.

"We're like that rock, *Ne' hyo,*" Raven Heart pointed out. "Not even the force of the stream can move us."

"Look closer," Wolf suggested. "See how the water's eating away at the soft earth beneath the rock. Gradually it will loosen it, and the boulder will roll to the shore. It's not always possible to stop a stream."

"And the bluecoats?" Broken Wing asked. "Won't we stop them either?"

"There aren't enough of us," Wolf declared. "When a single one of us dies, it's a calamity. *Wihio* are like grains of sand—endless. We may divert them. We may even defeat them for a time. They have the power, though. They grow ever stronger, and we lose what strength we have."

"Are you saying we should make peace?" Stands Long asked.

"There's no treating with *Wihio,*" Wolf insisted. "No, it's better to fight while we can and know that if our path leads to a young death, it can be a brave one."

"Yes," Crazy Horse agreed. "There's been enough talking of dying, though. Let's speak of what we'll do with the horses we've earned. Each man can claim three from the stolen herd. Give thought to which ones you want. When we join the others tonight, we should voice our choice."

"Has everyone agreed to this?" Wolf asked. "Even though the decoys had prevented pursuit and possible recapture of the horse herd, few raiders were likely to offer ponies to men who never stood at their sides during the greatest peril.

"It's only fair," Crazy Horse declared. "It's not necessary for everyone to agree. I have decided it's fair, so that's what we'll do."

It happened just that way, too. Each decoy accepted three ponies. Those who had waited in ambush took a single mount, and the raiders kept two each. Twelve remained when all the men had made their claims. Those ponies were given to people in need.

That night Wolf led his three animals past his camp circle. Wind's Whisper raced out to see, and he was glad to observe that his father had chosen a dark paint with good feet and a strong back. The other two animals were smaller, just ponies really.

"For my brothers?" Whisper asked.

"They're of an age to have their own mounts," Wolf said, nodding. "Your buckskin still serves you well?"

"Yes, *Ne' hyo*," the boy declared. "My brothers will be glad."

"What would make *you* glad?" Wolf asked.

"A quiet night," Wind's Whisper added. "Hunting these hills with my father."

"We'll enjoy both," Wolf vowed. It was a promise he was unable to keep, though. That same evening Wolf stirred fitfully. His hands flayed the air, and his voice cried out in the dark.

The dream followed quickly. It was a familiar one, seen often by Wolf in the old, troubled times of his childhood.

Snow Wolf was there, howling. The creature's voice was hollow, mournful. It filled Wolf's entire body with an icy chill no sun could warm.

"Brother, what's wrong?" Wolf heard his own voice call.

"The sacred hoop," Snow Wolf howled. "It's broken."

"How?" Wolf asked.

"Come and see," the phantom creature said, leaping from a rock onto a slope filled with eerie white sheets. Each seemed to cover the face of a man. Wolf felt his heart pound as he knelt beside the first one. He lifted the sheet with trembling hands, praying he would not see the face of a brother or son. Instead he found himself staring into what had once been a white man's face.

It was a ghastly sight. The eyes were gone. One ear was sliced away. A few feet away the naked body lay armless and legless. Where a heart should have been, there was only a bloody hole. The skin had turned an odd shade of bluish-white.

Wolf stepped to the next sheet. When he lifted it, he

saw still another mutilated *Wihio*. Ragged blue cloth clung to this man's arms, though. It was one of the soldiers who had escorted the chiefs through the camp.

Wolf tried to count the sheets, but there were too many, and each one lay close to another. Most of the bodies were broken and torn. Some were cut. Fingers, noses, and ears were missing. Some of the men's bowels had been opened, and several had had their manhood cut away. Finally Wolf reached a naked man whose body remained untouched. The corpse bore a solitary wound in the temple. Particles of black powder embedded in the bloody flesh testified to the manner of death.

Wolf recognized the man at once. So, here rested the impulsive, boastful little eagle chief, Fetterman. Had he tried to run the *Lakotas* with these men? Had Carrington ordered him to retrieve the stolen ponies? What had happened?

Snow Wolf resumed his howling, and Wolf stared above at the sky. No stars shined in the midnight darkness. The wind carried an icy bite, and he shivered. Suddenly something clasped Wolf's shoulder. What was it? A claw? Was a panther tearing at him?

"Wolf?" a voice cried.

"*Ne' hyo?*" someone else called.

Wolf blinked the vision from his eyes and clasped the paw that was tearing at his flesh. It lost its power instantly, and Wolf saw that it was only Wind's Whisper, trying to rouse him from his nightmare.

"What did you see, Wolf?" Sun Walker Woman asked.

"Death," he explained.

"Whose death?" Raven Heart asked. "Yours? Ours?"

"Two hundred bluecoats," Wolf declared.

"Where?" Raven Heart asked. "Near here?"

"Near here," Wolf said, frowning. "Near here and a world away."

chapter
20

WOLF SAID LITTLE ABOUT HIS dream. There was so much to do that summer, and he himself didn't fully understand what he'd seen. How was it possible that so many bluecoats could be dead? Who had cut the bodies so savagely? And why were sheets covering the bodies?

The dream nevertheless filled Wolf with high expectations of winning some great victory. He did share the dream with Sun Walker Woman. Although she continued to worry about his safety and the future of the children, she accepted his decision to remain near the new *Wihio* fort. Stands Long, too, agreed that the people had to continue their fight with the eagle chief Carrington.

Crazy Horse, although still viewed as a young man by most of the *Oglala* headmen, was growing tall in the eyes of the warriors. Wolf's cousin, upon hearing of the dream, invited him to join the decoys. They frequently attacked the fort's wood and water details, hoping to lure some hotheaded soldiers into an ambush.

When Wolf wasn't fighting or raiding, he was hunting. The warriors camped along the stolen road didn't organize

a formal buffalo hunt that year. Instead they relied on the
country's abundant deer and elk to meet their needs. Wolf
was glad to present three warm elk robes to his sons.

"To drive away the bite of the winter wind," he explained.

He also brought in elk roasts and venison. He smiled as
he noted the boys growing taller and stronger. Sun Walker
dried the venison and put it away for the cold weather
months when game grew scarce and hunting became impossible.

As the last breath of summer left the land, snowflakes
signaled the onset of winter. The countryside around Big
and Little Piney creeks had already changed. The bluecoats
finished their fort. It was clearly strong enough to withstand even a determined attack. Moreover, such an attack
would leave dozens, even hundreds, dead or crippled.

Red Cloud had a different plan.

"If we can't strike the bluecoats in their lair," he declared, "we must lure them out into the country where we
can kill them."

Red Cloud called on his fellow *Oglalas* and their allies
to camp nearby, in the Big Horn Mountains. Thousands
came. Small bands, led by Red Cloud or one of the soldier
society chiefs, struck every bluecoat patrol that left the
fort. Arapahos, still burning with the recollection of their
burned camp, raided the thieves' road and ambushed
woodcutters. Even the hang-arounds at Fort Laramie
helped by supplying rifles, lead, and powder bartered from
post traders like Walker Logan.

When the Moon of the Popping Trees appeared overhead, Wolf sensed a change in the air. It wasn't just the
hard cold that now touched his very bones. No, there was
a sense of anticipation in the air.

"Soon," the warriors whispered to one another.

That was also when Wolf's dream returned. It didn't fill
his head every night, but it did come often. Afterward he
would walk out onto the hillside and sit alone for a time,
trying to discover what truth *Heammawihio* was sending.

"Why the sheets?" he asked the clouds. "Why was the

younger chief, Fetterman, there and not Carrington?''

Wind's Whisper helped his father unravel one mystery.

"*Ne' hyo*," the boy asked, "what's a sheet?"

"A piece of cloth," Wolf explained. "The *Wihio* use them in their beds."

"So perhaps the bluecoats are only sleeping."

"No, I saw that part plainly. The *Wihios* were hacked into pieces."

"The way Broken Wing's brothers were cut at Sand Creek?" Whisper asked. Wolf nodded, and the boy frowned. "Southern people did it then. To punish the murderers of their relatives."

"Maybe," Wolf admitted.

"I don't understand the sheets, though. Were they bloody?"

"They were white as . . . ," Wolf began. He swallowed the words unspoken, though, and looked at a clearing in the woods beyond the hill. The snow! It was smooth, unwrinkled like one of the sheets he had seen in Walker Logan's quarters at the trading store.

"*Ne' hyo?*" Whisper asked when his father remained silent.

"Sheets," Wolf mumbled. "I was stupid not to see it before. Sometimes *Wihios* cover their dead with sheets, but then they *would* be bloody."

"I don't understand then," Wind's Whisper said, clasping his father's hand. "Are they sheets?"

"No," Wolf said, pointing to the clearing. "It's the snow. That's what's covering the bodies. It's why the dream's returned, too. Soon we'll fight the bluecoats. Soon many of them will die."

Wolf rode out to confer with his *Oglala* cousin that next morning. Crazy Horse was involved in organizing a raiding party, but he took time to see Wolf.

"I understand the dream," Wolf explained. As he shared his vision, Crazy Horse smiled approvingly.

"I've had dreams myself," Crazy Horse explained. "Mine are never as clear as yours, but I've also seen signs of such a battle. Today I ride out to decoy the woodcutters' escort. Others are hiding along the trail, eager to fall on them. Come, let's you and me lead the bluecoats to their deaths. We've been idle too long.''

Wolf couldn't recall a day since arriving at the Pineys when he or Crazy Horse either one had been idle. No one struck so many times or demanded less glory.

"Now?" Wolf asked.

"When we spy bluecoats," Crazy Horse explained. "Now. Tomorrow. Who can say?"

"I must prepare myself first," Wolf explained. "Stands Long isn't here."

"You and I'll be brother-friends today," Crazy Horse replied. "There's little danger of either of us being hurt. Your dream showed only dead bluecoats."

"They're never the only ones to die, though," Wolf pointed out.

He nevertheless joined Crazy Horse's decoys that day. There was a stiff breeze flowing off the Big Horns as they rode out at the head of a handful of determined men. Wolf nodded approvingly as Crazy Horse described his companions. All except the cousins, who shared the habit of riding modestly to battle, wore well-deserved coup feathers in their hair. Wolf spied no hot bloods. These were confident fighters, men who understood a decoy's purpose and were willing to expose themselves to danger in order to deliver the enemy into the hands of their well-concealed comrades.

Red Cloud himself led one of the parties lurking along the ridges that lined Big Piney Creek. Other men dismounted and hid in the brush along the treacherous frozen trails the bluecoats used when they cut pines from the thick forests nearby. Wolf himself spied less than fifty, but he knew others were hidden.

"This time a few hundred are here," Crazy Horse boasted. "Soon thousands will join the ambushers. Already most of the Arapahos have joined us. More *Tsis tsis tas* arrive each morning."

"When I fought Sumner's bluecoats at Red Shield River, we were many," Wolf pointed out. "We lacked medicine strong enough to break our enemies, and they ran us.''

"Bluecoats aren't the only ones with rifles now," Crazy Horse growled. "We only have a few guns, but they're good ones. Here, in the mountains, Carrington's thunder guns are worthless. We know these mountains, the trails, and the weather. They're strangers. That's our real advantage.''

"We're better led, too," Wolf said, grinning at his cousin. "Men will willingly follow a great man, and Red Cloud stands high in everyone's eyes. Even so, we should speak the medicine prayers and hope that *Heammawihio* grants us a victory.''

"You've seen it already," Crazy Horse remarked. "We'll run the bluecoats and regain this land for the people.''

Wolf knew that the first was no guarantee that the second would come to pass. You could kill a thousand bluecoats, but more of them would still come. It was useless to argue such a thing that day. It wouldn't hurry the bluecoats from the Big Horns and it could only trouble the younger men.

Once the decoys started toward the fort, Wolf saw for himself the elaborate preparations that the *Lakota* chiefs had taken. Watchers were scattered throughout the hills. Using mirrors, they signaled any bluecoat movements through the surrounding countryside. Others then relayed the messages to the chiefs and to decoy leaders such as Crazy Horse.

"What do we do if clouds swallow the sun?" Wolf asked.

"The watchers also have strips of black cloth," Crazy Horse explained. "They use them to wave back and forth, passing on similar messages.''

Of course, none of that mattered if Carrington's men remained within the strong walls of their fort. While the bluecoats could melt snow into drinking water, they could not warm their lodges with it. The hundreds of men, not to mention the women and children, who passed the frigid

nights of a Big Horn winter inside the fort's drafty wooden
dwellings, required wagons filled with firewood every day.
Pine, the most abundant wood, burned rapidly, and it provided only a modest amount of heat. The harder cottonwood and oak required greater effort by the cutters.

At least one detail seemed to leave each day to cut trees.
The bluecoats quickly cut most of the timber close to the
fort. By winter they had to ride farther and farther from
the safety of the thunder guns. That suited Red Cloud's
plan.

"Look there," Crazy Horse suddenly cried, and Wolf
followed his cousin's pointing fingers to a distant ridge.
The flashes came in a slow, irregular manner. It was a code
of sorts, and Crazy Horse quickly read it, turned to the
others, and announced that a wood detail was riding out
from the fort.

"So, these are the ones we'll run," Wolf muttered.

"No," Crazy Horse said, grinning. "These are the ones
who will run us."

The *Oglala* shirt wearer dismounted and pointed his
companions to a large boulder standing beside the narrow
trail. Once the decoys assembled, Crazy Horse began
speaking old, well-remembered warrior prayers. Wolf sang
the less familiar ancient *Suhtai* chant. Each man then
smeared paint on his own face or painted his pony. Those
who had a shield, as Wolf did, drew it out and invoked its
individual power. Men also tied charms behind their ears
or in their hair. Crazy Horse tied a red-tailed hawk atop
his head. When each man was satisfied that his preparations were complete, Crazy Horse remounted his pony.
The others followed his example, and the decoys rode toward the fort.

It wasn't difficult to locate woodcutters. Carrington had
dispatched several details from the fort that morning, and
Crazy Horse's band soon came upon a group of fifteen
soldiers who were chopping cottonwoods not far from the
frigid creek. Wolf wasn't the first to hear the sounds of
axes striking pine, but he did spy the bluecoats before anyone else.

"There," he called, pointing to four *Wihio* soldiers posted as guards.

"Follow me!" Crazy Horse shouted. Wolf Running and the others raised an earsplitting cry and charged toward the shallows of Big Piney Creek.

Wolf picked out one of the bluecoats and charged. The *Wihio* jumped to his feet and fired his rifle wildly. The shot tore a branch from a pine on the far side of the creek. Wolf fared somewhat better. Balancing his lance in his right hand and holding the medicine shield on his left, he got to within three feet of the bluecoat before striking. The point of the lance tore through the soft flesh of the soldier's right side, and he collapsed, bleeding, in the snow.

"I'm first!" Wolf shouted as he searched for a new enemy. The woodcutters had discarded their tools and fled into the trees. Two youngish bluecoats made a brief stand at the creek, but five *Oglalas* surrounded them. The bluecoats' dying cries were terrible to hear.

It had happened quickly, too quickly to suit Crazy Horse's purpose. Seeing no one left to chase him, Crazy Horse dismounted.

"We'll have to wait for someone to reach the fort," the shirt wearer declared. "Maybe the eagle chief will send someone for the bodies."

"Maybe," Wolf muttered. While most of the young *Oglalas* busied themselves collecting the bluecoats' horses, two of the younger men began mutilating the corpses. Seeing the anger in his companions' eyes, Wolf didn't believe there would be much left of the soldiers for anyone to find.

Red Cloud sent raiders after other details, too, but none of them had much luck drawing bluecoats into the well-planned ambush. Crazy Horse grew restless, and Wolf suggested leaving.

"They've had time," Wolf said, staring at the bloody smears that stained the snow. "The eagle chief's a prudent man. I saw the younger one, Fetterman, in my dream. He doesn't like his chief. At least that's how it seems to me. He might chase us. Do you want to go?"

"Not yet," Crazy Horse said, lifting his ear to the wind. "No, someone's coming after all."

Wolf paused to listen, and he, too, heard the whine of a bugle in the distance. Crazy Horse formed his little band and started in that direction.

They rode with rare energy toward the haunting sound of that distant horn. It seemed to take forever. Wolf had to whip his pony to keep up with his cousin and the others. When they finally topped a snowy rise, they found themselves confronting an entire column of bluecoats.

"Wait!" Crazy Horse called frantically as he halted his horse. Wolf pressed his knees against his lathered animal, and it slowed to a canter. Two of the younger *Oglalas* sped past, only to vanish in a withering swirl of gunfire and snow dust.

"Wolf!" Crazy Horse called out in alarm when Wolf urged his horse onward. He could just glimpse the stricken decoys through a white mist. Neither was badly hurt, but one was trapped by a dying horse, and the other fought frantically to free him.

"Nothing lives long!" Wolf shouted as he hurried toward the *Oglalas.* "Only the earth and the mountains!"

He hugged his buckskin's neck and extended his right hand. The trapped *Oglala* managed to free himself at that instant, and Wolf pulled the young man up behind him.

"I'll come back!" Wolf promised the second young man.

By then the bluecoats had halted. Instead of charging in a ragged line, they appeared to be forming a column. Wolf spied the little chief, Carrington, barking at his subordinates. He appeared none too eager to fight.

"They're not charging," the rescued *Oglala,* Swift Hare, muttered. "Why not?"

"The mist," Wolf said, pointing to a fog that was climbing skyward from the creek. It had been but a shadow all morning. Now it thickened.

"Look," Swift Hare said, pointing to where Crazy Horse rode beside the river. He shouted insults to the cavalry and even turned his back on them, as if to say, "Strike my back if you can find the courage."

By the time Wolf carried Swift Hare back to the others, an *Oglala* had gone out to rescue the other dismounted decoy. Crazy Horse continued to distract the cavalry, performing amazing tricks on horseback until Carrington lost patience. He waved his men toward the shirt wearer. Crazy Horse finally turned toward his companions.

"Take one of the *Wihio* ponies," Wolf told Swift Hare. "Pick a rested one."

In fact most of the party climbed onto a second mount. Normally raiders rode their horses in relays anyway, but the decoys had a second motive. They hoped the bluecoats would chase if for no other reason than to recover the stolen animals.

If decoying was an art, then Crazy Horse was its most talented craftsmen. He would hang back tantalizingly close to an enemy, daring them to fire a shot or mount a charge. Then he would race out of range. Wolf enjoyed watching his cousin's antics. For a time Crazy Horse pretended that his horse was lame. He dismounted and looked at the animal's right foreleg. Later it would be the back left foot. It was a masterpiece of deception and annoyance, and the bluecoats raged and fumed in frustration.

Wolf marked each ridge they crossed, counting down to the ambushers' positions.

"Just a little farther," he whispered. "Cross that next ridge."

Despite his anger, Carrington was no fool. As the chase drew him farther away from the fort, he ordered a halt. Eyeing the clouds overhead, the mists rising from the creeks, and the dense cover on the surrounding ridges, any soldier would see peril. Moreover, the bluecoats were no stranger to ambushes.

Crazy Horse saw Carrington hesitate.

"Wolf?" the *Oglala*'s strange one called.

"They won't follow," Wolf observed as he studied the *Wihio* eagle chief. Carrington was again barking orders.

This time the column was turning around. The pursuit was over.

"Where's Red Cloud?" Wolf asked. "Maybe I could ride out and urge him to attack."

"It's no use," Crazy Horse declared. "If we chase them, then they become the decoys, and we'll be the ones lying under those snowy blankets. No, we must try another time."

Wolf wanted to argue, but it was pointless. No man rose to high command without some skill, some talent. Carrington was a clever man. He never let his personal feelings overwhelm his judgment.

"Maybe next time we'll be able to draw them farther out," Wolf suggested that night when around a small cook fire the cousins discussed the failed plan.

"Perhaps," Crazy Horse said, staring into the flame. "There's another way, of course."

"Yes?"

"If the bluecoats won't ride far, we must plan the ambush close to their fort."

"They're watchful there," Wolf argued. "The thunder guns, after all, fire far."

"There's a good place nevertheless," Crazy Horse insisted. "Hundreds, perhaps even a thousand men, could hide there."

When Crazy Horse told Red Cloud of the plan, the *Oglala* chief simply grinned.

"We know that place," the chief said, laughing. "I spoke with the other chiefs a short time ago about trapping the bluecoats there."

"It's a good notion," Wolf later told Sun Walker Woman. "From the ridge, the ambushers can see the bluecoat fort. We decoys can bring the enemy up and let the others swarm upon them. There can be no escape once the bluecoats pass Lodge Trail Ridge."

chapter
21

F OR SEVERAL DAYS FOLLOWING THE failure of the decoys, Wolf Running remained near his lodge. His cousin and the others continued to harass wood details, but they had little to celebrate. The bluecoats were content to stay close to the fort. Twice its big guns fired shells at groups of *Lakota* watchers. The scouts had the good sense to leave before the cannons could find the range.

Twelve times the sun made its slow trek across the heavens. Each day Wolf made the morning prayers with Stands Long, Raven Heart, and Broken Wing.

"You'll not ride alone this time, *Nah nih,*" Raven Heart declared. "There's going to be a big fight, and we should be with you there."

Wolf didn't argue. The dream flooded his thoughts every night, and as snowflakes danced in the wintry air, he sensed that a fight was, indeed, coming.

"Soon," the warriors continued to whisper. But when?

Despite being busy raiding the wood details, Crazy Horse often passed the afternoons or evenings with Wolf.

One day the cousins would craft arrows. The next they would hunt rabbits for the cooking pot.

"When does your dream say that we will strike?" an increasingly impatient Crazy Horse finally asked.

"It doesn't show me the day," Wolf explained. "It will be soon."

"Soon!" Crazy Horse barked. "We all know it's coming. Is that all a man of your power can determine?"

"It will happen close to the fort," Wolf explained.

"I know that. Cousin, I'm going there again tomorrow. Will you come?"

Wolf examined the sky. It was sure to snow, and he disliked being away from the lodge with threatening weather coming. There was something in Crazy Horse's eye, though. Need. Urgency. Wolf agreed to come.

He announced his intentions, and Stands Long sent Raven Heart and Broken Wing to collect suitable ponies. As word of Wolf's plans spread, a handful of young men appeared. Each pleaded to go along, but Wolf refused every one of them.

"This is not a young man's fight," he explained. "It requires patience to ride as a decoy. Young men would be tempted to strike a blow and spoil the ambush."

Actually the war party *was* young, frightfully so. Most of the *Oglalas* were passing their first winter on Man's Road, and two of them had not yet plucked hairs from their chins.

"They should stay behind," Wolf argued.

"Would you?" Crazy Horse asked. "I wouldn't. They're better here, where I can control them, than among the ambushers. I want no ten or twenty of these bluecoats. I want them all!"

It was odd that Crazy Horse should have said that. When a *Tsis tsis tas* named Horned Owl joined them, he shared a peculiar tale. That morning a *he e man eh'*, a he-she, visited Owl's camp. Wearing a black cloth upon his head, this peculiar person blew shrill notes on an eagle bone whistle and darted about the camp, shouting and acting crazy. Finally he called to the assembled *Tsis tsis tas* and

Lakota camp, "Look! I have ten of our enemies in each of my hands. Do you want them?" The startled warriors said, "No!"

"The *he e man eh'* rode around the camp before returning," Horned Owl explained. "He offered us fifty this time, but we told him we didn't want them. Only on his fourth visit, when he offered us a hundred or more, did we agree to take them."

"The *he e man eh'* is a strange sort," Stands Long noted. "Some consider them crazy. It's certain they're close to the spirits. We should believe this one. Wolf's dream has promised such a victory over the *Wihio,* and now this odd man says it will be today."

Crazy Horse howled, and the others agreed that it was a good time to strike a hard blow. Each man dismounted and painted his face. Stands Long kindled a fire, and Wolf performed the pipe ritual. The warriors then spoke prayers and invoked their personal spiritual power.

By the time Crazy Horse led his little decoy band toward the fort, the fighting had already started. A party of *Oglalas* attacked a wood detail on the far side of Lodge Trail Ridge. Carrington sent bluecoats to help their besieged comrades. Forty-nine foot soldiers marched out of the fort. Twenty-seven mounted men followed.

"Look who leads them," Crazy Horse whispered as he topped the ridge. A smile slowly spread across his face.

"Yes," Wolf replied as he joined his cousin. They both stared hard at the arrogant bluecoat chief, Fetterman.

"You've lived too long!" Horned Owl shouted.

"No, not yet," Crazy Horse said as the young *Tsis tsis tas* raised his bow. "We're decoys, remember? Our task is to draw them into the trap."

The bluecoats approached cautiously. Crazy Horse motioned for his companions to leave, but he remained, taunting the cavalry. Wolf watched, wondering if the bluecoats would turn back to the fort or attack. Fetterman waved his horsemen onward. They charged.

It was a whirl of snow and confusion at first. The cavalrymen drove the decoys past the woodcutters while the infantrymen struggled to catch up. The horse soldiers pursued as long as the decoys remained within rifle range. Whenever Crazy Horse appeared ready to break away, though, Fetterman slowed his pace. Three times the decoys left the bluecoats behind. Each time Crazy Horse, accompanied by Wolf and Stands Long, raced back to challenge the enemy.

Crazy Horse's measured flight prolonged the chase. It also served to keep the cavalry and their dismounted comrades close together. Gradually the bluecoats approached Lodge Trail Ridge. Beyond that point, the ambushers waited.

"Just a little farther," Wolf whispered. "Only a little more."

By then the bluecoats had their blood up. They seemed intent on running down every Indian left in the Big Horns. Wolf simply laughed as the bluecoats shouted insults and vowed to perform all manner of unspeakable torture on the fleeing decoys.

"You'll be the ones to die," Horned Owl called. "Come and find your death, *Wihio!*"

It was almost humorous. Only a few of the *Tsis tsis tas* and *Lakota* raiders could understand English, and even fewer bluecoats had an inkling of the meaning of the words spoken by the plains tribes. A few on each side used signs to indicate their contempt, and a young *Lakota* called Winter Elk bared his backside. That was hard to misinterpret. Fetterman raised himself in his stirrups and waved his men forward. The bluecoats charged.

"We have them!" Crazy Horse shouted gleefully as he darted skillfully behind his companions. He dodged a handful of rifle shots before resuming his flight. By then the cavalrymen were closing rapidly. Their infantry cohorts were struggling to stay close, but the entire bluecoat band was beginning to lose cohesion. Men fell out here and there, and the once compact group was becoming a long uneven line.

Wolf's sharp eyes detected the lurking warriors. The largest force, mostly *Lakotas,* spread out in the high grasses lining the trail. Another band of *Lakotas,* all of them mounted, waited just to the west of the ridge. *Tsis tsis tas* riders similarly assembled to the east. Wolf wasn't certain how to signal the general attack, but he knew it was coming momentarily.

The honor of starting the fighting went to a *Tsis tsis tas,* Little Horse. He was a member of the contrary society, a group of odd men whose medicine required them to perform their ordinary activities in confusing, often opposite ways. Contraries developed extraordinary powers, especially in driving away lightning and other misfortunes. Some were actually called to the contraries by strikes of lightning. Others suffered other misfortunes and turned to the society to escape the ghosts of the past.

Little Horse carried a contrary lance, and as he rode out toward the bluecoats, he shifted it from his left hand to his right. The *Tsis tsis tas* riders rushed up the ridge. The decoys themselves split. Crazy Horse led most toward his *Lakota* kinsmen. Wolf led his little band eastward.

The very sky seemed to explode as hundreds of horses sprang into action, throwing a cloud of snow dust into the air. A mixed chorus of shrill young voices mixed with the deeper howls of older men. The startled bluecoats paused only a moment before falling back. The foot soldiers crowded into an area of flat rocks and tried to form a defensive circle. The cavalry reached the crest of the ridge and halted.

Wolf respected the marksmanship of the foot soldiers, and he knew that if they got organized, they could be difficult to dislodge. He waved Stands Long toward the rocks. As they approached, they saw Winter Elk, whose insult had induced the *Wihio* to continue their pursuit, ride past. He was singing a death chant and braving himself to make a suicide charge.

"Someone has to do it," Stands Long said, shouting encouragement.

Wolf nodded. He understood how suicide soldiers would charge the enemy, drawing their fire so that others could approach in relative safety and overwhelm the enemy. Of-

ten a man had vowed to make such a charge when mourning a dead relation or praying for a healing cure. It was a
remembered thing, but it usually won the charger a brave
death.

Elk's ride began well enough. He caught the confused
bluecoats by surprise, and they seemed unable to shoot him
from his horse. He leapt over the outer wall of rocks, rode
through the frantic foot soldiers, and escaped out the far
side. For just an instant it appeared as though Elk had done
the impossible. He had escaped! Then three shots pierced
the air. Elk threw his hands back and fell from his horse,
dead.

A second young *Lakota* walked toward the rocks, firing
his rifle in a slow, deliberate fashion. The *Wihio* soldiers
returned fire, but their aim was wild. Only when a whole
line of infantry rose and fired in a volley did the *Lakota*
fall.

As the bluecoats began reloading, *Tsis tsis tas* and *Lakota* war chiefs screamed loudly. The voices seemed to rise
from everywhere, and men fired a cascade of arrows into
the rocks. Others charged.

"Ayyyy!" Wolf howled as he climbed down from his
horse and joined the attack. The snowdrifts slowed him
considerably, and he had difficulty getting to, much less
through, the rocks. Once over the makeshift wall, he found
himself facing a thin-faced bluecoat with a jagged scar on
his right cheek. The *Wihio* fired his rifle at Wolf's chest,
but the gun was empty. Wolf laughed.

"It's no use," he said, clubbing the man with his lance.
"I'm first!" he added.

Raven Heart, who was on Wolf's left, drove a lance
through the bluecoat's belly, and Broken Wing finished the
pitiful wretch as he would have dispatched a wounded
deer, by making a throat cut.

When Broken Wing tore open the dead bluecoat's shirt
and started to mark the body, Wolf grabbed the young
man's hand.

"No," Wolf whispered. "Don't take his ghost with
you."

Wing recalled the killing of the Chivington soldiers at Platte River and closed his eyes. He cut only the scalp.

The fighting in the rocks quickly became confused. Even as the bluecoats fell under the onslaught of perhaps five or six hundred warriors, arrows fired by *Lakotas* on one side and by *Tsis tsis tas* on the other began striking their friends. One cut a slice from Wolf's left elbow. Another killed Snipe, the young *Sicangu* who had promised to return and fight the bluecoats if the treaty talk turned sour.

Wolf used his shield to deflect another volley of arrows, and he sent Broken Wing back to stop the archers. Meanwhile the last surviving infantrymen struggled up the ridge toward the horse soldiers. He pleaded for mercy, cried for water, and crawled away. Stands Long walked up to him, grabbed the rifle from the terrified bluecoat's hands, and clubbed him senseless.

"I would have let him go," Stands Long insisted, "but he wasn't a man."

Wolf understood his brother-friend's feelings. Those who had fought and died bravely merited respect and consideration. Cowards were worthless.

"It's finished here!" Wolf heard Crazy Horse call. "We must attack the others."

By that time the cavalrymen had run off their ponies or shot them to form a defensive wall. Riders had tried to follow up the narrow ridge trail, but dead horses and two fallen bluecoats blocked the path. The ground itself was frozen, and men trying to climb toward the bluecoats found themselves slipping and sliding. Most chose to remain below and fire arrows in high arcs into the remnant of Fetterman's command.

That proved more perilous to the attackers than the sporadic bluecoat gunfire coming from the hillside above them. Arrows knew neither friend nor enemy, and they struck both. Angry *Lakotas* shouted when *Tsis tsis tas* arrows fell close by. The *Tsis tsis tas* replied with angry words when *Lakota* arrows landed near them.

After a short time Little Horse, the contrary, reappeared.

Waving his contrary lance as a boy might wave a burning stick plucked from a fire, he ascended the hill and raced toward the bluecoats. Little Horse's medicine was strong that day, and no bullet or arrow touched him. His example stirred others to action. Soon handfuls of determined *Tsis tsis tas* and *Lakota* warriors crept toward the summit. Arrows thick as swarming bees smothered Fetterman's shrinking command, and more than one drove its stone or iron point into an attacker.

Wolf and Stands Long led one group of climbers. They made slow progress, but after easing their way through two icy patches, they reached firm ground a stone's throw from the *Wihio*. Just ahead, a tall, bearded bluecoat seemed firmly in command. Wolf nocked an arrow, steadied himself, and fired it. It struck the bearded bluecoat in the forehead. His eyes glazed over, and he fell back onto the hard ground. The other bluecoats stepped back. As Stands Long raised an ancient *Suhtai* war cry, the *Wihio* line collapsed. Men ran everywhere, and soon the fighting became a series of hand-to-hand duels between individual warriors and bluecoats.

Wolf picked his own enemies carefully. The first was a burly man of perhaps forty summers. He didn't look like a soldier at all. His tobacco-stained teeth spit juice as he talked, and his new Winchester rifle was a much better weapon than the soldiers carried.

"I've got no fight with the Cheyenne!" he shouted as Wolf circled closer. "Nor Sioux, neither. The general hired me to chop wood and hammer nails. You let me go, and you can have this rifle."

Wolf ignored the offer, and the *Wihio* did his best to repeat the offer in awkward *Lakota* phrases.

"You can't go," Wolf barked to him in English. "You come into our country. You won't leave."

"I got a wife and little ones, mister," the *Wihio* pleaded.

"You should have stayed with them," Wolf announced as he jabbed the man's side with the heavy stone point of the lance. The *Wihio* winced. He swung the new rifle like a club, and Wolf guessed it was out of ammunition. It was a poor way to fight a lance, and Wolf slashed the *Wihio's* forearm, causing him to drop the rifle.

"Please!" the *Wihio* cried, dropping to his knees. "Don't kill me!"

Wolf touched the man's shoulder with the tip of the lance. "I'm first!" he shouted. He then tore the *Wihio's* heavy coat open. Underneath was a soldier coat. A scalp dangled from the man's belt.

"You only chopped wood?" Wolf asked, driving the lance into the earth.

"It's the only one I have," the *Wihio* insisted. "I bought it off a fellow."

"A poor bargain," Wolf muttered as he drew out his knife.

"No, not that way," the terrified soldier screamed. He turned to one side. Then, quicker than Wolf imagined possible, he pulled a knife of his own and slashed at Wolf's face. The blade barely nicked Wolf's chin, but the sensation of his own blood trickling down his neck drove him crazy. Wolf leapt at the big man, knocked him down, and plunged his knife deep into the *Wihio's* considerable belly. The soldier moaned, tried to pull away, and finally went limp.

"Not yet," Wolf said, pulling his knife from a terrible deep gash. "You're not dead yet."

Wolf cut the soldier's belt and tossed the scalp away. He then tore the man's hat off, but there was no scalp to take. He was bald.

"This is for us to do," a youngish voice called. Wolf turned and gazed into the fiery eyes of a young *Tsis tsis tas* woman and an even smaller boy, perhaps her brother.

"Sand Creek," the boy mumbled.

"Leave it to them," Broken Wing said, helping Wolf rise. "They know what to do. They saw their own mother cut apart."

The youngsters nodded soberly, and Wolf left them to their task. Others were starting on the other dead cavalrymen, and the infantrymen down the slope were also receiving considerable attention.

"It's what you saw, *Nah nih*," Raven Heart whispered. "See how the snow's falling again?"

"It can cover the dead, but not the rage," Wolf said, pointing to the young people, the women, and the warriors butchering the corpses. Only two men remained unmarked, Fetterman and another officer. They lay side by side with solitary wounds on their foreheads.

"They caught the madness," Stands Long explained. "Perhaps it was the contrary lance that made them act so foolishly."

"They shot themselves?" Wolf asked.

"Each other," Stands Long explained. "They were maybe brother-friends. When they saw the death that was coming, they acted."

Wolf nodded. It seemed ironic to him that the men most responsible should escape the terrible brutality that followed the fighting. To *Lakotas* and *Tsis tsis tas,* lying there naked, untouched by the enemy, was shameful. It marked a coward's death.

Well, why not? Wolf wondered. Who could ever understand how human beings given the world to walk by *Heammawihio* could annihilate one another so savagely, so completely!

As the women and boys went among the dead, stripping their clothing, collecting their weapons, and mutilating their corpses, one or two sprang to life. It was almost humorous. One young *Wihio* ran around naked, bleeding from the thighs and shoulder. For a time no one would touch him.

"He's a ghost!" one woman cried. He was nearly blue from the cold, and he acted crazy.

"Leave him," someone suggested. "He's touched by spirits."

"I can go?" the young *Wihio* asked. "You won't kill me?"

That proved to be a fatal mistake. His clear thinking proved him to be a living being.

"He's only been pretending," a *Tsis tsis tas* boy declared. He nocked an arrow and fired it through the naked

Wihio's side. A *Lakota* then struck the staggered man in the face with a war ax, and three women fell on him, laughing as they cut flesh with their knives.

Finally there was only one survivor remaining from Fetterman's command. A solitary dog circled the corpses, barking and snapping at everyone.

"Only the dog's left alive," Raven Heart pointed out.

"Let him go," Broken Wing suggested.

"He can carry the news to the eagle chief Carrington," someone else added.

"No," Storm Eagle declared, standing near the body of his slain nephew, Winter Elk. "None of them should leave this place, not even the dog."

A boy nocked an arrow and killed the dog. Finally they were all dead, as were many good men killed by Fetterman's soldiers or stray arrows.

"It's time to leave," Stands Long declared.

"Yes," Wolf agreed. "It's growing cold."

Actually the midday sun stood overhead, and the morning mist was melting into memory.

"It was a good fight," Raven Heart declared.

"For once the hot bloods hung back," Broken Wing observed.

"We killed many bluecoats," Wolf muttered, gazing at the mutilated corpses. "There are more, though."

"We'll kill them later," Stands Long said, motioning toward the camps just to the north.

Wolf nodded. The brother-friends, accompanied by Broken Wing and Raven Heart, recovered their horses. It was time to seek the peace and comfort of a warm fire, to hear a child's laughter and enjoy a woman's touch. The fighting was over—at least for that day.

chapter
22

WOLF REMEMBERED IT AS THE killing of the eighty-one, but many *Tsis tsis tas* warriors called it Little Horse's fight. They claimed that the contrary's medicine brought success. After all, only two *Tsis tsis tas* fell while as many as fifty or sixty *Lakotas* died, many of them the victims of a friend's stray arrow.

It was difficult for Wolf to consider such a costly fight a great victory. Many *Oglala* camps were full of grieving mothers, fathers, wives, brothers, and sons. Nevertheless, he could not ignore the effect Fetterman's death would have on the *Wihio* eagle chief at the Piney fort.

Carrington had always been cautious. He soon prohibited any but the best-armed wood parties from leaving the fort. He abandoned the notion of escorting wagons on the stolen road, too. It was as if the dead bluecoats cast a shadow over the Big Horn country.

"It's said that the bluecoats hide in their fort, refusing to leave," Broken Wing told Wolf several days after the battle.

Crazy Horse told much the same story.

"We must put away our shields and hunt," Wolf's cousin told him. "There's no one left to run."

"They haven't gone away, though," Wolf noted. "There will be more fighting before we know peace."

Crazy Horse thought that likely. But as the hard face moons of winter painted the world white and froze the rivers, Wolf enjoyed as much peace as he could remember. He was with Wind's Whisper when the boy killed a rabbit with a well-aimed arrow. He held Sun Walker Woman close every night, and together they comforted the children when thunder shook the earth and lightning etched its brilliant lines across the sky.

Spring was the season of rebirth, of hope. It was no different in the Powder River country or up in the Big Horns. The great *Wihio* chiefs in Washington, perhaps feeling the sting of the Fetterman defeat, dispatched a new treaty maker to Fort Laramie. He made many promises, and a number of the *Sicangu* and *Tsis tsis tas* chiefs rode to the fort to receive presents and learn of the new proposals. Red Cloud remained in the Big Horns, though, refusing to talk of peace while bluecoats remained in his country.

"We could go back to the fort and speak with Walker Logan," Sun Walker suggested when Wolf broke down the lodge and prepared to join the *Lakotas* as they remade the earth. For the first time he would go there instead of joining the *Tsis tsis tas* in renewing *Mahuts,* the sacred medicine arrows.

"The fort's a long way to go," Wolf answered. "For what? The *Wihio* can have peace. They only have to keep their promises."

"I look around and see the women who've cut their hair," Sun Walker explained. "I think of my sons, of you. I gaze at Broken Wing's sad eyes and wonder if he will see another winter. What of Raven Heart and your other brothers? If we have to give up something, is it too high a price to be paid for your lives?"

"We don't have much left," Wolf mumbled. "We've given up enough."

And so Wolf Running accompanied the *Oglalas* that summer. After remaking the earth, the chiefs met in council with their allies and decided to take the fight to the bluecoats. The *Tsis tsis tas* vowed to destroy the northernmost fort, now called Fort C. F. Smith. Red Cloud promised to deal with the largest post, the walled stronghold on the Pineys named Fort Phil Kearny.

The *Tsis tsis tas* struck first, attacking a party of *Wihio* in an open field. One of their medicine men dreamed of destroying the whites with fire. After an initial charge failed to break the enemy line, the warriors set the prairie afire. Afterward the surviving warriors spoke in awe of how the flames had raced toward the bluecoats and then stopped. Nearby sixty good men died trying to kill only thirty *Wihios*. Unfortunately the whites had new, rapid-firing rifles that they could reload while lying prone.

The day after the *Tsis tsis tas* failure, Red Cloud's *Lakotas* tried to destroy the bluecoats at Fort Phil Kearny.

"It will be like before," Crazy Horse told Wolf. "We'll attack the woodcutters. When horse soldiers come to help, we'll run. The bluecoats will chase us. Our brothers, who will hide as before, can make another surround and kill the rest of the bluecoats."

"Carrington's not as foolish as Fetterman," Wolf argued. "He certainly won't send all of his men out to chase a handful of decoys. We'll still have to face the thunder guns at the fort."

"Maybe we'll use fire," Crazy Horse declared.

"Maybe lightning will burn the buildings. Anything's possible."

"Cousin, if you think it's a poor plan, you should remain in your lodge with your wife and children," Crazy Horse suggested.

"Why do you talk like that?" Wolf asked. "When did I ever turn away from danger? I'm Wolf Running. I rescue fools who ride into trouble."

"You also see things," Crazy Horse noted. "If your dreams . . ."

"I never turned away from a fight," Wolf growled. "I smoked your pipe. I'll ride with you."

"I'm glad," Crazy Horse confessed. "Many of our best men say that we cousins are certain to bring victory. We know the medicine prayers, and we see things in our dreams. I've seen many dead bluecoats lying naked under a summer sun. That will be our doing, Wolf."

"Perhaps," Wolf muttered. "I don't know whether we'll run Carrington or destroy his fort. I do believe we'll fight hard. And well."

"We always do," Crazy Horse boasted.

To be truthful, though, Wolf's heart never was in the fighting. For days he, too, had dreamed, but he saw no dead bluecoats. He saw very little at all. The dream began and ended in a cloud, and the vision was murky throughout.

In the beginning Wolf saw himself sitting alone in a dark, damp cave. Odd paintings of buffalo and horsemen covered the walls. Beside the embers of a cook fire sat a young boy of perhaps twelve years.

"Well, Brother?" Wolf whispered.

"I have no flute to play," the shadowy figure declared, holding out his empty hands. "I wanted to play the courting flute, but there's no one to make it for me."

"Your brothers . . ."

"Sickness took the last of them," the boy explained. "Ayyyy! There's someone I would follow, but he's lost his way."

"Yes," Wolf whispered, touching the youngster's shoulder. "It's difficult to know what to do."

The boy seemed to melt into the fire, and Wolf sat in his place. The cave filled with the sound of singing, and for a time Wolf felt the warmth of the fire flow through his bones. Then he recognized the song. It was an ancient *Suhtai* mourning prayer.

"No!" Wolf shouted through his dream. "No!"

The cave suddenly filled with light. It was as if the sun had stepped inside. Wolf stood, trembling. Behind him two shadows formed on the wall. Not one but two!

The sight terrified him, and he always awoke at that point. He dared not return to sleep for fear of seeing more.

"What did you see?" Raven Heart asked after Wolf shouted his way awake. "*Nah nih*, what's happened?"

Wolf never answered, but he understood all too well. Two shadows! One man. A close relation would soon die.

Before riding to the fort, Wolf had feared that it might be Sun Walker Woman or one of the children. Once he crossed Lodge Trail Ridge, he sensed what would happen. Dark clouds cast shadows over the world below. They even swallowed the crests of the towering mountains. Wolf had the sensation of being closed in, walled up as in the cave from his dream.

And the pictures? They were explained when he passed a band of Arapahos hunting a small buffalo herd. Wolf turned back and glanced at the others in his party. Stands Long, as always, was at his side. Raven Heart and Broken Wing followed. Up ahead Crazy Horse led *Oglalas* who had once been strangers. Suffering and fighting had forged a bond between them all.

Who would it be?

Wolf considered turning back, but that, of course, wasn't possible. He was an Elk, and his place was in the front. He could make the buffalo horn medicine, offer the ancient medicine prayers, and do his best to protect both the brother who shared the same mother and those related through hardship and shared struggles.

They halted near the site of the Fetterman fight. Scraps of cloth and a few arm and leg bones remained to mark the place. Carrington's men had carried what they could of the dead back to their fort for burial. Once Crazy Horse described the plan to his companions, Wolf kindled a fire. Stands Long took a long medicine pipe from its elk hide sheath, and Raven Heart brought tobacco.

"We must make strong medicine today," Wolf declared. "This fight will be different from the other one."

"How so?" Broken Wing asked as Wolf accepted the tobacco and began filling the pipe bowl.

Wolf gazed deeply into their faces. He couldn't tell

them, but perhaps they sensed it. Raven Heart sat closer
to his brother than usual, and Broken Wing took great care
to speak the unfamiliar *Suhtai* prayers.

When the last of the prayers ended, Wolf remained a
moment beside the fire. He spoke other, silent pleas to
Heammawihio. He then drew out bits of broken shell and
began tying them in his companions' hair.

"Our grandfather had these," Wolf told Raven Heart.
"Once our people camped in a place where shells were
plentiful. These hold great power."

"*Nah nih*, what did your dream tell you?" the young
man asked. "Will I die today?"

"I don't know," Wolf confessed. "But there's danger."

Broken Wing also asked the reason for the additional
precautions, but Wolf didn't answer. Instead he spoke of
the old ways and how men should never forget what had
gone before them.

Only Stands Long remained silent. The brother-friends
had faced peril so often there was no longer any counting
them. As Wolf applied the white buffalo horn paint, he
could only nod solemnly.

"Don't worry, Brother," Stands Long whispered. "I
won't be far. Together we'll protect them."

Wolf couldn't shake the shadows, though. Nevertheless
he followed his cousin along the well-traveled trail to the
fort. A dark flag waving from a nearby hillside revealed
the location of the wood detail, and the decoys turned in
that direction.

It began well enough. There were only a few bluecoats
guarding the cutters, and they quickly retreated. A bugler
sounded his horn, and other *Wihio* began readying their
ponies to give chase. Crazy Horse rode toward the wagons,
taunting the bluecoats to come out from the cover of their
wagon boxes and fight. The horse soldiers appeared to be
ready to do just that when a line of *Lakotas* rose from their
hiding places and raced toward the woodcutters' horses.

"No!" Crazy Horse shouted. He waved to Wolf, and
the two of them tried to cut off the onrushing raiders.
Wolf's pony was weary from the long ride to Big Piney

Creek, though, and he had to ease his pace. Crazy Horse continued a short way, but the raiders ignored both men. Instead they broke past the bluecoat guards and drove the horses from the creek.

"It's always the same!" Crazy Horse barked. "The hot bloods spoil our plans."

Wolf scowled. The horse stealers had raised dust, and Carrington would soon know this was no skirmish with a wood detail. He would have his walls manned and his cannons ready.

The cousins were not the only ones troubled by the spoiled plan. Red Cloud himself watched from the nearby hills. He rode down with a small party to see for himself what had gone wrong. He then decided to attack the woodcutters with his whole force.

"We'll kill these few," Crazy Horse agreed. "The effort won't be wasted after all."

Wolf grew cold. He was already troubled by the dream, and he didn't like the notion of attacking the woodcutters.

"Look," he told Crazy Horse. "There's no good way to get at them. Their boxes have high sides, and they're made of hard wood. Our arrows won't penetrate. We can't see the enemy without riding close. They'll find killing us easy."

"It's good we have the shell charms," Raven Heart declared.

"And the horn powder," Broken Wing added. "Besides, they'll have to expose themselves when they reload."

Others thought so, too, but they were proved wrong. The bluecoats in their wagon boxes had the same new rifles that had bloodied the *Tsis tsis tas* raiders at Fort C. F. Smith. The cover of the boxes and the new rifles afforded a great advantage, and the bluecoats used it to good effect.

A line of *Oglalas* made the first charge. They raced toward the woodcutters, but there was no way to break through the line of boxes. They circled around them instead, and the bluecoats began killing. It was not a matter of one or two men dying. Five, ten, fifteen fell in turn, and those *Oglalas* who remained mounted raced away. Others, wounded or trapped beneath crippled horses, cried for help.

"They require rescuing," Wolf said, easing his pony toward the wagon boxes.

"We're Elks," Raven Heart shouted. "It's for us to do this difficult thing."

Wolf turned and tried to stop his brother, but Broken Wing had already whipped his pony into motion, and Raven Heart was determined to follow.

"Ayyyy!" Wolf howled, kicking his horse into a gallop. "Nothing lasts long . . ."

Raven Heart and Broken Wing led a charmed life, darting in and out of volleys of rifle fire. One stopped to free a trapped warrior while the other shielded him with horse and body. They freed three men and carried two wounded men to safety.

Wolf did his best to divert the bluecoats' aim. He charged toward the boxes before turning at the last minute. He fired arrows at two men taking careful aim. They leapt back, losing their concentration. Wolf spotted a third bluecoat rifleman and fired an arrow through the man's side. He fell, screaming.

Retribution quickly followed. While his young companions escaped, Wolf's pony whined as three bullets tore through its side. One bullet nicked Wolf's right foot. Wolf winced, but the pain passed. The danger didn't. Wolf's horse managed to run despite its wounds, but the animal finally stumbled. Wolf jumped free, but the dying creature broke his bow and trapped the medicine shield beneath its rump.

As Wolf stared at the bluecoats still firing from their boxes, he heard the words of an old *Suhtai* war chant. That was when he spotted Stands Long.

"Today I'm the rescuer!" he shouted, raising his shield and nudging his horse forward. Raven Heart and Broken Wing started to follow, but Stands Long waved them back. "It's for me to do!" he yelled.

Even Wolf, who was well acquainted with his brother-friend's exploits, admired the ride. Stands Long galloped toward the boxes, then veered to one side as the bluecoat rifles barked. He then reversed his route until he appeared at Wolf's side.

"Come, Brother, it's time to go," he said, jumping down and helping Wolf onto the horse.

"You should have stayed back," Wolf scolded.

"I thought you'd be pleased to see me."

"I am," Wolf confessed as he reached down to help Stands Long onto the horse.

"Something's left undone," Stands Long said, stepping to the other side of the dead pony and freeing Wolf's shield. Snow Wolf's nose was covered with blood, and Wolf suddenly remembered his foot. The blood didn't come from that wound, though.

"Stands Long?" he called.

"Nobody lives forever," he said, opening his shirt so that Wolf could see an ugly bullet wound just below the left nipple. "Not even the mountains."

Wolf continued to extend his hands toward his brother-friend, but Stands Long ignored them.

"I won't cough out my life in your lodge, troubling your sons with my ghost," Stands Long explained as he balanced a lance in his right hand. Mine will be a remembered death."

"Take the horse," Wolf pleaded.

"Tell your sons . . ."

"Our sons," Wolf insisted.

"Tell them mine was a remembered charge," Stands Long said, slapping the horse's rump. Instinctively Wolf hugged the animal's neck as it sped toward safety. Stands Long flashed a final smile before stumbling toward the wagon boxes.

chapter
23

THOSE WHO SAW IT SAID that it was a remembered
thing. Stands Long crossed the open ground like a
whiskey drinker, stumbling and singing. The bluecoats
tried to kill him, but their bullets held no power. He
reached the wagon boxes and died killing a *Wihio* with
two yellow stripes on the arm of his coat.

Wolf Running felt as though a lance had pierced his
heart. He recalled the day Stands Long and he had left
their winter camp in search of meat to feed the people.
They were just boys, and no one considered them capable
of helping. Wolf had dreamed of game, though, and Stands
Long had trusted that dream. They had been brothers from
that day.

How many times had one of them rescued the other?
Ten times? Twenty? A hundred? Why count? There was
never to have been an end to the rescuing, but suddenly it
had come. Wolf felt a burden greater than a hundred
mountains descending upon him. Stands Long was gone.
The man who had always guarded Sun Walker Woman,

who helped Wolf's sons walk Man's Road, had begun the long walk up Hanging Road.

Following the fighting, Wolf had lingered on the ridge overlooking the wagon boxes. He waited until the blue-coats left before riding down to recover the body of his truest friend. Wolf expected the bluecoats to mark the body, but he discovered Stands Long resting peacefully beside a broken wagon wheel. Except for the bullet holes and blood, he was little different from when Wolf had applied the horn powder. The shells remained in his hair. Someone had pinned a hastily scrawled note to his buck-skin shirt.

A brave man, it said simply.

"Yes," Wolf had agreed as he lifted his brother-friend's body onto a waiting horse. "I won't meet a better one on this side."

Wolf saw to the mourning rites. There were no relatives to do it, and after all, Wolf was the one most saddened by the passing. He spoke the prayers and gave away five po- nies in honor of Stands Long's rescue.

"Little enough," he remarked when Raven Heart sug- gested presenting only three. "I would give ten ponies to have him back."

Wolf chose a resting place deep in the Big Horns. It was far from the stolen road and the curious *Wihios* who might steal a bow or a shield, defile the body, or otherwise dis- turb the ghost. Raven Heart and Broken Wing erected the scaffold, and the three of them raised the frail remains of their friend onto the framework and bid him farewell.

"*Heammawihio*, look down on us!" Wolf shouted as he stared through tears at the sky. "We're nothing. Hurry this good man to the other side where he can be with those he loved as a boy. Give him the peace he never found in life."

The others nodded reverently, but Wolf wasn't finished.

"Look here!" he shouted across the mountains. "This is Stands Long Beside Him, my brother-friend. No man stood taller on the day of his death. Remember him!"

The people who had ridden out to observe the final rites

howled their agreement. Wolf then allowed Broken Wing and Raven Heart to lead the way back to the *Oglala* camp. He remained beside the scaffold for a time. When he finally returned to camp, Sun Walker Woman was waiting.

"I know it's been a sad time," she told him, "but you must put it behind you. For three days you have been away. It was necessary. You had to help that man who was your brother-friend climb Hanging Road. Now you have to let him make the climb. If you hold onto his ghost, it can only cause trouble for both of you."

"Is that what I'm doing?"

"Aren't you? When I mourn, I cut my hair. It grows again. That's the way *Heammawihio* orders things. Within the sacred hoop, everything has its season. We plant and we reap. We're born and we die. I've seen you hurt before, but this time is different. The wound's festering, but it's too deep to lance."

"I'll try to put it behind me," Wolf promised.

"Good," she whispered, gripping his hands. "It's what a man does. Your sons need you, and our people require leaders."

"I lead no one," Wolf insisted.

"Raven Heart and Broken Wing remain at your side. Others join you when you ride to fight the bluecoats. You don't yet wear a chief's bonnet, but soon the Elks will invite you to accept one."

"I'm not certain I have eyes that see clearly enough to be a chief."

"Of all the men I know, you are the one most often called a man of the people. Who provides food for the hungry and hides to clothe those who need them? You give more ponies away in a season than anyone else captures. The *Oglalas* accept you as a brother. We all need you to guide our feet."

"I can only walk my own path, Sun Walker. It's for the others to choose."

"They will, choose, too. You can't remain in the darkness of your despair, though. You have to step into the

light and let us help you. Touch me. Let me know that I
have a husband. Be a father to your sons.''

"When haven't I?" Wolf asked.

"Often," she scolded. "We know that a man with far-
seeing eyes has unusual obligations, and we try to understand. It's difficult for them sometimes. They don't
consider the welfare of others. They only know their father's away, and they must hunt rabbits alone.''

"I'll put an end to that," Wolf vowed.

She smiled, stroked his wrinkled forehead, and left.
Wolf turned to follow, but stopped when Wind's Whisper
emerged from the lodge.

"Are you better, *Ne' hyo*?" the boy asked.

"Yes," Wolf replied. "Your mother says that I've ne-
glected you and your brothers.''

"Our uncles used to show us things," Whisper said,
looking at his toes. "Now that they've gone to ride with
the *Arapahos,* only Raven Heart's left.''

"He's also your uncle," Wolf pointed out.

"He's only a young man himself, *Ne' hyo*. He rides off
with you most days, too.''

"We'll hunt tomorrow.''

"Yes?" Wind's Whisper asked. "You've said it before.
I know that some days you must go to fight the bluecoats,
but so often?"

"It seems often," Wolf confessed.

"The sun's high in the sky," the boy pointed out. "Who
can say what tomorrow will bring? Maybe rain. Maybe
bluecoats. We could go today.''

Wolf frowned. He felt weak, humorless. It wasn't a
good time to take a son into the mountains.

"Go," Whisper pleaded. "There are deer and elk to kill
nearby.''

"You carry a boy's bow," Wolf noted. "Do you have
good arrows?"

"Many," Whisper answered. "My uncles showed me
how to make them. Raven Heart says that you carry stone
points on your arrows, and he taught me how to put flint
points on mine. We'll hunt in the old, sacred way.''

"Raven Heart's a good teacher."

"Not so good as my father. Heart said so. You, after all, taught him."

"Mostly we teach ourselves," Wolf explained, pulling his eldest son closer. "I'll show you what I know, though."

That afternoon Wolf readied two ponies. He and Wind's Whisper rode out from the camp and continued northward into the Absaroka country of the Crows. With *Tsis tsis tas* bands watching Fort C. F. Smith, no Crows camped there that summer, though. They passed a few abandoned camping places, but Wolf could tell by the seedlings sprouting in the center of old campfire rings that no one had kindled a log there recently.

"This is a good place," Wind's Whisper announced when they neared a thicket beside a small pond. "See the deer tracks?"

"I thought we came to shoot rabbits," Wolf objected.

"Ah, a rabbit won't feed many people. A man of the people should always bring something back for the helpless ones."

"So you are a man now?"

"I was speaking of you, *Ne' hyo*," the youngster insisted. "String your bow and follow me."

Wolf grinned. Who was guiding whom?

After stringing their bows, the two hunters entered the thicket. Wind's Whisper walked as silently as his name suggested, and they wove their way through the thick underbrush with barely a sound. Eventually they came upon a handful of deer chewing leaves. Wolf nodded to his son, and Whisper nocked an arrow. The nine-year-old studied the deer and picked a target, a young buck.

"Why not him?" Wolf asked, waving to a tall, thick-necked buck.

"You taught me to honor the old ones," the nine-year-old replied. "Besides, I'm not certain my arrows will pierce his thick hide."

Wolf grinned. He then drew the boy back, and they spoke the required hunting prayers. Wolf motioned Whis-

per to shoot, and the youngster drew the arrow back until
it almost touched his ear. He steadied the bow. Finally he
released it, and the arrow split the air. The buck glanced
up at the faint sound, but it was dead before realizing what
had happened. The other deer scampered away.

"Do you know how to make the throat cut?" Wolf
asked.

"Yes," the boy said, drawing his knife. He stepped to
the buck and cut the delicate flesh of the neck. Blood began to drain, and Wolf began skinning the animal while
his son severed the head. They were just beginning the
butchering when a pair of quail scurried through the underbrush. Moments later several crows announced an in-
truder. Wolf instinctively nudged Whisper toward the
safety of a nearby boulder.

"Look!" a voice called. "Someone's shot a deer."

Wolf turned in that direction and spied a white-bearded
Wihio leading a boy that might have been his grandson.
The old man carried a rifle, and when Wolf stepped out to
confront him, the old *Wihio* aimed the gun. Wolf had only
an instant to leap away as the rifle spit a bullet past his
head.

"Jeremy, run!" the white hair shouted as Wolf nocked
an arrow.

This isn't necessary, Wolf thought. When the old man
aimed a second time, though, Wolf fired. The arrow struck
the *Wihio* just above the breastbone.

"Oh," the white hair gasped as he stared in surprise as
the arrow shaft now protruding from his chest. Blood
poured out, and he fell backward, dead.

"Grandpa!" the boy screamed, racing to the fallen
man's side. The boy tried to lift the rifle, but by then Wolf
was standing beside him.

"You don't belong here," Wolf said, tearing the rifle
from the youngster's hands.

"Go ahead, kill me, too," the young *Wihio* suggested.
"We'll all of us die now. I don't know the way."

"No," Wind's Whisper said, joining his father. The two
boys eyed each other with a mixture of suspicion and cu-

riosity. They were about the same age, and their stern eyes mirrored similar hard experiences. Whisper gazed up into Wolf's eyes and said, "Let him go, *Ne' hyo*. He can't hurt us."

"If I let these boys go, they'll come back grown, eager to kill us," Wolf explained, using the *Tsis tsis tas* words the stranger couldn't understand.

"Don't make me stand here, waiting," the *Wihio* pleaded. "Make it quick."

"You're here alone?" Wolf asked. The boy didn't answer, but his eyes betrayed a secret. "Go and see," Wolf told Wind's Whisper.

Whisper was gone only a short time. He returned with news that a woman and two smaller children sat beside a wagon an arrow's shot farther on.

"Don't hurt them," the *Wihio* cried, dropping to his knees. "Ma's done nobody any harm. Josh and Johnny are just kids."

Wolf smiled for the first time since meeting the *Wihio*. Just kids? And what was this youngster, a grown man?

"They're starving," Whisper mumbled. "Their horses have broken down, and their wagon's an old one."

"You're lost?" Wolf asked.

"Yessir," the boy admitted. "I'm Jeremy Bradshaw. My pa's gone and died, and we planned to go back to Kansas. Then the horses stopped, and nothing we did got 'em going. Grandpa said maybe we could shoot something. We're pretty hungry."

"This isn't your country," Wolf declared.

"Grandpa said Crows camp here. They've been helpful more'n once. Grandpa thought you Sioux, but . . ."

"We are with them," Wolf announced.

"Oh," Jeremy muttered. "Thought there was . . . a chance."

"No, *Ne' hyo*," Whisper said when Wolf fingered an arrow. "The deer. They can have it. You can show them how to leave the Big Horns."

"Your first kill?" Wolf asked. "You want to give it to these thieves?"

"To him," Whisper explained, pointing to the boy. "He's got little brothers. Like me. A mother. Like me. I have a father, though," he added, wrapping an arm around Wolf's waist. "It's hard, walking Man's Road without one."

Wolf nodded. He then told young Jeremy.

"I don't understand," Jeremy said, gazing down at his grandfather. The young *Wihio* didn't argue. Instead he raced back to tell his brothers.

After the wagon people dressed the deer and buried the slain old man, Wolf provided them with directions to Montana. He then gave them a stern warning.

"Don't return here," he growled. "You may not find someone with as generous a heart as my son next time."

Jeremy nodded, and his mother started the wagon northward. Wolf and Wind's Whisper turned to head in the opposite direction.

"You're not disappointed in me?" Whisper asked.

"It's a good thing, aiding the helpless," Wolf noted.

"They're enemies, though."

"Ask yourself this, *Naha','" Wolf advised. "Would another death, or four, restore the harmony of the sacred hoop? Would a thousand dead *Wihio* restore what we've lost?"

"No," Whisper declared. "If you feel this way, why don't you believe we should go to Fort Laramie and speak with the treaty makers?"

"I've met them before," Wolf explained. "Many of them. They promise peace but send soldiers to our country. They offer us things we've always had and later take them away, claiming we agreed. I don't trust any of them."

"So you'll fight until we all die?"

"It's a warrior's fate to die fighting," Wolf declared. "My father and his fell riding to battle."

"I'm too young to walk the world alone, *Ne' hyo*," Wind's Whisper insisted. "My brothers are even younger. We need you."

"I know," Wolf said, drawing the boy close. "All my life I've looked forward to the time I would lead my sons toward Bull Buffalo. Now Bull Buffalo's dying, though, and the land I walked as a boy is gone. *Wihio* roads and *Wihio* forts stand where we once built our summer camps. Soon towns and iron roads will reach even this valley."

"And the *Tsis tsis tas*?"

"Will be no more," Wolf confessed. "Already we camp near our cousins, the *Lakotas,* seeking their protection."

"The *Lakotas* will survive," Whisper boasted. "They're strong. I'll take an *Oglala* wife, and . . ."

"A storm's coming that will sweep even the *Lakotas* into memory."

"No, *Ne' hyo*," Wind's Whisper cried.

"Sweet Medicine saw it in a vision long ago," Wolf explained. "He warned us to avoid the pale people with the hairy faces, but few listened. The women liked the shiny beads and the looking glasses. The men coveted the long rifles and black powder. The traders brought us these good things. While we weren't watching, they stole our souls. We forgot the old ways, and we became lost within the sphere of the sacred hoop."

"I've heard you say it before," Whisper declared. "We can't change what's happened. We have to look to tomorrow. What can you do? What can I do?"

"Remember," Wolf suggested. "Observe the ancient prayers. Hunt in the old way. Find a brave heart death."

"Like he who was your brother-friend?"

"Yes," Wolf agreed. "Like him."

Wind's Whisper intertwined his small fingers with those of his father and gazed up into Wolf's eyes.

"It's not an easy path *Heammawihio* gives us to walk," the boy observed. "I have a guide to show me the way, though. What do you do, *Ne' hyo,* when you lose the way?"

"I grow sad," Wolf said, smiling at his son.

"Why?"

"Because I know that Wind's Whisper, my son, will find a way to cheer me."

"I do that?" the boy asked. "How?"

"You know," Wolf said, tickling the boy. "This time it was asking me to hunt rabbits. You bring me back from my heavy thoughts to the world I love best."

"*Nah' koa* proposed the hunt," Whisper explained.

"You let the *Wihio* go," Wolf pointed out. "You restored the harmony to this place."

Wind's Whisper smiled. Wolf lifted the youngster onto his shoulders, and they walked toward their ponies.

chapter
24

NOT LONG AFTER WOLF RETURNED, a handful of messengers arrived from Spotted Tail's *Sicangu* band. A new peace commissioner wanted the tribes to come down and talk. He promised to provide lead and powder to anyone arriving at the iron road east of Fort Laramie during the Moon of the Dry Grass. The bluecoats' great soldier chief, General Sherman, was coming out with six treaty makers.

"The *Wihio* are coming to listen," Hairy Robe told Wolf Running. "They say they are going to satisfy our concerns and end the war."

"They can end it tomorrow," Wolf insisted. "All they have to do is march away from our country and leave us alone. They can abandon the forts and close the stolen road. It's not difficult. It requires no words from us."

"They'll want us to give up something," Hairy Robe argued.

"We've given up enough!" Wolf exclaimed. "More than enough!"

Wolf was not the only one who thought so. Crazy Horse

and many other prominent young *Lakotas* refused to make any concessions. As for Red Cloud, he said that his mind hadn't changed. He would quit killing bluecoats when they left his country.

Red Cloud nevertheless dispatched Man Afraid of His Horses to the treaty council. Man Afraid was to represent Red Cloud and the other *Oglalas*. He would make sure that some of the other bands, especially those who had remained at Fort Laramie or farther south, did not sign away the land that had claimed the lives of so many good men.

Man Afraid returned from the iron rail gathering with disappointing news. The star chief Sherman proposed moving all the *Lakotas* to Missouri River. He said that the tribes were at fault for raiding the *Wihio* travelers on the stolen road. A council was going to be held that autumn at Fort Laramie, and chiefs wishing to make peace should come.

"So now we're to trade these good valleys for land already empty of game?" Wolf asked. "These commissioners will find few men to speak with when they hold their council."

Wolf proved prophetic. The council was a great failure. Few chiefs came, and even the headmen of the Crows criticized the bluecoat chiefs for ruining the country with their roads. When some of the *Lakotas* who were hanging around the fort learned what had happened, they sent word to Red Cloud.

"Perhaps we should talk with the *Wihio* after all," Red Cloud told his fellow warriors. "This time, though, we will be the ones to say what must happen before we hold a council."

Red Cloud was shrewd enough to sense he had an opportunity to gain a second great victory. This time it would be bloodless, too. The *Oglala* chief sent a messenger to Fort Laramie with word that he would meet with the treaty makers once the bluecoats abandoned their forts. The commissioners, in return, sent tobacco and asked Red Cloud to come to Fort Laramie to talk peace once the snows melted.

That winter Wolf sensed change was on the wind. The bluecoats rarely ventured from their forts, and then only to cut wood. Few miners dared to travel their stolen road, and so there was little killing on either side.

"Do you really think we can have peace, *Ne' hyo*?" Wind's Whisper asked Wolf.

"It's hard to forget all the killing," Wolf replied. "But if the *Wihio* stay away, we'll have no one to kill."

Winter that year was hard, both for the soldiers penned in their fort and the warriors camped on the surrounding hillsides. Wolf passed most of the season in his lodge, nestled beside Sun Walker Woman. He found time to hunt and time to share the old stories with his three sons. Once the snow began to melt, he passed more time in the hills, harassing the bluecoat woodcutters.

No sooner did the creeks begin to thaw than messengers again arrived with an invitation to Fort Laramie.

"The *Wihio* insist that they will only agree to meet with you," Man Afraid told Red Cloud. "You have to go."

Red Cloud promised to come only when he could see the bluecoats marching out of their forts.

"Then I'll come down and talk," Red Cloud announced. "Only then."

Wolf didn't really believe that the *Wihio* would agree to such a condition. The bluecoats remained in their fort, and the treaty makers began giving up and going east. By midsummer, only two remained. They had only a few minor chiefs' signatures, bartered for tobacco, and everyone knew that a paper Red Cloud had not signed was worthless.

"You could ride into the fort and talk with Walker Logan," Sun Walker said. "Not so long ago you dreamed of how the two of you brought peace and understanding between your people."

"I saw a meeting," Wolf admitted, "but there was no peace. You always believed we would find a way to bring about a treaty, but I knew better. I'm no treaty maker. I'll

take my brother to hunt Bull Buffalo. We'll consider treaties another time.''

Red Cloud, Crazy Horse, and most of the other *Oglalas*
were of similar mind. They devoted those burning days of
summer to hunting. They smoked meat and cured hides so
that no one would be hungry or cold when the snows next
came.

It was during the second big summer hunt that Wolf
dreamed of a great fire. It seemed as if the sky turned black
with smoke. Flames devoured everything.

Crazy Horse told his cousin that the dream warned of a
great clash with the *Wihio*.

"We must be prepared for it," Crazy Horse argued.
"That's what the dream urges."

"Maybe," Wolf admitted. "But it might simply warn
of a grass fire. Who can say for certain?"

If Wolf was not prepared for the dream, he certainly
wasn't ready for his second great surprise. He and Wind's
Whisper were stalking deer one afternoon not far from Big
Piney Creek when he heard a commotion on the far side
of the river. Perhaps twenty *Oglalas* were riding through
the shallows, shouting and flashing mirrors.

"Cousin, come and see it!" Crazy Horse howled.

Wolf gazed around in alarm. Once he realized that the
Oglalas were laughing, he relaxed.

"*Ne' hyo,* what should we do?" Whisper asked.

"Go along and see what's making these people crazy,"
Wolf explained.

He soon had his answer. Just ahead a column of bluecoats escorted a line of wagons. They were going south,
toward the *Wihio* fort. A band of *Tsis tsis tas* and *Lakota*
warriors trailed behind.

"It's the fort up north," one of the pursuers explained
when Crazy Horse called to them. "The bluecoats are
leaving. We own this country again."

"We always have," Crazy Horse insisted. "What's happened to the fort?"

"Red Cloud is burning it," a *Tsis tsis tas* explained.
"Look!"

To the north a plume of dark smoke rose skyward. It was a considerable distance away, but there was no mistaking the location. One fort, at least, would soon pass into memory.

Before another moon passed, the last bluecoats left Fort Phil Kearny, too. Red Cloud awarded the *Tsis tsis tas* the honor of burning the place, and Little Wolf directed its thorough destruction. Wolf didn't watch from afar this time. He carried one of the torches.

He also joined Crazy Horse and other *Oglalas* after the bluecoats abandoned the little post on Powder River. Fort Reno was already in a sad state, and flames quickly devoured its small cabins and stockade.

"It's finally finished," Wolf said as he watched the flames lick the dry wooden walls. "Now Red Cloud can talk to the treaty makers."

"That's a mistake," Crazy Horse growled. "We're strong now. We've broken the *Wihio* power. We should try to run them from Platte River."

"Once we might have done it," Wolf observed. "Now it's too late. There are too many of them."

Red Cloud understood that if Crazy Horse did not. Once the last white soldiers departed the Powder River country, he sent word to Fort Laramie that he would come in and talk. He had the autumn buffalo hunt to conduct, but afterward he would ride in and talk about peace. By then the dirt in the face moon was giving way to the hard face moon, and the air possessed an icy edge.

Wolf pondered making the journey. He wasn't asked to translate this time, and Crazy Horse urged him to stay in the mountains.

"There's nothing for us in that place," Wolf's cousin argued. "We walk the world modestly, in the old manner of our grandfathers. We need no cloth or woolen blankets. We drink no whiskey. The *Wihio* steal our hearts and corrupt our souls."

Sun Walker Woman saw it differently. She urged Wolf to take them along. "Don't forget your dreams," she said, gripping his shoulders. "Logan's still there."

"How do you know?" he asked. "His family went east. I told him he should also go there."

"His heart's here, on the plains," she insisted. "Wolf, you know that. You don't wear the silver eagle anymore, but do you think he's forgotten that he owes you his life? How many times have you told that story? A hundred? He'll be at the fort, and so should you. Your rescue marked the last treaty signing. Perhaps you will do something important this time, too."

Wolf doubted it, but he had never been any good arguing with Sun Walker. He reluctantly agreed to ride to the fort.

A strange parade of *Oglalas, Sicangus,* and *Tsis tsis tas* journeyed from Powder River to Fort Laramie that autumn. Red Cloud led the way, accompanied by his family and several prominent *Oglalas.* Lines of warriors guarded the flanks. Families completed the contingent. Some carried their lodges on pony drags while others packed their belongings on captured bluecoat mules and pack animals.

From time to time other bands appeared. Some would follow along. Others took their own route. One morning Wolf spied a dozen *Sicangus* racing along the fringe of the band. He was riding with Wind's Whisper that morning, and the boy pointed to them.

"Look!" Whisper shouted as the *Sicangus* rode by. Behind them a bearded *Wihio* galloped along ahead of two slight-shouldered young riders. "*Ne' hyo,* it's your friend, the trader."

"Logan?" Wolf called.

The trader waved a red cloth in his right hand, and Wolf motioned Wind's Whisper toward them. Together, they closed the distance until they were alongside Walker Logan.

"I feared you wouldn't come," Logan declared. "I wasn't even certain you were still alive."

"You didn't leave after all," Wolf noted.

"You were right, though, to believe a father should be with his sons. These are my boys, Wolf. Tom's the oldest."

The taller of the youngsters grinned. He had his father's sandy hair and thin face, but he was reluctant to take Wolf's hand.

"I'm Joe," the younger boy announced, nudging his horse between his brother and Wolf in order to shake the warrior's hand. "I'm only ten, but anybody'll tell you I'm the smart one. Handsomer, too."

"Only got a bigger mouth's all," Tom argued. The older boy finally accepted Wolf's hand.

"This is my oldest son," Wolf told the young Logans. "He's called Wind's Whisper, and he also has walked the world ten summers."

"Whisper, huh?" Joe said, waving. Both *Wihio* youngsters appeared surprised at Wolf's command of English.

"Guess you're quiet, huh?" Tom said. "Come around for a visit. Maybe my brother'll catch a case of it."

"The name comes from a dream," Whisper explained. "My father asked for a vision the night I was born, but mostly he heard the wind. I'll win a better name when I'm old enough to fight."

"I thought the fighting was over," Joe said, turning to his father.

"We hope it is," Logan explained. "No agreement's been made yet, though."

"It will be settled soon, though," Wolf declared. "Red Cloud's satisfied that the bluecoats have left Powder River, so we can set aside our lances."

Wolf certainly hoped so. For days the treaty makers had talked and discussed wording for the agreement despite the fact that the tribes believed that the old Horse Creek Treaty remained in effect.

"Many of the old words fail to say clearly which land belongs to which tribe," Logan explained. "Instead of changing a bad paper, it's better to start anew."

Wolf didn't see the logic of that, but he didn't wish to argue with his old friend. As for the treaty council, it faced serious challenges. Red Cloud had arrived like a conqueror, and he believed he had earned the right to dictate terms. The commissioners insisted that the *Wihio* father-president should be the one to decide.

"Do what you want," one of Red Cloud's nephews finally shouted. "We'll ride back to Powder River and hunt."

The bluecoats declared that such a a thing wasn't possible. They had no fight left in them, and neither did the father-president. He ordered an agreement drawn up and signed as quickly as was possible.

The morning the treaty was signed, Wolf was out at Horse Creek, swimming with a mixed group of boys. Some were sons of commissioners and post traders. Others camped with *Lakota* or *Tsis tsis tas* bands. Few understood one another's tongues, but they nevertheless conversed, raced, and laughed. Only when Joe Logan jumped from the bank into deep water did anyone voice concern.

"Joe!" Tom called. "Where'd my brother go?"

"River," Wind's Whisper cried as he swam toward the spot.

Wolf instinctively ordered all swimmers to the banks, then hurried toward the outcropping from which Joe had jumped. He and Logan arrived at virtually the same instant, and both began searching frantically for the vanished ten-year-old. Neither had any luck, and their common despair drew nods of sympathy from onlookers, whether they were *Wihio* or Indian.

It was Wind's Whisper who located young Joe. Age-mates often had a sixth sense for spotting each other, or so it seemed. It certainly worked that day. Joe had caught his foot on a root, and now the tree was trying to take the boy under.

"Wait!" Wolf called as Whisper started to dive beneath the surface.

There could be no waiting, though. Joe was already sputtering and breathing heavily. Whisper dived down and freed the trapped foot. The two then swam together toward the fort.

As had been the case seventeen long years before when Wolf had rescued Walker Logan, Wind's Whisper's act appeared as an omen of future good relations between white people and the plains tribes. Joe even presented the same silver eagle charm to Whisper that had long graced Wolf's neck.

"I did nothing unusual," Wind's Whisper explained later, after the Elks celebrated his rescue by presenting him with a coup feather.

"Perhaps," Wolf admitted. "There were many close by, though, and no one else acted."

"You did."

"I arrived too late. Had the boy gone under, he would have been dead."

"You would have performed some cure," Whisper insisted. "I know it."

"A man can only do so much," Wolf told his son. "Soon you'll be older, and you'll see yourself that men can only try to walk the world in harmony, keep their family safe, and show their sons the few secrets that they've discovered."

"Such as?"

"There is some good and some bad in most men. Look for the good and try to forgive the bad. You'll make many friends that way."

"Is it a bad thing to have *Wihio* friends? You have one."

"A bad thing?" Wolf mused. "No. It's hard, though."

"Winter Pup and Deer Foot believe I did a bad thing, giving a *Wihio*'s life back to him."

"That answer can only come when both of you have finished walking the world," Wolf explained. "I don't believe this would be a better place for his dying."

"Or for the boy we saw in the mountains?"

"No, and perhaps the memory of compassion will draw our peoples closer."

As the treaty negotiations continued, though, it was hard to remain open-minded or optimistic. The *Wihio* words confused the people, and even when the pens were touched to the paper, many signers were unsure what was settled.

A passer-by would never have suspected the problems,

though. Thousands of plains people shared in the feasting, and the *Oglalas* demonstrated amazing tricks on horseback. Wolf raced ponies with three Arapahos, winning twice. Raven Heart outshot a hundred bowmen. Even Winter Pup drew attention for setting the women's privy alight.

Wolf tried to keep those last, happy days in mind as he rode from the store, but it wasn't entirely possible. When Red Cloud left, Wolf rode along. Once they were safely back in the Powder River country, Crazy Horse asked his cousin to speak of the treaty. Wolf spelled out the terms, and Wolf noticed his brow darken.

All this talk of peace is a waste of time," Crazy Horse declared. "We have gained nothing in our struggle. The *Wihio* take too much. They never admit who started the fighting."

"Yes, but even the treaty makers, who are famous soldiers, know they failed to run us. They'll keep the peace because they don't want to fight us."

"You're wrong, Wolf," Crazy Horse argued. "Some of the *Wihio* may be tired, but others are eager to fill the empty ranks. They want to pen us up in a reservation. I'll not do it."

"Nor will I," Wolf vowed. "I don't believe we have to fight a war over this country, though. I have sons who would also have to fight such a war, and I don't like to think of them dying."

"We'll teach them the medicine prayers, Wolf. We'll craft them good arrows and well-balanced bows. Best of all, we're rescuers. We'll save them."

Just then a band of *Sicangus* raised a huge howl. Others joined in, saluting an end to the war.

"It's not the end, though," Crazy Horse told Wolf. "It's only a warm summer before another long winter ensues."

Wolf tried to digest the words, but he couldn't. To fight on and on with no hope of discovering something better was pointless. Stands Long had won a brave death, but the world was a bleaker place without him. Was it to be the same for Wind's Whisper, Winter Pup, and Deer Foot? No! He couldn't bear the thought.

"What's wrong?" Sun Walker asked as Wolf sat in the soft meadow grass, recalling other times, other people.

"The world," he told her. "When the old ones were here, they found answers for everything. Now there's only confusion."

"Are you certain?" she asked. "It seems to me that things are clear enough. We only have to recall the old ways. We walk the world in harmony, disturbing nothing. We harm no one, and we help those we can. You're a man of the people, Wolf Running. Confusion? It's for you to explain things to the rest of us."

"And if I can't?"

"Then we'll be left with false prophets and a world we can't possibly understand. I wouldn't wish to know a world like that. Don't let that happen."

Wolf wanted to promise her that it wouldn't, but what had Crazy Horse said? This was the summer. Winter lies ahead.

A man can only do what he can. He must walk his own path. Wolf's grandfather had told him that. It was true. He tried to take comfort from the fact as he glanced at his sons running with the other boys beside Horse Creek. He could only hope that Crazy Horse's summer would last long enough that he would be able to share such wisdom with grandchildren. It was the only way to complete the circle, to restore the sacred hoop.